The Sign of the Grail

The seventh volume in
a collection of writings by

C.J.S. Hayward

C.J.S. Hayward Publications, Wheaton

1. Orthodox Eastern Church--literature. 2. Orthodox Eastern Church--humor. 3. Liturgical theology. 4. Icons--theology. 5. Arthurian literature.

ISBN 978-0-6152-0219-8

The reader is invited to visit CJSHayward.com.

Contents

Archdruid of Canterbury Visits Orthodox Patriarch

The Archdruid of Canterbury appeared as head of a delegation to His All Holiness THOMAS, Patriarch of Xanadu.

The Archdruid bore solemn greetings and ecumenical best wishes. He presented gifts, including an oak and holly icon, portraying St. Francis of Assisi as the pioneer of "I-Thou" existentialism. The icon was "not made by hands" ("all done by paw," in the memorable words of Paddington Bear).

The Druidic leader spoke of the Orthodox Church with the most solemn reverence. "The Orthodox Church is not only Oriental and exotic, but has the most hauntingly beautiful liturgy achieves has what we are trying to engineer in our liturgical reform, and the Orthodox Church would make the perfect partner for the most dynamic and progressive forces that keep the C of E a living spiritual power in this world. St. Alban and St. Sergius *are* Anglican saints, but they are first and foremost Orthodox saints, and are only Anglican saints because they are Orthodox saints. I have personally blended the most excellent traditions of Druidic Bard and occupant of the See of Canterbury. We would be most deeply honoured if the existing profound (if invisible) bond uniting Orthodox, Anglican, and Druid were made explicit."

After the Druid spoke for an hour, he paused in thought a moment, turned to His All Holiness THOMAS and said, "But I fear I have done too much talking, while you have said nothing. Isn't there anything you'd like to say? Don't you have questions we could speak to?"

The Patriarch coughed, sat in silence for a moment, and began to squirm. "Have you considered pursuing ecumenical relations with the African majority in your own communion? I've dealt with some of them and they're really quite solid people, with good heads on their shoulders."

The Archdruid made no reply.

The Eighth Sacrament

"Holy" is an important word in the Bible, and there are many holy actions described in the Bible: Communion, prayers, and worship, to pick some of the larger ones. But there is only one act in the Bible that is called holy, and it is one we might not think of. What is it? "Greet one another with a holy kiss," which is repeated four or five times. "Holy" is *not* just another way of saying "appropriate," or rather it means "appropriate" but also something much stranger, much wilder. "Holy" means set apart to God, an element of Heaven here on earth.

The New Testament's main word for a profound display of respect in fact means "kiss", even if our translations hide it. Bowing and kissing have some interesting similarities throughout the Bible, and they mean something similar. Kissing has one meaning in American culture, but it has a very different set of colors in the Bible, and we are missing something of the holy kiss until we can see it as a display of profound reverence for one who is living in the life of Christ and becoming a little Christ. Is giving a kiss to an Orthodox Christian really different from kissing an icon?

The holy kiss is an opportunity to meet others in love. Do you know how someone gives you a greeting, a gift, or *something* and you know it isn't fake, you know another person has put his heart into it? That's what the holy kiss should be, and for many people here, *is*. Why? There was one tenth degree black belt in karate who was asked what he thought our society could learn from his martial art. He didn't give any of the answers we find so obvious: exercise, self-defense, discipline, and the like. What he said, very emphatically, was "to bow," at which point he stood up and gave a great, courteous, and majestic bow. Bowing was bigger to him than any of the things that draw us, and that is what the holy kiss should be. What's the connection? Bowing and giving a kiss are never very far in the Bible, and once you understand them, you understand that they are a place where quite a lot come together. Furthermore, some of the warmest kisses I've received have been from bishops and other devout Orthodox Christians, and then the kisses have been worthy of that bow. How you give the holy kiss is related to your spiritual state.

The holy kiss is tied to holy communion. It is part of the eucharistic liturgy, and the Fathers draw interesting connections. St. Ambrose of Milan said, "We kiss Christ with the kiss of Communion:" we embrace Christ when we embrace each other, and yet there's something that the holy kiss adds. The kiss is itself an image for the Eucharist: even our prayers before communion say more than that. Yet the holy kiss is not just something indirectly connected to Holy Communion. The holy kiss is an act of communion between persons, and if we pray before Communion, "Neither like Judas will I give thee a kiss," this means not only that love must be in our reception of Holy Communion, but that we must not like Judas kiss our brethren without the love of Communion. There is difference between an embrace to someone who is Orthodox and someone who is not, because as with Holy Communion the kiss does not stand by itself: full communion makes a difference.

There are many other things one could say; the holy kiss takes different forms in different cultures and in my home parish is usually a hug. But the holy kiss is, in its way, the eighth sacrament, and is a window that opens out onto the whole of Orthodoxy. It is well worth living.

Do We Have Rights?

As we [Paul and Silas] were going to the place of prayer, we were met by a slave girl who had a spirit of divination and brought her owners much gain by soothsaying. She followed Paul and us, crying, "These men are servants of the Most High God, who proclaim to you the way of salvation." And this she did for many days. But Paul was annoyed, and turned and said to the spirit, "I charge you in the name of Jesus Christ to come out of her." And it came out that very hour.

But when her owners saw that their hope of gain was gone, they seized Paul and Silas and dragged them into the market place before the rulers; and when they had brought them to the magistrates they said, "These men are Jews and they are disturbing our city. They advocate customs which it is not lawful for us Romans to accept or practice."

The crowd joined in attacking them; and the magistrates tore the garments off them and gave orders to beat them with rods. And when they had inflicted many blows upon them, they threw them into prison, charging the jailer to keep them safely. Having received this charge, he put them into the inner prison and fastened their feet in the stocks.

But about midnight Paul and Silas were praying and singing hymns to God, and the prisoners were listening to them, and suddenly there was a great earthquake, so that the foundations of the prison were shaken; and immediately all the doors were opened and every one's fetters were unfastened. When the jailer woke and saw that the prison doors were open, he drew his sword and was about to kill himself, supposing that the prisoners had escaped. But Paul cried with a loud voice, "Do not harm yourself, for we are all here."

And he called for lights and rushed in, and trembling with fear he fell down before Paul and Silas, and brought them out and said, "Men, what must I do to be saved?"

And they said, "Believe in the Lord Jesus, and you will be saved, you and your household." And they spoke the word of the Lord to him and to all that were in his house. And he took them the same hour of the night, and washed their wounds, and he was baptized at once, with all his family. Then he brought them up into his house, and set food before them; and he rejoiced with all his household that he had believed in God.

Acts 16:16-34, RSV

As [Jesus] passed by, he saw a man blind from his birth. And his disciples asked him, "Rabbi, who sinned, this man or his parents, that he was born blind?"

Jesus answered, "It was not that this man sinned, or his parents, but that the works of God might be made manifest in him. We must work the works of him who sent me, while it is day; night comes, when no one can work. As long as I am in the world, I am the light of the world."

As he said this, he spat on the ground and made clay of the spittle and anointed the man's eyes with the clay, saying to him, "Go, wash in the pool of Silo'am" (which means Sent). So he went and washed and came back seeing.

The neighbors and those who had seen him before as a beggar, said, "Is not this the man who used to sit and beg?" Some said, "It is he"; others said, "No, but he is like him." He said, "I am the man."

They said to him, "Then how were your eyes opened?"

He answered, "The man called Jesus made clay and anointed my eyes and said to me, `Go to Silo'am and wash'; so I went and washed and received my sight."

They said to him, "Where is he?" He said, "I do not know."

They brought to the Pharisees the man who had formerly been blind. Now it was a sabbath day when Jesus made the clay and opened his eyes. The Pharisees again asked him how he had received his sight. And he said to them, "He put clay on my eyes, and I washed, and I see."

Some of the Pharisees said, "This man is not from God, for he does not keep the sabbath." But others said, "How can a man who is a sinner do such signs?" There was a division among them.

So they again said to the blind man, "What do you say about him, since he has opened your eyes?" He said, "He is a prophet."

The Jews did not believe that he had been blind and had received his sight, until they called the parents of the man who had received his sight, and asked them, "Is this your son, who you say was born blind? How then does he now see?"

His parents answered, "We know that this is our son, and that he was born blind; but how he now sees we do not know, nor do we know who opened his eyes. Ask him; he is of age, he will speak for himself." His parents said this because they feared the Jews, for the Jews had already agreed that if any one should confess him to be Christ, he was to be put out of the synagogue. Therefore his parents said, "He is of age, ask him."

So for the second time they called the man who had been blind, and said to him, "Give God the praise; we know that this man is a sinner."

He answered, "Whether he is a sinner, I do not know; one thing I know, that though I was blind, now I see."

They said to him, "What did he do to you? How did he open your eyes?"

He answered them, "I have told you already, and you would not listen. Why do you want to hear it again? Do you too want to become his disciples?"

And they reviled him, saying, "You are his disciple, but we are disciples of Moses. We know that God has spoken to Moses, but as for this man, we do not know where he comes from."

The man answered, "Why, this is a marvel! You do not know where he comes from, and yet he opened my eyes. We know that God does not listen to sinners, but if any one is a worshiper of God and does his will, God listens to him. Never since the world began has it been heard that any one opened the eyes of a man born blind. If this man were not from God, he could do nothing."

They answered him, "You were born in utter sin, and would you teach us?" And they cast him out.

Jesus heard that they had cast him out, and

having found him he said, "Do you believe in the Son of man?"

He answered, "And who is he, sir, that I may believe in him?"

Jesus said to him, "You have seen him, and it is he who speaks to you."

He said, "Lord, I believe"; and he worshiped him.

John 9:1-38, RSV

The Gospel today deals with physical blindness, but it is about much more than physical blindness. In this passage, the man who was blind from birth received his physical sight. That is an impressive gift, but there's more. The passage deals with the Pharisees' spiritual blindness, but the Church has chosen to end today's reading with the blind man saying, "Lord, I believe," and worshipping Christ. When he did this, the blind man demonstrated that he had gained something far more valuable than physical sight. He had gained spiritual sight. The Bible actually gives a few more chilling words about the Pharisee's spiritual blindness, but the Church, following the Spirit, is attentive to spiritual sight and ends its reading with the man demonstrating his spiritual sight by adoring Christ in worship.

What is spiritual sight? We see a glimmer of it in the passage from Acts, where we read something astonishing. We read that Paul and Silas were stripped, savagely beaten, and thrown into what was probably a dungeon. And how do they respond to their "reward" for a mighty good deed? Do they say, "Why me?" Do they rail at God and tell him he's doing a lousy job at being God? Do they sink into despair?

In fact none of these happen; they pray and sing to God. Like the man born blind, they turn to God in worship. As should we.

That is advanced spiritual sight. I'm not there yet and you're probably not there either. But let me suggest some basic spiritual sight: Next time someone cuts you off on the road and you almost have an accident, instead of fuming and maybe thinking of evil things to do the other driver, why don't you thank God?

What do you have to be thankful for? Well, for starters, your eyes work and so do your driver's reflexes, you have a car, and your brakes work, and probably your horn. And God just saved you from a nasty scrape that would have caused you trouble. Can't you be thankful for some of that?

In the West, we think in terms of rights. Almost all of the ancient world worked without our concept of rights. People then, and some people now, believed in things we should or should not do--we should love others and we shouldn't steal, cheat, or murder--but then there was a queer shift to people thinking "I have an entitlement to this." "This is something the universe owes me." Now we tend to have a long list of things that we're entitled to (or we think God, or the universe, or someone "owes me"), and if someone violates our rights, boy do we get mad.

But in fact God owes none of the things we take for granted. Not even our lives. One woman with breast cancer responded to what the women's breast cancer support group was named ("Why me?"), and suggested there should be a Christian support group for women with breast cancer called "Why not me?"

That isn't just a woman with a strong spirit speaking. That is the voice of spiritual sight. Spiritual sight recognizes that we have no right to things we take for granted. We have no right to exist, and God could have created us as rocks or fish, and that would have been generous. We have no right to be free of disease. If most of us see, that is God's generosity at work. He doesn't owe it to us. Those of us who live in the first world, with the first world's luxuries, do not have those luxuries as any sort of right.

I am thinking of one friend out of many who have been a blessing. I stop by his house, and he receives me hospitably. Usually he gives me a good conversation and I can hold his bunny Smudge on my lap and tell Smudge that my shirt is not edible. This is God's generosity and my friend's. Not one of these blessings is anything God owes me, or for that matter my friend owes me. Each visit is a gift.

It isn't just first world luxuries that none of us are entitled to. We have no right to live in a world where a sapphire sky is hung with a million constellations of diamonds. If there is a breathtaking night sky, God chose to create it in his goodness and generosity. Not only do I have no right to be a man instead of a butterfly or a bird (or to exist in the first place), I have no right to be in community with other people with friendships and family. God could have chosen to make me the only human in a lonely world. Instead, in his sovereignty, he chose to place me in a world of other people where his love would often come through them. I have no right to that. I'm not entitled to it. If I have friends and family, that is because God has given me something better than I have any right to. God isn't concerned with giving me the paltry things I have a right to. He is generous, and gives all of us things that are better than our rights. We have no right to join the seraphim, cherubim, thrones, dominions, powers, authorities, principalities, archangels, and angels--rank upon rank of angels adoring God. Nor do we have any right to live in a world that is both spiritual and material, where God who gives us a house of worship to worship him in, also truly meets us as we work, garden, play, visit with our friends, and go about the business of being human.

Isn't it terrible if we don't have rights? It's not terrible at all. It means that instead of having a long list of things we take for granted as "Here's what God, or the universe, or somebody owes me," we are free not to take it for granted and to rejoice at God's generosity and recognize that everything we could take for granted, from our living bodies to the possessions God has given us to God placing us at a particular point in place in time and choosing a here and now for us, with our own cultures, friendships, languages, homelands, sights and sounds, so that we live as much in a particular here and now as Christ, to a world carpeted with life that includes three hundred and fifty thousand species of beetles, to the possibility of rights. Every single one of these is an opportunity to turn back in praise and worship God. It is an opportunity for joy, as we were created for worship and we find our fullest joy in worshipping God and thanking him. Would you rather live in a world where you only have some of the things that can be taken for granted, or in a world where God has created for you so many more blessings than he or anyone else owes you?

There is, actually, one thing that we have a right to, and it's a strange thing to have a right to. Hell. We have a right to go to Hell; we've earned a ticket to Hell with our sins, and we've earned it so completely that it cost God the death of his Son to let us choose anyone else. But Hell is not only a place that God casts people into; it is also where he leaves people, with infinite reluctance, after he has spent a lifetime telling people, "Let go of Hell. Let go of what you think you have a right to, and let me give you something better." Hell is the place God reluctantly leaves people when they tell him, "You can't take my rights away from me," and the gates of Hell are barred and bolted from the inside by people who will not open their hands to the Lord's grace. The Lord is gracious, and if we allow him, he will give us something infinitely better than our rights. He will give us Heaven itself, and God himself, and he will give us the real beginnings of Heaven in this life. The good news of God is not that he gives us what we think we have a right to, but that he will pour out blessings that we will know we have no right to, and one of these blessings is spiritual sight that recognizes this cornucopia as an opportunity for joyful thanksgiving and worship.

When I was preparing this homily, there's one word in the Greek text that stood out to me because I didn't recognize it. When the blind man says that Christ must be from God and have healed him as a "worshiper of God," the word translated "worshiper of God" is *theosebes*, and it's a very rare word in the Orthodox Church's Greek Bible. Another form of the word appears in Acts but this is the only time this word appears in either the Gospels or the books John wrote. It is also rare in the Greek Old Testament, the Septuagint. It occurs only four times: once in IV Maccabees 15:28 where the mother of seven martyred sons sees past even her maternal love "because of faith in God" (15:24) and is called "the daughter of God-fearing [*theosebes*] Abraham," and three times in Job where the blameless Job is called a *theosebes*, or "worshiper of God." In Job, this word occurs once in the book's opening verse, then Job is twice called a "worshiper of God" by God himself. The Maccabees' mother is not even called *theosebes* herself, but "the daughter of *theosebes* Abraham."

What does this mean? I'm not sure what it all means, but John didn't use very many unusual words. Unlike several New Testament authors, he used simple language. In the Greek Old Testament, this word is reserved for special occasions, it seems to be a powerful word, and it always occurs in relation to innocent suffering. Job is the very image of innocent suffering and the Maccabees mother shows monumental resolve in the face of innocent suffering--the text is very clear about what it means for a mother to watch her sons be tortured to death. The Gospel passage is about innocent suffering as well as spiritual sight. When the blind man calls Christ a "worshiper of God," he is speaking about a man who would suffer torture for a miracle, before Paul and Silas, and this little story helps move the Gospel towards the passion. But Christ says that the blind man suffered innocently, and I'm not sure that we recognize all of what that meant.

People believed then, as many people believe now, that sickness is a punishment for sin. The question, "Who sinned? Who caused this man's blindness?" was an obvious question to ask. And Jesus says explicitly that neither this man nor his parents sinned to bring on his blindness. Jesus, in other words, says that this man's suffering was innocent, and he was saying something shocking.

What does this have to do with spiritual sight?

Spiritual sight is not blind to evil. The Son of God came to destroy the Devil's work, and that includes sin, disease, and death. Sin, disease, and death are the work of the Devil. The woman who survived breast cancer who suggested there should be a

Christian support group called "Why not me?" never suggested that cancer is a good thing, and would probably never tell a friend, "I wish you could have the sufferings of cancer." When Paul and Silas were beaten with rods, being spiritual didn't mean that they didn't feel pain. I believe the beatings hurt terribly. Sin is not good. Disease is not good. Death is not good. Spiritual sight neither ignores these things, nor pretends that they are blessings from God. Instead, God transforms them and makes them part of something larger. He transformed the suffering of Paul and Silas into a sharing of the sufferings of Christ, a sharing of the sufferings of Christ that is not only in the Bible but is written in Heaven. I've had sufferings that gave terrifying reality to what had always seemed a trite exaggeration that "Hell is a place you wouldn't wish on your worst enemy." My sufferings are something I wouldn't wish on my worst enemy, and it is terrifying to realize that Hell is worse. So why then is spiritual sight joyful?

C.S. Lewis in The Great Divorce describes a journey. This journey begins in an odd place, and one that is not terribly cheerful. Anyone can have anything physical he wants just by wishing, only it's not very good. The ever-expanding borders of this place are pushed out further and further as people flee from each other and try to get what they want.

A bus Driver takes anyone who wants into his bus, which ascends and ascends into a country that is painfully beautiful to look at, where not only are the colors bright and full but heavy, rich, and deep. It is painful to walk on the ground because the people who got off the bus are barely more than ghosts, devoid of weight and substance, and their feet are not real enough to bend the grass. This is in fact a trip from Hell to Heaven, where Hell is mediocre and insubstantial, and Heaven is real and hefty beyond measure, not only beautiful and good but colorful and rich and deep--and infinitely more real than Hell. One part that really struck me was that when Lewis's Heavenly guide (George MacDonald) explains why a woman in Heaven, whom MacDonald said had gone down as far as she could, did not go so far as descending to Hell:

"Look," he [MacDonald] said, and with the word he went down on his hands and knees. I did the same (how it hurt my knees!) and presently saw that he had plucked a blade of grass. Using its thin end as a pointer, he made me see, after I had looked very closely, a crack in the soil so small that I could not have identified it without his aid.

"I cannot be certain," he said, "that this is the crack ye came up through. But through a crack no bigger than that ye certainly came."

"But--but" I gasped with a feeling of bewilderment not unlike terror. "I saw an infinite abyss. And cliffs towering up and up. And then this country on top of the cliffs."

"Aye. But the voyage was not mere locomotion. That buss, and all you inside it, were increasing in size."

"Do you mean then that Hell--all that infinite empty town--is down some little crack like this?"

"Yes. All Hell is smaller than one pebble of your earthly world: but it is smaller than one atom of this world, the Real World. Look at yon butterfly. If it swallowed all Hell, Hell would not be big enough to do it any harm or have any taste."

"It seems big enough when you're in it, Sir."

"And yet all loneliness, angers, hatreds, envies and itchings that it contains, if rolled into one single experience and put into the scale against the least moment of the joy that is felt by the least in Heaven, would have no weight that could be registered at all. Bad cannot succeed even in being bad as truly as good is good."

Bad cannot succeed even in being bad as truly as good as good is good, and spiritual sight knows this. To have spiritual sight is not to close your eyes so tight they don't even see evil, but to let God open your eyes wider. Our eyes can never open wide enough to see God as he truly is, but God can open our eyes wide enough to see a lot. Why were Paul and Silas able to turn from being viciously beaten and imprisoned to singing and praying to God? For the same reason a butterfly from Heaven could swallow all of Hell without it even registering. In that image of Heaven, not just the saints but the very birds and butterflies could swallow up Hell. This is just an image; the Real Place, real Heaven, is far more glorious.

Death is swallowed up in victory. Let us let spiritual blindness be swallowed up by spiritual sight that begins to see just how much God's generosity, grace, mercy, kindness, love, and 1001 other gifts we have to be thankful for. Let us worship God.

Lesser Icons

Reflections on Faith, Icons, and Art

C.S. Lewis's The Voyage of the Dawn Treader opens with a chapter called "The Picture in the Bedroom," which begins, "There was a boy called Eustace Clarence Scrubb, and he almost deserved it." Not long into the chapter, we read:

> They were in Lucy's room, sitting on the edge of her bed and looking at a picture on the opposite wall. It was the only picture in the house that they liked. Aunt Alberta didn't like it at all (that was why it was put away in a little back room upstairs), but she couldn't get rid of it because it had been a wedding present from someone she did not want to offend.
>
> It was a picture of a ship--a ship sailing straight towards you. Her prow was gilded and shaped like the head of a dragon with a wide-open mouth. She had only one mast and one large, square sail which was a rich purple. The sides of the ship--what you could see of them where the gilded wings of the dragon ended--were green. She had just run up to the top of one glorious blue wave, and the nearer slope of that wave

came down towards you, with streaks and bubbles on it. She was obviously running fast before a gay wind, listing over a little on her port side. (By the way, if you are going to read this story at all, and if you don't know already, you had better get it into your head that the left of a ship when you are looking ahead is *port*, and the right is *starboard.*) All of the sunlight fell on her from that side, and the water on that side was full of greens and purples. On the other, it was darker blue from the shadow of the ship.

"The question is," said Edmund, "whether it doesn't make things worse, *looking* at a Narnian ship when you can't get there."

"Even looking is better than nothing," said Lucy. "And she is such a very Narnian ship."

"Still playing your old game?" said Eustace Clarence, who had been listening outside the door and now came grinning into the room. Last year, when he had been staying with the Pevensies, he had managed to hear them all talking of Narnia and he loved teasing them about it. He thought of course that they were making it all up; and as he was far too stupid to make anything up himself, he did not approve of that.

"You're not wanted here," said Edmund curtly.

"I'm trying to think of a limerick," said Eustace. "Something like this:

Some kids who played games about Narnia
Got gradually balmier and balmier--"

"Well, *Narnia* and *balmier* don't rhyme, to begin with," said Lucy.

"It's an assonance," said Eustace.

"Don't ask him what an assy-thingummy is," said Edmund. "He's only longing to be asked. Say nothing and perhaps he'll go away."

Most boys, on meeting a reception like this, would have either cleared out or flared up. Eustace did neither. He just hung about grinning, and presently began talking again.

"Do you like that picture?" he asked.

"For Heaven's sake don't let him get started about Art and all that," said Edmund hurriedly, but Lucy, who was very truthful, had already said, "Yes, I do. I like it very much."

"It's a rotten picture," said Eustace.

"You won't see it if you step outside," said Edmund.

"Why do you like it?" said Eustace to Lucy.

"Well, for one thing," said Lucy, "I like it because the ship looks as if it were really moving. And the water looks as if it were really wet. And the waves look as if they were really going up and down."

Of course Eustace knew lots of answers to this, but he didn't say anything. The reason was that at that very moment he looked at the waves and saw that they did look very much indeed as if they were going up and down. He had only once been in a ship (and then only so far as the Isle of Wight) and had been horribly seasick. The look of the waves in the picture made him feel sick again. He turned rather green and tried another look. And then all three children were staing with open mouths.

What they were seeing may be hard to believe when you read it in print, but it was almost as hard to believe when you saw it happening. The things in the picture were moving. It didn't look at all like a cinema either; the colours were too real and clean and out-of-doors for that. Down went the prow of the ship into the wave and up went a great shock of spray. And then up went the wave behind her, and her stern and her deck became visible for the first time, and then disappeared as the next wave came to meet her and her bows went up again. At the same moment an exercise book which had been lying beside Edmund on the bed flapped, rose and sailed through the air to the wall behind him, and Lucy felt all her hair whipping round her face as it does on a windy day. And this was a windy day; but the wind was blowing out of the picture towards them. And suddenly with the wind came the noises--the swishing of waves and the slap of water against the ship's sides and the creaking and the overall high steady roar of air and water. But it was the smell, the wild, briny smell, which really convinced Luch that she was not dreaming.

"Stop it," came Eustace's voice, squeaky with fright and bad temper. "It's some silly trick you two are playing. Stop it. I'll tell Alberta--Ow!"

The other two were much more accustomed to adventures but, just exactly as Eustace Clarence said, "Ow," they both said, "Ow" too. The reason was that a great cold, salt splash had broken right out of the frame and they were breathless from the smack of it, besides being wet through.

"I'll smash the rotten thing," cried Eustace; and then several things happened at the same time. Eustace rushed towards the picture. Edmund, who knew something about magic, sprang after him, warning him to look out and not be a fool. Lucy grabbed at him from the other side and was dragged forward. And by this time either they had grown much smaller or the picture had grown bigger. Eustace jumped to try to pull it off the wall and found himself standing on the frame; in front of him was not glass but real sea, and wind and waves rushing up to the frame as they might to a rock. There was a second of struggling and shouting, and just as they thought they

> had got their balance a great blue roller surged up round them, swept them off their feet, and drew them down into the sea. Eustace's despairing cry suddenly ended as the water got into his mouth.

I don't know that C.S. Lewis was thinking about icons or Orthodoxy when he wrote this, and I am reluctant to assume that C.S. Lewis was doing what would be convenient for the claims I want to make at icons. Perhaps there are other caveats that should also be made: but the caveats are not the whole truth.

I am not aware of a better image of what an icon is and what an icon does than this passage in Lewis. Michel Quenot's The Icon: A Window on the Kingdom is excellent and there are probably more out there, but I haven't come across as much of an evocative image as the opening to The Voyage of the Dawn Treader.

I don't mean that the first time you see an icon, you will be swept off your feet. There was a long time where I found them to be clumsy art that was awkward to look at. I needed to warm to them, and appreciate something that works very differently from Western art. I know that other people have had these immediate piercing experiences with icons, but appreciating icons has been a process of coming alive for me. But much the same could be said of my learning French or Greek, where I had to struggle at first and then slowly began to appreciate what is there. This isn't something Orthodoxy has a complete monopoly on; some of the time Roman Catholic piety can have something much in the same vein. But even if it's hard to say that there's something in icons that is nowhere else, there is something in icons that I had to learn to appreciate.

Icon of the Holy Transfiguration, Anonymous

A cradle Orthodox believer at my parish explained that when she looks at an icon of the Transfiguration, she is there. The Orthodox understanding of presence and memory is not Western and not just concerned with neurons firing in the brain; it means that icons are portals that bring the spiritual presence of the saint or archetypal event that they portray. An icon can be alive, some more than others, and some people can sense this spiritually.

Icons are called windows of Heaven. Fundamental to icon and to symbol is that when the Orthodox Church proclaims that we are the image of God, it doesn't mean that we are a sort of detached miniature copy of God. It doesn't mean that we are a detached *anything*. It is a claim that to be human is to be in relation to God. It is a claim that we manifest God's presence and that the breath we breathe is the breath of God. What this means for icons is that when the cradle Orthodox woman I just mentioned says that she is there at the Transfiguration, then that icon is like the picture of the Narnian ship. If we ask her, "Where are you?" then saying "Staring at painted wood" is like saying that someone is "talking to an electronic device" when that person is using a cell phone to talk with a friend. In fact the error is deeper.

Icon of the Glykophilousa (Sweetly-Kissing) Mother of God, Anonymous

An icon of a saint is not intended to inform the viewer what a saint looked like. Its purpose is to connect the viewer with Christ, or Mary the Theotokos, or one of the saints or a moment we commemorate, like the Annunciation when Gabriel told humble Mary that she would bear God, or the Transfiguration, when for a moment Heaven shone through and Christ shone as Christians will shine and as saints sometimes shine even in this life. I don't know all of the details of how the art is put together--although it *is* art--but the perspective lines vanish not in the depths of the picture but behind the viewer because the viewer is part of the picture. The viewer is invited to cross himself, bow before, and kiss the icon in veneration: the rule is not "Look, but don't touch." any more than the rule in our father's house is "Look, but don't touch." The gold background is there because it is the metal of light; these windows of Heaven are not simply for people to look into them and see the saint radiant with Heaven's light, but Heaven looks in and sees us. When I approach icons I have less the sense that I am looking at these saints, and Heaven, than that they are looking at me. The icon's purpose is not, as C.S. Lewis's picture, to connect people with Narnia, but to draw people into Heaven, which in the Orthodox understanding must begin in this life. It is less theatrical, but in the end the icon offers something that the Narnian picture does not.

It is with this theological mindset that Bishop KALLISTOS Ware is fond, in his lectures, of holding up a photograph of something *obviously* secular--such as a traffic intersection--and saying, "In Greece, this is an icon. It's not a holy icon, but it's an icon."

Door (*KPOYETE*), C.J.S. Hayward
(Not a holy icon, but an icon)

That, I believe, provides as good a departure as any for an Orthodox view of art. I would never say that icons are inferior art, and I would be extremely hesitant to say that art is equal to icons. But they're connected. Perhaps artwork is lesser icons. Perhaps it is indistinct icons. But art is connected to iconography, and ever if that link is severed so that art becomes non-iconic, it dies.

Another illustration may shed light on the relation between iconography and other art. The Eucharist is the body and blood of Christ to Orthodox. It is not simply a sacrament, but the sacrament of sacraments, and the sacrament which all other sacraments are related. And there are ways the Orthodox Church requires that this Holy Communion be respected: it is to be prepared for with prayer and fasting, and under normal circumstances it is only received by people who are of one mind as the early Church. It encompasses, inseparably, mystic communion with God and communion with the full brothers and sisters of the Orthodox Church.

How does an ordinary meal around a table with family compare? In one sense, it doesn't. But to say that and stop is to miss something fundamental. Eating a meal around a table with friends and family is communion. It is not Holy Communion, but it is communion.

A shared meal is a rite that is part of the human heritage. It persists across times, cultures, and religions. This is recognized more clearly in some cultures than others, but i.e. Orthodox Jewish culture says that to break bread is only something you do when you are willing to become real friends. The term "breaking of bread" in the New Testament carries a double meaning; it can mean either the Eucharist or a common meal. A common meal may not have Orthodox making the same astounding claims we make about the Eucharist, but it is a real communion. This may be why a theologian made repeatedly singled out the common meal in the Saint Vladimir's Seminary Education Day publication to answer questions of what we should do today when technology is changing our lives, sometimes for the better but quite often not. I myself have not made that effort much, and I can say that there is a difference between merely eating and filling my animal needs, and engaging in the precious ritual, the real communion, of a common meal around a table.

If we compare a common meal with the Eucharist, it seems very small. But if we look at a common meal and the community and communion around that meal (*common*, *community*, and *communion* all being words that are related to each other and stem from the same root), next to merely eating to serve our animal needs, then all of the sudden we see things that can be missed if we only look at what separates the Eucharist from lesser communions. A common meal is communion. It is not Holy Communion, but it *is* communion.

In the same sense, art is not the equal of sacred iconography. My best art, even my best religious art, does not merit the treatment of holy icons. But neither is art, or at least good art, a separate sort of thing from iconography, and if that divorce is ever effected (it has been, but I'll wait on that for how), then it generates from being art as a meal that merely fills animal, bodily needs without being communion degenerates from what a common meal should be. And in that sense I would assert that art is lesser iconography. And the word "lesser" should be given less weight than "iconography." I may not create holy icons, but I work to create icons in all of my art, from writing to painting to other creations.

In my American culture--this may be different in other areas of the world, even if American culture has a strong influence--there are two great obstacles to connecting with art. These obstacles to understanding need to be denounced. These two obstacles can be concisely described as:

- The typical secular approach to art.
- The typical Christian approach to art.

If I'm going to denounce those two, it's not clear how much wiggle room I am left over to affirm--and my goal is not merely to affirm but embrace an understanding of art. Let me begin to explain myself.

Let's start with a red flag that provides just a glimpse of the mainstream Christian view of art. In college, when I thought it was cool to be a cynic and use my mind to uncover a host of hidden evils, I defined "Christian Contemporary Music" in Hayward's Unabridged Dictionary to be "A genre of song designed primarily to impart sound teaching, such as the doctrine that we are sanctified by faith and not by good taste in music."

May God be praised, that was not the whole truth in Christian art then, and it is even further from being the whole truth today--I heartily applaud the "Wow!" music videos, and there is a rich stream of exceptions. But this doesn't change the fact that the #1 selling Christian series today is the *Left Behind* series, which with apologies to Dorothy Parker, does not have a *single* book that is to be set aside lightly. (They are all to be hurled with great force!)

If I want to explain what I would object to instead of simply making incendiary remarks about Christian arts, let me give a concrete example. I would like to discuss something that I discussed with a filmmaker at a Mennonite convention a couple of years I converted to Orthodoxy. I did not set out to criticize, and I kept my mouth shut about certain things.

What I did do was to outline a film idea for a film that would start out indistinguishably from an action-adventure movie. It would have one of the hero's friends held captive by some cardboard-cutout villains. There is a big operation to sneak in and deftly rescue him, and when that fails, all Hell breaks loose and there is a terrific action-adventure style firefight. There is a dramatic buildup to the hero getting in the helicopter, and as they are leaving, one of the villain's henchmen comes running with a shotgun. Before he can aim, the hero blasts away his knee with a hollow-nosed .45.

The camera surprisingly does not follow the helicopter in its rush to glory, but instead focuses on the henchman for five or ten excruciating minutes as he curses and writhes in agony. Then the film slows down to explore what that one single gunshot means to the henchman for the remaining forty years of his life, as he nursed a spiritual wound of lust for vengeance that was infinitely more tragic than his devastating physical wound.

The filmmaker liked the idea, or at least that's what he thought. He saw a different and better ending than what I envisioned. It would be the tale of the henchman's journey of forgiveness, building to a dramatic scene where he is capable of killing the hero and beautifully lets go of revenge. And as much as I believe in forgiveness and letting go of revenge, this "happy ending" (roughly speaking) bespoke an incommensurable gulf between us.

The difference amounts to a difference of love. Not that art has to cram in as much love, or message about love or forgiveness, as it can. If that happens, it is fundamentally a failure on the part of the artist, and more specifically it is a failure of a creator to have proper love for his creation. My story would not show much love in action, and it is specifically meant to leave audiences not only disturbed but shell shocked and (perhaps) sickened at how violence is typically shown by Hollywood. The heartblood of cinematic craft in this film would be an effort to take a character who in a normal action-adventure movie is faceless, and which the movie takes pains to prevent us from seeing or loving as human when he is torn up by the hero's cool weapon, and give him a human face so that the audience feels the pain not only of his wounded body but the grievous spiritual wound that creates its deepest tragedy. That is to say that the heartblood of cinematic craft would be to look lovingly at a man, unloving as he may be, and give him a face instead of letting him be a faceless henchman whose only purpose is to provide conflict so we can enjoy him being slaughtered. And more to the point, it would not violate his freedom or his character by giving him a healing he would despise, and announce that after his knee has been blasted away he comes to the point of forgiving the man who killed his friends and crippled him for life.

Which is to say that I saw the film as art, and he saw it as a container he could cram more message into. That is why I was disturbed when he wanted to tack a happy ending on. There is a much bigger problem here than ending a story the wrong way.

I don't mean to say that art shouldn't say anything, or that it is a sin to have a moral. This film idea is not only a story that has a moral somewhere; its entire force is driven by the desire to give a face, a human face, to faceless villains whose suffering and destruction is something we rejoice in other words. In other words, it has a big moral, it doesn't mince words, and it makes absolutely no apologies for being driven by its moral.

Then what's the difference? It amounts to love. In the version of the story I created, the people, including the henchmen, are people. What the filmmaker saw was a question of whether there's a better way to use tools to drive home message. And he made the henchman be loving enough to forgive by failing to love him enough.

When I was talking with one professor at Wheaton about

how I was extremely disappointed with a Franklin Peretti novel despite seeing how well the plot fit together, I said that I couldn't put my finger on what it was. He rather bluntly interrupted me and simply said that Peretti didn't love his characters. And he is right. In *This Present Darkness*, Franklin Peretti makes a carefully calculated use of tools at his disposal (such as characters) to provide maximum effect in driving home his point. He does that better than art does. But he does not love his characters into being; he does not breathe into them and let them move. It's not a failure of technique; it's a failure of something much deeper. In this sense, the difference between good and bad art, between A Wind in the Door and *Left Behind*, is that in A Wind in the Door there are characters who not only have been loved into being but have a spark of life that has been not only created into them but loved into them, and in *Left Behind* there are tools which are used to drive home "message" but are not in the same sense *loved*.

There is an obvious objection which I would like to pause to consider: "Well, I understand that elevated, smart people like you can appreciate high art, and that's probably better. But can't we be practical and look at popular art that will reach ordinary people?" My response to that is, "Are you sure? Are you *really* sure of what you're assuming?"

Perhaps I am putting my point too strongly, but let me ask the last time you saw someone who wasn't Christian and not religious listening to Amy Grant-style music, or watching the *Left Behind* movie? *If it is relevant, is it reaching non-Christians?* (And isn't that what "relevant" stuff is supposed to do?) The impression I've gotten, the strong impression, is that the only people who find that art relevant to their lives are Evangelicals who are trying to be relevant. But isn't the world being anti-Christian? My answer to that is that people who watch *The Chronicles of Narnia* and people who watch *Star Wars* movies are largely watching them for the same reason: they are good art. The heavy Christian force behind *The Chronicles of Narnia*, which Disney to its credit did not edit out, has not driven away enough people to stop the film from being a major success. *The*

Chronicles of Narnia is relevant, and it is relevant not because people calculated how to cram in the most message, but because not only C.S. Lewis but the people making the film loved their creation. Now, there are other factors; both *The Chronicles of Narnia* and *Star Wars* have commercial tie-in's. And there is more commercial muscle behind those two than the *Left Behind* movie. But to only observe these things is to miss the point. The stories I hear about the girl who played Lucy walking onto the set and being so excited she couldn't stop her hands from shaking, are not stories of an opportunistic actress who found a way to get the paycheck she wanted. They are stories of people who loved what they were working on. *That* is what makes art powerful, not budget.

There's something I'd like to say about love and work. There are some jobs--maybe all--that you really can't do unless you really love them. How? Speaking as a programmer, there's a *lot* of stress and aggravation in this job. Even if you have no difficulties with your boss, or co-workers, the computer has a sort of perverse parody of intelligence that means that you do your best to do something clearly, and the computer does the strangest things.

It might crash; it might eat your work; it might crash and eat your work; it might show something weird that plays a perverted game of hide and seek and always dodge your efforts to find out what exactly is going wrong so you can fix it. Novices' blood is boiling before they manage to figure out basic errors that won't even let you run your program at all. So programmers will be fond of definitions of "Programming, n. A hobby similar to banging your head against a wall, but with fewer opportunities for reward."

Let me ask: What is programming like if you do not love it? There are many people who love programming. They don't get there unless they go through the stress and aggravation. There's enough stress and aggravation that you can't be a good programmer, and maybe you can't be a programmer at all, unless you love it.

I've made remarks about programming; there are similar remarks to be made about carpentry, or being a mother (even if being a mother is a bigger kind of thing than programming or carpentry). This is something that is true of art--with its stress and aggravation--precisely because art is work, and work can have stress and aggravation that become unbearable if there is no love. Or, in many cases, you can work, but your work suffers. Love may need to get dirty and do a lot of grimy work--you can't love something into being simply by feeling something, even if love can sometimes transfigure the grimy work--but there absolutely *must* be love behind the workgloves. It doesn't take psychic powers to tell if something was made with love.

I would agree with Franky Schaeffer's remark in Addicted to Mediocrity: 20th Century Christians and the Arts, when he pauses to address the question "How can I as a Christian support the arts?" the first thing he says is to avoid Christian art. I would temper that remark now, as some Christian art has gotten a lot better. But he encouraged people to patronize good art, and to the question, "How can I afford to buy original paintings?" he suggests that a painting costs much less than a TV. But Schaeffer should be set aside another work which influenced his father, and which suggests that if Christian art is problematic, that doesn't mean that secular art is doing everything well.

Penny, Edward the Confessor (1042-1066)
An example of coinage that shows icon-like medieval *figures*, instead of photograph-style modern *portraits*. Other ancient and medieval examples abound.

When I was preparing for a job interview with an auction house that deals with coins and stamps, I looked through the

2003(?) *Spink's Catalogue of British Coins*. (Mainly I studied the pictures of coins to see what I could learn.) When I did that, a disturbing story unfolded.

The Spink's catalogue takes coins from Celtic and Roman times through medieval times right up through the present day. While there are exceptions in other parts of the world, the ancient and early medieval coins all had simple figures that were not portraits, in much the way that a drawing in a comic strip like Foxtrot differs from Mark Trail or some other comic strip where the author is trying to emulate a photograph. Then, rather suddenly, something changes, and people start cramming in as much detail as they could. The detail reaches a peak in the so-called "gold penny", in which there is not a square millimeter of blank space, and then things settle down as people realize that it's not a sin to have blank space as well as a detailed portrait. (On both contemporary British and U.S. coinage, the face of the coin has a bas-relief portrait of a person, and then there is a blank space, and a partial ring of text around the edge, with a couple more details such as the year of coinage. The portrait may be detailed, but the coinmakers are perfectly willing to leave blank space in without cramming in more detail than fits their design. In the other world coinage I've seen, there can be some differences in the portrait (it may be of an animal), but there is a similar use of portrait, text, and blank space.

This is what happened when people's understanding of symbol disintegrated. The effort to cram in detail which became an effort to be photorealistic is precisely an effort to cram some reality into coins when they lost their reality as symbols. There are things about coins then that even numismatists (people who study coins) do not often understand today. In the Bible, the backdrop to the question in Luke 20 that Jesus answered, "Show me a coin. Whose likeness is it, and whose inscription? ... Give what is Caesar's to Caesar, and what is God's to God," is on the surface a question about taxes but is not a modern gripe about "*Must* I pay my hard-earned money to the Infernal Revenue Service?", It is not the question some Anabaptists ask today about whether it is OK for Christians' taxes to support things they believe are unconscionable, and lead one pastor to suggest that people earn less money so they will pay less taxes that will end up supporting violence. It's not a question about anything most Christians would recognize in money today.

It so happens that in traditional fashion quarters in the U.S. today have a picture of George Washington, which is to say not only a picture but an authority figure. There is no real cultural reason today why this tradition has to be maintained. If the government mint started turning out coins with a geometric design, a blank surface, or some motto or trivia snippet, there would be no real backlash and people would buy and sell with the new quarters as well as the traditional ones. The fact that the quarter, like all commonly circulated coins before the dollar coin, has the image of not simply a-man-instead-of-a-woman but specifically the man who once held supreme political authority within the U.S., is a quaint tradition that has lost its meaning and is now little more than a habit. But it has been otherwise.

The Roman denarius was an idol in the eyes of many Jewish rabbis. It was stamped with the imprint of the Roman emperor, which is to say that it was stamped with the imprint of a pagan god and was therefore an idol. And good Jews shouldn't have had a denarius with them when they asked Jesus that trapped question. For them to have a denarius with them was worse on some accounts than if Jesus asked them, "Show me a slab of bacon," and they had one with them. The Jewish question of conscience is "Must one pay tax with an idol?" and the question had nothing to do with any economic harship involved in paying that tax (even though most Jews then were quite poor).

Jesus appealed to another principle. The coin had Caesar's image and inscription: this was the one thing he asked them to tell him besides producing the coin. In the ancient world people took as axiomatic that the authority who produced coinage had the authority to tax that coinage, and Jesus used that as a lever: "Then render to Caesar the things that are Caesar's, and to God's the thing that are God's."

This last bit of leverage was used to make a much deeper point. The implication is that if a coin has Caesar's image and we owe it to Caesar, what has God's image--*you and I*--are God's and are owed to God. This image means something deep. If it turns out that we owe a tax to Caesar, how much more do we owe our very selves to God?

Augustine uses the image of "God's coins" to describe us. He develops it further. In the ancient world, when coins were often made of precious and soft metals instead of the much harder coins today, coins could be "defaced" by much use: they would be rubbed down so far that the image on the coin would be worn away. Then defaced coins, which had lost their image, could be restruck. Augustine not only claims that we are owed to God; he claims that the image in us can be defaced by sin, and then restruck with a new image by grace. This isn't his whole theology for sin and grace, but it says something significant about what coins meant not just to him but to his audience.

During the Iconoclastic Controversy, not only in the East but before the overcrowded "gold penny", one monk, who believed in showing reverence to icons, was brought before the emperor, who was trying to suppress reverence to icons. The emperor asked the monk, "Don't you know that you can walk on an icon of Christ without showing disrespect to him?" and the monk asked if he could walk on "your face", meaning "your face as present in this coin," without showing the emperor disrespect. He threw down a coin, and started to walk on it. The emperor's guards caught him in the act, and he was brutally assaulted.

These varying snapshots of coins before a certain period in the West are shapshots of coins that are icons. They aren't holy icons, but they are understood as icons before people's understanding of icons disintegrated.

When I explained this to one friend, he said that he had said almost exactly the same thing when observing the development or anti-development of Western art. The story I was told of Western art, at least until a couple of centuries ago, was a story of progress from cruder and more chaotic art. Medieval art was sloppy, and when perspective came along, it was improved and made clearer. But this has a very different light if you understood the older art's reality as symbol. In A Glimpse of Eastern Orthodoxy, I wrote:

> Good Orthodox icons don't even pretend to be photorealistic, but this is not simply because Orthodox iconography has failed to learn from Western perspective. As it turns out, Orthodox icons use a reverse perspective that is designed to include the viewer in the picture. Someone who has become a part of the tradition is drawn into the picture, and in that sense an icon is like a door, even if it's more common to call icons "windows of Heaven." But it's not helpful to simply say "Icons don't use Renaissance perspective, but reverse perspective that includes the viewer," because even if the reverse perspective is there, reverse perspective is simply not the point. There are some iconographers who are excellent artists, and artistry does matter, but the point of an icon is to have something more than artistry, as much as the point of visiting a friend is more than seeing the scenery along the way, even if the scenery is quite beautiful and adds to the pleasure of a visit. Cramming in photorealism is a way of making more involved excursions and dredging up more exotic or historic or whatever destinations that go well beyond a scenic route, after you have lost the ability to visit a friend. The Western claim is "Look at how much more extravagant and novel my trip are than driving along the same roads to see a friend!"--and the Orthodox response shows a different set of priorities: "Look how lonely you are now that you no longer visit friends!"

Photorealistic perspective is not new life but an extravagance once symbol has decayed. That may be one problem, or one thing that I think is a problem. But in the centuries after perspective, something else began to shift.

The Prophet Elias, Anonymous
Before photorealistic perspective.

There is rich detail and artistry in this icon of the Prophet Elias. To those making their first contacts with Orthodox iconography, it may seem hard to appreciate--the perspective and proportions are surprising--but the things that make it something you need to learn are precisely the gateway to what an icon like this can do that mere photographs can never do.

The Dream of Joachim, Giotto
Medieval art is beginning to become photorealistic.

In Giotto's painting of the dream of Joachim, one can see something probably that looks like an old icon to someone used to photorealistic art and probably looks photorealistic to someone used to icons. Not all medieval art is like this, but this specific piece of medieval art is at once a contact point, a bridge, and a hinge.

Madonna of the Rocks, Leonardo da Vinci
Renaissance photorealism.

Leonardo da Vinci's art is beginning to look very different from medieval art. In some ways Leonardo da Vinci's art is almost more like a photograph than a camera would take--Leonardo da Vinci's perspective is all the more powerful for the fact that he doesn't wear his grids on the outside, and in this picture Leonardo da Vinci makes powerful use of what is called "atmospheric perspective", giving the faroff place and above the Madonna of the Rocks' shoulder the blue haze that one gets by looking through a lot of air. Hence Leonardo da Vinci's perspective is not just a precise method of making things that are further away look smaller.

When Renaissance artists experimented with more photorealistic perspective, maybe they can be criticized, but they were experimenting to communicate better. Perspective was a tool to communicate better. Light and shadow were used to communicate better. It's a closer call with impressionism, but there is a strong argument that their departure from tradition and even photorealism was to better communicate how the outsides of things looked in different lighting conditions and at different times of day. But then something dreadful happened: not only artists but the community of people studying art learned a lesson from history. They learned that the greatest art, from the Renaissance onwards, experimented with tradition and could decisively break from tradition. They did not learn that this was always to improve communicate with the rest of us. And so what art tried to do was break from tradition, whether or not this meant communicating better to "the rest of us".

The Guitar Player, Pablo Picasso
Art that has disintegrated from photorealism.

In at least some of Pablo Picasso's art, the photorealistic has vanished. Not that all Pablo Picasso art looks this way: some looks like a regular or perhaps flattened image. But this, along with Picasso's other cubist art, tries to transcend perspective, and the effect is such that one is told as a curiosity the story of a museumgoer recognizing someone from the (cubist) picture Picasso painted of him. Of all the pictures I've both studied and seem live, this kind of Pablo Picasso art is the one where I have the most respect for the responses of people considered not to be sophisticated enough to appreciate Pablo Picasso's achievement.

Some brave souls go to modern art museums, and look at paintings that look nothing like anything they can connect with, and walk away humbled, thinking that they're stupid, or not good enough to appreciate the "elevated" art that better people are able to connect with. There's something to be said for learning to appreciate art, but with most of these people the problem is *not* that they're not "elevated" enough. The problem is that the art is not trying to communicate with the world as a whole. Innovation is no longer to better communicate; innovation at times sneers at communication in a fashion people can recognize.

The Oaths of the Horatii, Jacques Louis David
"High" art that communicates to ordinary people.

In an age before television, Jacques Louis David's depiction of the oaths of the Horatii was extraordinarily powerful political communication, even political propaganda. Jacques Louis David combines two things that are separate today: elevated things from classical antiquity, and a message that is meant to communicate to ordinary people. A painting like one of Jacques Louis David's was the political equivalent of a number of television news commentaries in terms of moving people to action.

The Franky Schaeffer title I gave earlier was Addicted to Mediocrity: 20th Century Christians and the Arts; the title I did not give is Modern Art and the Death of a Culture, which has disturbing lettering and a picture of a man screaming on its cover art. If there is a deep problem with the typical Christian approach to arts (and it is *not* a universal rule), there is a deep problem with the typical secular Western approach to arts (even if that is *not* a universal rule either). A painting like "The Oaths of the Horatii" is no more intended to be a private remark among a few elite souls than Calvin and Hobbes; Calvin and Hobbes may attract the kind of people who like other good art, but this is never because, as Calvin tells Hobbes about his snowman art which he wants lowbrows to have to subsidize, "I'm trying to criticize the lowbrows who can't appreciate this."

The concept of an artist is also deeply problematic. When I was taking an art history class at Wheaton, the professor asked people a question about their idea of an artist, and my reaction was, "I don't have any preconceptions." Then he started talking, and I realized that I did have preconceptions about the matter.

If we look at the word "genius" across the centuries, it has changed. Originally your "genius" was your guardian angel, more or less; it wasn't connected with great art. Then it became a muse that inspired art and literature from the outside. Then "genius" referred to artistic and literary giftedness, and as the last step in the process of internalization, "genius" came to refer to the author or artist himself.

The concepts of the artist and the genius are not the same, but they have crossed paths, and their interaction is significant. Partly from other sources, some artists take flak today because they lead morally straight lives. Why is this? Well, given the kind of superior creature an artist is supposed to be, it's unworthy of an artist to act as if they were bound by the moral codes that the common herd can't get rid of. The figure of the artist is put up on a pedestal that reaches higher than human stature; like other figures, the artist is expected to have an enlightened vision about how to reform society, and be a vanguard who is above certain rules.

That understanding of artists has to come down in the Christian community. Artists have a valuable contribution; when St. Paul is discussing the Spirit's power in the Church, he writes (I Cor 12:7-30, RSV):

> To each is given the manifestation of the Spirit for the common good. To one is given through the

Spirit the utterance of wisdom, and to another the utterance of knowledge according to the same Spirit, to another faith by the same Spirit, to another gifts of healing by the one Spirit, to another the working of miracles, to another prophecy, to another the ability to distinguish between spirits, to another various kinds of tongues, to another the interpretation of tongues. All these are inspired by one and the same Spirit, who apportions to each one individually as he wills. For just as the body is one and has many members, and all the members of the body, though many, are one body, so it is with Christ. For by one Spirit we were all baptized into one body -- Jews or Greeks, slaves or free -- and all were made to drink of one Spirit. For the body does not consist of one member but of many. If the foot should say, "Because I am not a hand, I do not belong to the body," that would not make it any less a part of the body. And if the ear should say, "Because I am not an eye, I do not belong to the body," that would not make it any less a part of the body. If the whole body were an eye, where would be the hearing? If the whole body were an ear, where would be the sense of smell? But as it is, God arranged the organs in the body, each one of them, as he chose. If all were a single organ, where would the body be? As it is, there are many parts, yet one body. The eye cannot say to the hand, "I have no need of you," nor again the head to the feet, "I have no need of you." On the contrary, the parts of the body which seem to be weaker are indispensable, and those parts of the body which we think less honorable we invest with the greater honor, and our unpresentable parts are treated with greater modesty, which our more presentable parts do not require. But God has so composed the body, giving the greater honor to the inferior part, that there may be no discord in the body,

> but that the members may have the same care for one another. If one member suffers, all suffer together; if one member is honored, all rejoice together. Now you are the body of Christ and individually members of it. And God has appointed in the church first apostles, second prophets, third teachers, then workers of miracles, then healers, helpers, administrators, speakers in various kinds of tongues. Are all apostles? Are all prophets? Are all teachers? Do all work miracles? Do all possess gifts of healing? Do all speak with tongues? Do all interpret?

I would suggest that the secular idea of an artisan is closer to an Orthodox understanding of an artist than the secular idea of artist itself. Even if an artisan is not thought of in terms of being a member of a body, the idea of an artisan is one that people can accept being one member of an organism in which all are needed.

An artisan can show loving craftsmanship, can show a personal touch, can have a creative spark, and should be seen as pursuing honorable work; however, the idea of an artisan carries less bad freight than the idea of an artist. They're also not too far apart: in the Middle Ages, the sculptors who worked on cathedrals were closer to what we would consider artisans who produced sculptures than being seen as today's artists. Art is or should be connected to iconography; it should also be connected to the artisan's craft, and people are more likely to give an artisan a place as a contributing member who is part of a community than artists.

If we look at technical documentation, then there are a number of believable compliments you could give if you bumped into the author. It would be believable to say that the documentation was a helpful reference met your need; that it was clear, concise, and well-written; or that it let you find exactly what you needed and get back to work. But it would sound odd to say that the technical writer had very distinctive insights, and even odder to say that you liked the author's personal self-expression about what the technology could do. Technical writing is not glorified self-expression, and if we venerate art that is glorified self-expression, then maybe we have something to learn from how we treat technical writing.

If this essay seems like a collection of distinctive (or less politely, idiosyncratic) personal insights I had, or my own personal self-expression in Orthodoxy, theology, and faith, then that is a red flag. It falls short of the mark of what art, or Orthodox writing, should be. (And it is intended as art: maybe it's minor art, but it's meant as art.) It's not just that most or all of the insights owe a debt to people who have gone before me, and I may have collated but contributed nothing to the best insights, serving much more to paraphrase than think things up from scratch. Michel Quenot's The Icon: A Window on the Kingdom, and, for much longer, Madeleine l'Engle's Walking on Water: Reflections on Faith and Art have both given me a grounding. But even aside from that, art has existed for long before me and will exist for long after me, and I am not the sole creator of an Orthodox or Christian approach to the arts any more than a technical writer has trailblazed a particular technique of creating such-and-such type of business report. Good art is freedom and does bear its human creator's fingerprints. Even iconography, with its traditional canons, gives substantial areas of freedom to the iconographer and never specify each detail. Part of being an iconographer is using that freedom well. However, if this essay is simply self-expression, that is a defect, not a merit. As an artist and writer, I am trying to offer more than glorified self-expression.

This Sunday after liturgy, people listened to a lecture taped from Bp. KALLISTOS Ware. He talked about the great encounter at the burning bush, when God revealed himself to Moses by giving his name. At the beginning of the encounter, Moses was told, "Take off your shoes, for the place you are standing is holy ground." Bp. KALLISTOS went on to talk about how in those days, as of the days of the Fathers, people's shoes were something dead, something made from leather. The Fathers talked about this passage as meaning by implication that we should take off our dead familiarity to be able to encounter God freshly.

I was surprised, because I had reinvented that removal of familiarity, and I had no idea it was a teaching of the Orthodox Church. Perhaps my approach to trying to see past the deadness of familiarity--which you can see in Game Review: Meatspace--was not exactly the same as what Bp. KALLISTOS was saying to begin a discussion about receiving Holy Communion properly. Yet I found out that something I could think of as my own private invention was in fact a rediscovery. I had reinvented one of the treasures of Orthodoxy. Part of Orthodoxy is surrender, and that acknowledgment that anything and everything we hold, no matter how dear, must be offered to God's Lordship for him to do with as we please. Orthodoxy is inescapably a slow road of pain and loss. But there is another truth, that things we think are a private heresy (I am thinking of G.K. Chesterton's discussion) are in fact a reinvention, perhaps a crude reinvention, of an Orthodox treasure and perhaps an Orthodox treasure which meets its best footing, deepest meaning, and fullest expression when that jewel is set in its Orthodox bezel.

There are times when I've wanted to be an iconographer (in the usual sense). I don't know if that grace will ever be granted me, but there was one point when I had access to an icon painting class. When I came to it and realized what was going on, I shied away. Perhaps I wanted to learn to write icons (Orthodox speak of writing icons rather than painting them), but there was something I wasn't comfortable with.

Parishes have, or at least should have, a meal together after worship, even if people think of it as "coffee hour" instead of thinking of it as the communion of a common meal. The purpose is less to distribute coffee, which coffee drinkers have enough of in their homes, than to provide an opportunity (perhaps with a social lubricant) for people to meet and talk. That meeting and talking is beautiful. Furthermore, a parish may have various events when people paint, seasonally decorate, or maintain the premises, and in my experience there can be, and perhaps should be, an air of lighthearted social gathering about it all.

But this iconography class had lots of chatter, where people gathered and learned the skill of icon painting that began and ended with a prayer but in between had the atmosphere of a casual secular gathering that didn't involve any particularly spiritual endeavor or skill. Now setting my personal opinions aside, the classical canons require that icons be written in prayer, concentration, and quiet. There are reasons for this, and I reacted as I did, not so much because I had heard people were breaking such-and-such ancient rule, but more because I was affronted by something that broke the rule's spirit even more than its letter, and I sensed that there was something askew. The reason is that icons are written in silence is that you cannot make a healthy, full, and spiritual icon simply by the motions of your body. An icon is first and foremost created through the iconographer's spirit to write what priests and canons have defined, and although the iconographer is the copyist or implementor and not original author, we believe that the icon is written by the soul of the iconographer--if you understand it as a particular (secular) painting technique, you don't understand it. That class, like that iconographer, have produced some of the dreariest and most opaque icons, or "windows of Heaven", that I have seen. I didn't join that class because however much I wanted to be an iconographer, I didn't want to become an iconographer like that, and in the Orthodox tradition you become an iconographer by becoming a specific iconographer's disciple and becoming steeped in that iconographer's spiritual characteristics.

Years ago, I stopped watching television, or at least started making a conscious effort to avoid it. I like and furthermore love music, but I don't put something on in the background. And, even though I love the world wide web, I observe careful limits, and not just because (as many warn) it is easy to get into porn. The web can be used to provide "noise" to keep us from coming face to face with the silence. The web (substitute "television"/"music"/"newspapers"/"movies"/for that matter, "Church Fathers" for how this temptation appears to you) can be used to anesthetize the boredom that comes when we face silence, and keep us from ever coming to the place on the other side of boredom. When I have made decisions about television, I wasn't thinking, on conscious terms, about being more moral and spiritual by so doing. I believe that television is a pack of cigarettes for the heart and mind, and I have found that I can be creative in more interesting ways, and live better, when I am cautious about the amount of noise in my life, even if you don't have to be the strictest "quiet person" in the world to reap benefits. Quiet is one spiritual discipline of the Orthodox Church (if perhaps a lesser spiritual discipline), and the spiritual atmosphere I pursued is a reinvention, perhaps lesser and incomplete, of something the Orthodox Church wants her iconographers to profitably live. There is a deep enough connection between icons and other art that it's relevant to her artists.

When I write what I would never call (or wish to call) my best work, I have the freedom to be arbitrary. If I'm writing something of no value, I can impose my will however I want. I can decide what I want to include and what I want to exclude, what I am going to go into detail about what I don't want to elaborate on, and what analogies I want to draw. It can be as much dictated by "Me! Me! Me!" as I want. When I am creating something I value, however, that version of freedom hardly applies. I am not free, if I am going to create fiction that will resonate and ring true, to steamroll over my characters' wishes. If I do I diminish my creation. What I am doing is loving and serving my creations. I can't say that I never act on selfish reasons, but if I am doing anything of a good job my focus is on loving my creation into being and taking care of what it needs, which is simultaneously a process of wrestling with it, and listening to it with the goal of getting myself out of the way so I can shape it as it needs to be shaped.

There is a relationship that places the artist as head and lord of his creation, but if we reach for some of the most readily available ideas of headship and lordship, that claim makes an awful lot of confusion. Until I began preparing to write this essay, it didn't even occur to me to look at the human creator-creation connection in terms of headship or lordship. I saw a place where I let go of arbitrary authority and any insistence on my freedoms to love my creation, to listen to and then serve it, and care for all the little details involved in creating it (and, in my case, publishing it on the web). All of this describes the very heart of how Christians are to understand headship, and my attitude is hardly unique: Christian artists who do not think consciously about headship at all create out of the core of the headship relation. They give their works not just any kind of love, but the particular and specific love which a head has for a body. If art ends by bearing the artist's fingerprints, this should not be because the artist has decided, "My art must tell of my glory," but because loved art, art that has been served and developed and educed and drawn into manifest being, cannot but be the image, and bear the imprint, of its creator. That is how art responds to its head and lord.

To return to spiritual discipline: Spiritual discipline is the safeguard and the shadow of love. This applies first and foremost to the Orthodox Way as a whole, but also specifically to art. Quiet is a lesser discipline, and may not make the front page. Fasting from certain foods can have value, but it is only good if saying no to yourself in food prepares you to love other people even when it means saying no to yourself. There are harsh warnings about people who fast and look down on others who are less careful about fasting or don't fast at all and judging them as "less spiritual". Perhaps fasting can have great value, but it is better not to fast than to fast and look down.

Prayer is the flagship, the core, and the crowning jewel of spiritual discipline. The deepest love for our neighbor made in God's image is to pray and act out of that prayer. Prayer may be enriched when it is connected with other spiritual disciplines, but the goal of spiritual discipline and the central discipline in creating art is prayer.

There is a passage in George MacDonald where a little girl stands before an old man and looks around an exquisite mansion in wonder. After a while the old man asks her, "Are you done saying your prayers?" The surprised child responds, "I wasn't saying my prayers." The old man said, "Yes you were. You just didn't realize it."

If I say that prayer drives art, I don't just mean that I say little prayers as I create art (although that should be true). I mean that when I am doing my best work, part of why it is my best work is that the process itself is an act of prayer. However many arbitrary freedoms I would not dare to exercise and deface my own creation, I am at my freest and most alive when I am listening to God and a creation about how to love it into being. It is not the same contemplation as the Divine Liturgy, but it is connected, part of the same organism. The freedom I taste when I create, the freedom of service and the freedom of love, is freedom at so deep a level that a merely arbitrary freedom to manipulate or make dictatorial insistences on a creation pales in comparison to the freedom to listen and do a thousand services to art that is waiting for me to create it.

"He who does not love his brother whom he has seen, cannot love God whom he has not seen." (I Jn 4:20, RSV). If an artist does not love God and the neighbors whom he can see and who manifest the glory of the invisible God, he is in a terrible position to healthily love a creation which--at the moment, exists in God's mind and partially in its human creator, but nowhere else. This is another way of saying that character matters. I have mentioned some off-the-beaten-track glimpses of spiritual discipline; this leaves out more obvious and important aspects of love like honesty and chastity. The character of an artist who can love his works into being should be an overflow of a Christian life of love. Not to say that you must be an artist to love! Goodness is many-sided. This is true of what Paul wrote (quoted above) about the eye, hand, and foot all belonging to the body. Paul also wrote the scintillating words (I Cor 15:35-49, RSV):

> But some one will ask, "How are the dead raised? With what kind of body do they come?" You

> foolish man! What you sow does not come to life unless it dies. And what you sow is not the body which is to be, but a bare kernel, perhaps of wheat or of some other grain. But God gives it a body as he has chosen, and to each kind of seed its own body. For not all flesh is alike, but there is one kind for men, another for animals, another for birds, and another for fish. There are celestial bodies and there are terrestrial bodies; but the glory of the celestial is one, and the glory of the terrestrial is another. There is one glory of the sun, and another glory of the moon, and another glory of the stars; for star differs from star in glory.
>
> So is it with the resurrection of the dead. What is sown is perishable, what is raised is imperishable. It is sown in dishonor, it is raised in glory. It is sown in weakness, it is raised in power. It is sown a physical body, it is raised a spiritual body. If there is a physical body, there is also a spiritual body. Thus it is written, "The first man Adam became a living being"; the last Adam became a life-giving spirit. But it is not the spiritual which is first but the physical, and then the spiritual. The first man was from the earth, a man of dust; the second man is from heaven. As was the man of dust, so are those who are of the dust; and as is the man of heaven, so are those who are of heaven. Just as we have borne the image of the man of dust, we shall also bear the image of the man of heaven.

These are words of resurrection, but the promise of the glorious and incorruptible resurrection body hinge on words where "star differs from star in glory". An artist's love is the glory of one star. It is no more the only star than the eye is the only part of the body. It is part of a scintillating spectrum--but not the whole spectrum itself!

I would like to also pause to respond to an objection which careful scholars would raise, and which some devout Orthodox would sense even if they might not put it in words. I have fairly uncritically used a typically Western conception of art. I have lumped together visual arts, literature, music, film, etc. and seem to assume that showing something in one case applied to every case. I would acknowledge that a more careful treatment would pay attention to their differences, and that some stick out more than others.

I am not sure that a better treatment would criticize this assumption. However, let's look at one distinctive of Orthodoxy. One thinks of why Western Christians talk about how the superficial legend goes that the leaders of (what would become) Russia went religion-shopping, and they saw that the Orthodox worship looked impressive, and instead of deciding based on a good reason, they went with the worship they liked best. Eastern Christians tend to agree about the details of what people believe happened, but we do not believe the aesthetic judgments were something superficial that wasn't a good reason. We believe that something of Heaven shone through, and if that affected the decision, people weren't making a superficial decision but something connected with Truth and the Light of Heaven and of God. We believe that worship, and houses of worship, are to be beautiful and reflect not only the love but the Light and beauty of Heaven, and a beautiful house of worship is no more superfluous to light than good manners are superfluous to love. The "beauty connection" has not meant that we have to choose between good homilies, music, liturgy, and icons. A proper Orthodox listing of what constituted real, iconic art may differ from a Western listing, and there's more than being sticks in the mud behind the fact that Orthodox Churches, by and large, do not project lyrics with PowerPoint. Part of what I have said about icons is crystallized in a goal of "transparency", that the goal of a window of Heaven is to be transparent to Heaven's light and love. Not just icons can be, or fail to be, transparent. Liturgical music can be transparent or fail to be transparent. Homilies can be transparent or fail to be transparent.

I've heard just enough bad homilies, that is opaque homilies that left me thinking about the homilist instead of God--to appreciate how iconically translucent most of the homilies I've heard are, and to realize that this is a privelege and not a right that will automatically be satisfied. The opaque Orthodox homilies don't (usually) get details wrong; they get the details right but don't go any further. But this is not the whole truth about homilies. A homily that is written like an icon--not necessarily written out but drawn into being first and foremost by the spirit, out of love, prayer, and spiritual discipline, can be not only transparent but luminous and let Heaven's light shine through.

Some wag said, "A sermon is something I wouldn't go across the street to hear, but something I'd go across the country to deliver." I do not mean by saying this to compete with, or replace, the view of homilies as guidance which God has provided for our good, but a successful homily does more than inform. It edifies, and the best homilies are luminously transparent. They don't leave the faithful thinking about the preacher--even about how good he is--but about the glory of God. When icons, liturgy, and homilies rise to transparency, they draw us beyond themselves to worship God.

My denser and more inaccessible musings might be worth reading, but they should never be read as a homily; the photographs in my slideshow of Cambridge might capture real beauty but should never be mounted on an icon stand for people to venerate; my best cooking experiments may be much more than edible but simply do not belong in the Eucharist--but my cooking can belong at coffee hour. The Divine Liturgy at its best builds up to Holy Communion and then flows into a common meal (in my culture, coffee hour) that may not be Holy Communion but is communion, and just as my more edible cooking may not be fit for the Eucharist but belongs in a common meal, I am delighted to tell people I have a literature and art website at **Jonathan's Corner** which has both short and long fiction, musings and essays, poetry, visual art, and (perhaps I mention) computer software that's more artistic than practical. I have put a lot of love into my website, and it gives me great pleasure to share it. If its contents should not usurp the place of holy icons or the Divine Liturgy, I believe they do belong in the fellowship hall and sacred life beyond the sanctuary. Worshipping life is head and lord to the everyday life of the worshipping faithful, but that does not mean a denigration of the faithful living as lesser priests. The sacramental priesthood exists precisely as the crystallization and ornament of our priestly life in the world. As I write, I am returning from the Eucharist and the ordination of more than one clergy. Orthodox clergy insist that unless people say "Amen!" to the consecration of the bread and wine which become the holy body and the holy blood of Christ, and unless they say, "Axios!" ("He is worthy!") to the ordination, then the consecration or the ordination doesn't happen. Unlike in Catholicism, a priest cannot celebrate the Divine Liturgy by himself in principle, because the Divine Liturgy is in principle the work of God accomplished through the cooperation of priest and faithful, and to say that a priest does this himself is as odd as saying that the priest has a hug or a conversation by himself. The priest is head and even lord of the parish, but under a richer, Christian understanding of headship and lordship, which means that as the artist in his care he must listen to the faithful God has entrusted to his inadequate care, listening to God about who God and not the priest wants them to become, and both serve them and love them into richer being. (And, just as it is wrong for an artist to domineer his creation, it is even more toxic for a priest to domineer, *ahem*, work to improve the faithful in his parish. The sharpest warning I've heard a bishop give to newly ordained clergy is about a priest who decided he was the best thing to happen to the parish in his care, and immediately set about improving all the faithful according to his enlightened vision. It was a much more bluntly delivered warning than I've said about doing that to art.) The priest is ordained as the crystallization and crown of the faithful's priestly call. The liturgy which priest (and faithful) is not to be cut off when the ceremony ends; it is to flow out and imprint its glory on the faithful's life and work. Not only the liturgical but the iconic is to flow out and set the pace for life.

Art is to be the broader expression of the iconic.

Icon of the Trinity, Rublev
One of the greatest icons in the Orthodox treasury

Our Crown of Thorns

I remember meeting a couple; the memory is not entirely pleasant. Almost the first thing they told me after being introduced was that their son was "an accident," and this was followed by telling me how hard it was to live their lives as they wanted when he was in the picture.

I do not doubt that they had no intent of conceiving a child, nor do I doubt that having their little boy hindered living their lives as they saw fit. But when I heard this, I wanted to almost scream to them that they should look at things differently. It was almost as if I was speaking with someone bright who had gotten a full ride scholarship to an excellent university, and was vociferously complaining about how much work the scholarship would require, and how cleanly it would cut them off from what they took for granted in their home town.

I did not think, at the time, about the boy as an icon of the Holy Trinity, not made by hands, or what it means to think of such an *icon* as "an accident." I was thinking mainly about a missed opportunity for growth. What I wanted to say was, "This boy was given to you for your deification! Why must you look on the means of your deification as a curse?"

Marriage and monasticism are opposites in many ways. But there are profound ways in which they provide the same thing, and not only by including a community. Marriage and monasticism both provide--in quite different ways--an opportunity to take up your cross and follow Christ, to grow into the I Corinthians 13 love that says, "When I became a man, I put childish ways behind me"--words that are belong in this hymn to love because love does not place its own desires at the center, but lives for something more. Those who are mature in love put the childish ways of living for themselves behind them, and love Christ through those others who are put in their lives. In marriage this is not just Hollywood-style exhilaration; on this point I recall words I heard from an older woman, that you don't know understand being in love when you're "a kid;" being in love is what you have when you've been married for decades. Hollywood promises a love that is about having your desires fulfilled; I did not ask that woman about what more there is to being in love, but it struck me as both beautiful and powerful that the one thing said by to me by an older woman, grieving the loss of her husband, was that there is much more to being in love than what you understand when you are young enough that marriage seems like a way to satisfy your desires.

Marriage is not just an environment for children to grow up; it is also an environment for parents to grow up, and it does this as a crown of thorns.

The monastic crown of thorns includes an obedience to one's elder that is meant to be difficult. There would be some fundamental confusion in making that obedience optional, to give monastics more control and make things less difficult. The problem is not that it would fail to make a more pleasant, and less demanding, option than absolute obedience to a monastic elder. The problem is that when it was making things more pleasant and less demanding, it would break the spine of a lifegiving struggle--which is almost exactly what contraception promises.

Rearing children is not required of monastics, and monastic obedience is not required married faithful. But the spiritual struggle, the crown of thorns by which we take up our cross and follow Christ, by which we die to ourselves that we live in Christ, is not something we can improve our lives by escaping. The very thing we can escape by contraception, is what all of us--married, monastic, or anything else--need. The person who needs monastic obedience to be a crown of thorns is not the elder, but the monastic under obedience. Obedience is no more a mere aid to one's monastic elder than our medicines are something to help our doctors. There is some error in thinking that some people will be freed to live better lives, if they can have marriage, but have it on their own terms, "a la carte."

What contraception helps people flee is a spiritual condition, a sharpening, a struggle, a proving grounds and a training arena, that *all* of us need. There is life in death. We find a rose atop the thorns, and the space which looks like a constricting prison from the outside, has the heavens' vast expanse once we view it from the inside. It is rather like the stable on Christmas' day: it looks on the outside like a terrible little place, but on the inside it holds a Treasure that is greater than all the world. But we need first to give up the illusion of living our own lives, and "practice dying" each day, dying to ideas, our self-image, our self-will, having our way and our sense that the world will be better if we have our way--or even that *we* will be better if we have our way. Only when we have given up the illusion of living our own lives… will we be touched by the mystery and find ourselves living God's own life.

The Horn of Joy

A Meditation on Eternity and Time, Kairos and Chronos

As I write, I am in a couch in a large parlor looking out on an atrium with over a dozen marble pillars, onto another parlor on the other side. I have spent the day wandering around a college campus and enjoying the exploration. I've gotten little of the homework done that I meant to do (reading and writing about a theologian), and spent most of my energies trying to dodge the sense that the best way to explain what I want to explain about time is to begin with a classical form of alchemy. (The other alternative to lead into the discussion would be to start talking about Augustine, but that could more easily create a false familiarity. Alchemy is a more jarring image.)

Alchemy is one of those subjects most people learn about by rumor, which means in that case that almost everything we "know" about it is false. Trying to understand it through today's ideas of science, magic, and proto-science is like trying to understand nonfiction reference materials, like an encyclopedia, through the categories of fiction and poetry, or conversely trying to understand fictional and poetic works through (the non-fiction parts of) the Dewey Decimal system.

It is much more accurate to say that alchemy is a particular religious tradition, perhaps a flawed religious tradition, which was meant to transform its practitioners and embrace matter in the process. It may be rejected as heresy, but it is impossible to really understand heresy until you understand that heresy is impressively similar to orthodox Christianity, confusingly similar, and 'heresy' does *not* mean "the absolute opposite of what Christians believe." (Heresy is *far* more seductive than that.) Perhaps you may have heard the rumor that alchemists sought to turn lead into gold. The verdict on this historical urban legend, as with many urban legends, is, "Yes, *but*..."

Alchemy sought a way to turn lead into gold, but it has absolutely nothing to offer the greedy person who wants money to indulge his greed. Alchemy is scarcely more about turning lead into gold than astronomy is about telescopes. A telescope is a tool an astronomer uses to observe his real quarry, the stars as best they can be observed, and the alchemist, who sought to make matter into spirit and spirit into matter was trying to establish a spiritual bond with the matter so that the metals were incorporated into the person being performed. An Orthodox Christian might say the alchemist was seeking to be transfigured, even if that was a spiritually toxic way of seeking transfiguration or transformation--which is to say that the alchemist sought a profound and spiritual good. The alchemist sought gold that was above 24 karat purity, which is absurd if you think in today's material terms about a karat gold that was chemically up to 100% (24k) pure)... but what we call a "chemist" today is the successor to what alchemists called "charcoal blowers", and chemistry today is a more sophisticated form of what the "charcoal blowers" were doing, not the alchemists. But the desire for purer-than-24k-gold becomes a much clearer and more intelligible desire when you understand that gold was not seen by the alchemists as simply a "container" for economic value, but the most noble substance in the material world. (And a "material" world that is not just "material" as Americans today would understand it.) If you look at Jesus' words in the Sermon on the Mount about "Store up treasures in Heaven," and "Do not store up treasures on earth," the alchemists' desire to transmute metals and eventually produce gold is much more of a treasure in Heaven than merely a treasure on earth. (Think about why it is better to have a heart of gold and no merely physical gold than have all the merely physical gold in the world and a heart of ice with it.)

Newton, introduced to me as one of the greatest physicists, spent more time on alchemy than on the science he is remembered for today. He was also, among other things, an incredibly abrasive person and proof that while alchemy promises spiritual transformation it at least sometimes fails miserably, and there are a lot of other scathing things one could say about alchemy that I will refrain from saying. But I would like to suggest one way we could learn something from the alchemists:

When I wanted to explain the term "charcoal blower" by giving a good analogy for it, I searched and searched and couldn't find the same kind of pejorative term today. I don't mean that I couldn't find another epithet that was equally abrasive; we have insults just as insulting. But I couldn't find another term that was pejorative *for the same reason.* The closest parallels I found (and they were reasonably close parallels) to what lie behind the name of "charcoal blower" would be how a serious artist would see a colleague who produced mercenary propaganda for the highest bidder, or how a clergyman who chose the ministry to love God and serve his neighbor would view people who entered the clergy for prestige and power over others. (It may be a sign of a problem on our side that while we can understand why people might be offended in these cases, we do not (as the alchemists did) have a term that embodies that reprobation. The alchemists called proto-chemists "charcoal blowers" because the alchemists had a pulse.)

To an alchemist, a "charcoal blower" was someone merely interested in what we would today call the science of chemistry and its applications--and someone who completely failed to pursue spiritual purification. Calling someone a "charcoal blower" is akin to calling someone an "irreligious, power hungry minister." Whether they were right in this estimation or not, alchemists would not have recognized chemistry as a more mature development of alchemy. They would have seen today's chemistry as a completely unspiritual parody of their endeavor: perhaps a meticulous and sophisticated unspiritual parody, but a parody none the less.

This provides a glimpse of a thing, or a kind of thing, that can be very difficult to see today. "Alchemy is a crude, superstitious predecessor to real chemistry" or "Chemistry is alchemy that's gotten its act together" is what people often assume when the only categories they have are shaped by our age's massive scientific influence.

Science is a big enough force that young earth Creationists deny Darwinian evolution by assuming that Genesis 1 is answering the same kind of questions that evolution is concerned with, namely "What were the material details of how life came to be?"/"What was the mechanism that caused those details to happen?" That is to say, young earth Creationism still assumes that if Genesis 1 is true, that could only mean that it is doing the same job as evolution while providing different answers. It is very difficult for many people to see that Genesis 1-2 might address questions that evolution never raises: neo-Darwinian evolution is silent or ambivalent about all questions of meaning (if it does not answer "There is no meaning and that is not a question mature scientists should ask."). It is a serious problem if young earth proponents can read Genesis 1 and be insensitive to how the texts speak to questions of "What significance/meaning/purpose/goal does each creation and the whole Creation live and breathe?" This may be a simplification, but we live in enough of a scientific age that many people who oppose the juggernaut (in this case, neo-Darwinian evolution) still resort to disturbingly scientific frameworks and can show a pathological dependence of scientific ways of looking at the world, even when there is no conscious attempt to be scientific. Perhaps evolutionists may accuse young earth Creationists of not being scientific enough, but I would suggest that the deepest problem is that they are *too* scientific: they may not meet the yardstick in non-Creationist biology departments, but they try to play the game of science hard enough that whatever critique you may offer of their success in gaining science's sight, nobody notices how perfectly they gain science's blind spots--even when they are blind spots that make more sense to find in a neo-Darwinist but are extremely strange in a religiously motivated movement.

This is symptomatic of today's *Zeitgeist*, and it affects our understanding of time.

Time is something that I don't think can be unraveled without being able to question the assumed science-like categories and framework that define what is thinkable when we have no pretensions of thinking scientifically, along lines like what I have said of alchemy. I'm not really interested in calling chemists "charcoal blowers": the Pythagoreans would probably censure me in similar vein after finding I ranked such-and-such in a major math competition, did my first master's in applied math, and to their horror studied a mathematics that was *completely* secularized and had absolutely nothing of the "sacred science"/"spiritual discipline" character of their geometry left.

I may not want to call scientists "charcoal blowers", but I *do* want to say and explore things that cannot be said unless we appreciate something else. That something else... If you say that alchemy disintegrated to become chemistry, that something else disintegrated in alchemy with its secrets and something else purportedly better than what was in the open. Alchemy has a host of problems that need to be peeled back; they may be different problems than those of our scientific age, and it may make a helpful illustration before the peeling back further and cutting deeper that is my real goal, but it is a problematic illustration.

I once would have said that classical (Newtonian) physics was simply a mathematical formalization of our common sense. My idea of this began when I was taking a class that dealt with modern physics (after covering Einstein's theory of relativity). I grappled with something that many budding physicists grapple with: compared to classical physics, the theory of relativity and modern physics are remarkably counter-intuitive. One wag said, "God said, 'Let there be light!' And there was Newton. The Devil howled, 'Let darkness return!' And there was Einstein [and then modern physics], and the status quo was restored." Modern physics may describe our world's behavior more accurately, but it takes the strangest route to get to its result: not only is light both a particle and a wave, but everything, from a sound wave to you, is both a particle and a wave; nothing is exactly at any one place (we're all spread throughout the whole universe but particularly densely concentrated in some places more than others); it can depend on your frame of reference whether two things happen simultaneously; Newton's mathematically simple, coherent, lovely grid for all of space no longer exists, even if you don't consider space having all sorts of curvatures that aren't *that* hard to describe mathematically but are impossible to directly visualize. (And that was before superstring theory came into vogue; it seems that whatever doesn't kill physics makes it *stranger.*)

I would make one perhaps subtle, but important, change to what I said earlier, that classical Newtonian physics is a mathematical expression of common sense: I had things backwards and *the Western common sense I grew up with is a non-mathematical paraphrase of classical physics*.

One thing Einstein dismantled was a single absolute grid for space and a single timeline that everything fit on. That was something Newton (and perhaps others--see the chapter "The Remarkable Masculine Birth of Time" in Science as Salvation, Mary Midgley) worked hard to establish. What people are not fond of saying today is that "It's all relative" is something people might like to be backed by Einstein's theory, but *relativity* is no more *relativism* than 'lightning' is 'lightning bug'. In that sense the theory of relativity makes a far smaller difference than you might expect... Einstein if anything fine-tuned Newton's timeline and grid and left behind something practically indistinguishable. But let's look at Newton's timeline and not look at almost equivalent replacements later physics has fine-tuned. All of space fits on a single absolute grid and all of time is to be understood in terms of its place on a timeline. This is physics shaping the rest of its culture. *It's also something many cultures do not share.* I do not mean that the laws of physics only apply where people believe in them; setting aside miracles, a stove works as Newtonian physics says it should whether you worship Newton, defy him and disbelieve him whenever you can, or simply have never thought of physics in connection with your stove. I don't mean that kind of "subjective reality". That's not what I'm saying. But the experience of space as "what fits on a grid", so that a grid you cannot touch is a deeper reality than the things you see and touch every day, and the experience of time as "what fits on a timeline" is something that can be weaker or often nonexistent in other cultures. It's not an essential to how humans automatically experience the world.

There is a medieval icon of two saints from different centuries meeting; this is not a strange thing to portray in a medieval context because much as space was not "what fills out a grid" but spaces (plural) which were more or less their own worlds, enclosed as our rooms are, time was not defined as "what clocks measure" even if people just began to use clocks.

Quick--what are the time and date? I would expect you to know the year immediately (or maybe misremember because the year has just changed), and quite possibly have a watch that keeps track of seconds.

Quick--what latitude and longitude you are at? If you didn't or don't know the Chicago area and read in a human interest news story that someone took an afternoon stroll from Homewood to Schaumburg, IL, would those two names make the statement seem strange?

What if you continued reading and found out that Homewood is at 41°34'46"N and 87°39'57"W and Schaumburg is at 42°01'39"N and 88°05'32W? Setting aside the quite significant fact that most of us don't tell latitude and longitude when we see a place name, what would that say?

If you do the calculations, you see that saying someone walked from Homewood to Schaumburg and back in an afternoon is like a newspaper saying that the President was born in 671.

Schaumburg and Homewood are both Chicago suburbs, but in almost opposite directions, and to the best of my knowledge no distance runner could run from Homewood to Schaumburg to Homewood in an afternoon--even in good traffic the drive would chew up more than a little bit of an afternoon.

Do you see the difference between how we approach and experience our position on the time-grid on the one-hand, and our latitudinal and longitudinal position on the other? Setting aside various questions about calendars, I would suggest that the way most of us neither know nor care what latitude and longitude we're at, can give a glimpse into how a great many people neither know nor cared not only what a watch says but what century they're in. (*Quick*--does your country include the "turn of the century" for degrees latitude or longitude?)

There are other things to say; I want to get into chronos or kairos, and some of the meaning of "You cannot kill time without injuring eternity." (One facet, besides the wordplay, is that time is an image of not only eternity but the Eternal One.) There are several images of time, or names of time, that I wish to explore; none of them is perfect, but all of them say something. But first let me give the question I am trying to answer.

The Question

Before I say more about time in the sense of giving names to it, I would like to explain the question I am trying to answer, because it is perhaps idiosyncratically my own question, and one that may not be entirely obvious.

There is a book on college admissions essays that listed cliché student essays that almost immediately make an admissions reader's eyes glaze over. Among these was The Travel Experience, which went something like this:

> In my trip to ________, I discovered a different way of life that challenged many of my assumptions. It even challenged assumptions I didn't know I had!

> Yet I discovered that their way of life is also valid and also human.

Note that this boiled down essay is ambiguous, not only about what region or what country, but for that matter what continent the writer has been to. And thus, however deep and interesting the experience itself may have been, the writeup is cliché and uninteresting.

This, in my opinion, is because the experience is deep in a way that is difficult to convey. If something funny happened yesterday on the way to the store, it is perfectly straightforward to explain what happened, but a deep cross-cultural counter is the sort of thing people grasp at words to convey. It's like the deepest gratitude that doesn't know how to express itself except by repeating the cliché, "Words cannot express my gratitude to you."

I'm from the U.S. and have lived in Malaysia, France, and England (in that order). I was only in Malaysia for a couple of months, but I was baptized there, and I have fond memories of my time there--I understand why a lot of Westerners come to Malaysia and want to spend the rest of their lives there.

One thing I changed there was how quickly I walked. Before then, I walked at a swift clip. But walking that way comes across somewhere between strange and bothersome, and I had to learn to walk slowly--and that was the beginning of my encounter with time in Malaysia. In the cliché above, I learned that some things that were to me not just presuppositions but "just the way things were" were in fact not "just the way things were" but cultural assumptions and a cultural way of experiencing time, which could be experienced very differently.

Some of this is an "ex-pat" experience of time in Malaysia rather than a native Malaysian experience of Malaysian time (there are important differences between the two), but the best concise way I can describe it is that there are people in the U.S. who try and want to escape the "tyranny of the clock," and the tyranny of the clock is frequently criticized in some circles, but in Malaysia there is much less tyranny of the clock--I was tempted to say the tyranny of the clock didn't exist at all. People walk more slowly because walking is not something you rush through just to get it done, even if it's important that you arrive where you're walking to.

Every place I've lived I've taken something away. The biggest personal change I took from Malaysia had to do with time. That experience gave me something I personally would not have gained from hearing and even agreeing with complaints about the tyranny of the clock. The first domino started to topple in Malaysia, and the chain continued after I returned to the U.S.

What I tried to do on the outside was move more slowly and rebel against the clock, and on the inside to experience, or cultivate, a different time more slowly. (I was trying to be less time-bound, but interacted with time in ways I didn't do before Malaysia.) I still tried (and still try) to meet people on time, but where I had freedom, the clock was as absent as I could make it. And it was essentially an internal experience, in a sort of classically postmodern fashion. I wore a watch, but changed its meaning. Augustine regarded there being something evil about our existence being rationed out to us, God having his whole existence in one "eternal moment"; I equated time with the tyranny of the clock and "what a clock measures", and called timelessness a virtue. If we set aside the inconsistency between trying to "escape" time as not basically good and digging more and more deeply into time, you have something that was growing in me, with nuance, over the years since I've been in Malaysia.

That sets much of the stage for why I began to write this. In one sense, this is an answer to "What can time be besides what the tyranny of the clock says it is?" In another sense it is recognizing that I took something good from Malaysia, but didn't quite hit the nail on the head: I regarded time as basically evil, something to neutralize and minimize even as I was in it, which I now repent of. That is an incorrect way of trying to articulate something good. I would like to both correct and build upon my earlier living-of-time, beginning with what might be called **the flesh of the Incarnation**.

The Flesh of the Incarnation

One time several friends and I were together, and one of them, who is quite strong but is silver-haired, talked about how he couldn't put a finger on it, but he saw a sadness in the fact that the closest place for him to be buried that would satisfy certain Orthodox concerns was a couple of states over. I said that there were Nobel prizes for literature and economics, but there would never be a Nobel prize for scamming seniors out of their retirement. In that sense the Nobel prize is not just an honor for the negligible handful of physicists who receive that accolade, but every physicist. Perhaps there are a great many more honorable professions than there are Nobel prizes, but the Nobel prize doesn't vacuously say that physics is a good thing but specifically recognizes one physicist at a time, and by implication honors those who share in the same labor.

I said that "God does not make any generic people," and I clarified that in the Incarnation, Jesus was not a sort of "generic person" ("I went to the general store and they wouldn't sell me anything specific!") who sort of generically blessed the earth and in some generic fashion sympathized with those of us specific people who live in time. God has never made a specific person, and when Christ became incarnate, he became a specific man in a specific place at a specific time. As much as we are all specific people who live in a specific place at a specific time, he became a specific person who lived in a specific place at a specific time, and by doing that he honored every place and time.

"The flesh of the Incarnation," in Orthodox understanding, is not and cannot be limited to what an atheist trying to be rigorous would consider the body of Christ. The Incarnation is a shock wave ever reaching out in different directions. One direction is that the Son of God became a Man that men might become the Sons of God. Another direction is that Christ the Savior of man or the Church can never be separated from Christ the Savior of the whole cosmos, and for people who are concerned with ecology, Christ's shockwave cannot but say something profound from the Creation which we must care for. Sacraments and icons are part of this Transfigured matter, and the Transfiguration is a glimpse of what God is working not only for his human faithful but the entire universe he created to share in his glory.

To me at least, "the flesh of the Incarnation" is why, while the Catholic Church is willing to experiment with different philosophies and culture, because they are not part of the theological core, the Orthodox Church has preserved a far greater core of the patristic philosophy and culture. It is as if the Catholic Church, getting too much Augustine (or even worse, DesCartes), said "Spirit and matter are different things; so are theology and philosophy. We must keep the spirit of theology, but matter is separate and can be replaced." An Orthodox reply might be "Spirit and matter are connected at the most intimate level; so are theology, philosophy and culture. We must keep the spirit of theology without separating it from the philosophy and culture which have been the flesh of the Incarnation from the Church's origin."

If Jesus was not a "generic person", and I am not supposed to be a "generic person", then the place in time he made for you is to be transfigured as the flesh of the Incarnation. What I mean by "the flesh of the Incarnation" is that Christ became Incarnate at a specific time and place, and by so doing he honored not only your flesh and mine--he is as much a son of Adam as you and me--but every time and place.

There is a major Orthodox exegesis which looks at the Gospels and says that when Pilate presented Christ to the crowd and said, "*Idou ton anthropon.*" ("Behold the man", Jn 19.5), he was prophesying like Caiphas and (perhaps without knowing it) completing the Genesis story; when Christ on the cross said, "It is finished," he announced that the work of Creation which was begun in Genesis had come to its conclusion--not, perhaps, the end of history, but the beginning of the fulness which Creation always needed but is only found at the cross. There are theologians today which answer the question "When did God create the earth?" by giving the date of the crucifixion: not that nothing existed before then, but then it was made complete. 25 March 28 AD is, in commercial terms, not the beginning of when prototypes began to be assembled and plans began to be made towards a product release, but the date that the finished product is released and thereafter available to the public. The Cross is the axis of the world, so that the Incarnation is not simply the central event in history but the defining event, not only in the time and place that we falsely consider remote which Jesus lived in, but your time and mine.

A Paradox: Historical Accuracy and Timelessness

I read a cultural commentary on the Bible cover to cover, and in one sense I'm glad I read it, but in another sense, I think I would have been better off reading the Bible cover to cover another time. Or, for that matter, creating computer software or pursuing some other interest outside of the Bible and theology.

Years earlier, I said I wished I could read a cultural commentary on the Bible, but reading it drove home a point in a Dorothy Sayers essay. The essay suggested that "period awareness", our sharp sense of "That was then and this is now" that puts such a sharp break between the past and the present, is a product of the Enlightenment and something a great many periods do not share. When one reads the Canterbury Tales and asks what they thought about cultures, the answer is that though the stories begin in classical times there is no modern sense of "These people lived in another time so I need to try to be historically accurate and keep track of lots of historical context to take them seriously."

What I have realized, partly in writing my first theology thesis in Biblical studies, was that a lot of cultural commentary is spiritually inert when it is not used as a tool to manipulate or neutralize the Bible for contradicting what's in vogue today. Even when the sizeable "lobbyist" misuse of cultural context is ignored, there is a big difference between scholarly cultural and historical inquiry and a cultural sermon illustration--and it's *not* that less scholarly pastors do a half-baked job of something "real" scholars do much better. Cultural sermon comments are selected from a vast body of knowledge specifically because they illuminate the text and therefore at least can enhance how the text speaks to us. "Serious", "real" scholarship tends to bury the text's meaning under a lot of details and result in the same kind of loss of meaning that would happen if someone asked what a Pulitzer Prize-winning novel meant and the answer was to explain try to explain everything about how the novel came to be, including how the author's food was prepared, how the editing process was managed, and perhaps a few notes on how a Pulitzer Prize novel, after the award is received, is marketed differently from novels that haven't received that award.

I would like to suggest that in this piece my opening historical illustration did not detail everything a "historical-critical" study would get bogged down in, and showed independence from the historical-critical version of what scholarly accuracy means *precisely as it challenged a popular historical misunderstanding of alchemy.*

How does this fit together? There are two things. First of all, I disagree with most scholarship's center of gravity. "Historical-critical" scholarship, in a bad imitation of materially focused science, has a material center of gravity, and almost the whole of its rigor can be described in saying, "Look down as carefully as you can!" There is a painting which shows two philosophers, Plato and Aristotle. You can tell them apart because Plato is pointing up with one finger, and Aristotle is pointing down to material particulars with one finger. The problem with "historical-critical" scholarship in theology--and not only "historical-critical" scholarship--is that it asks Aristotle to do Plato's work. It asks the details of history to provide theological meaning. (Which is a bit like using a microscope to view a landscape, only worse and having more kinds of problems.)

Dorothy Sayers points out that up until the Enlightenment, people producing Shakespeare plays made no more effort to have the actors dress like people did in Shakespeare's days than Shakespeare himself felt the need to dress ancient characters in authentic Roman styles of clothing. Shakespeare's plays were produced because they had something powerful that spoke to people, and people didn't have this rigid historical dictate that said "If you will produce Shakespeare authentically, that means you go out of your way to acquire costumes nobody wears today." In the Globe Theatre, people were dressed up like... well, *people*, whether that meant Rome or the "here and now". And now theatre companies will be provocative or "creative" and change the setting in a Shakespeare play so that things look like some romanticization of the Wild West, or classy 20's gangsters, or (*yawn*) contemporary to us, but if you exclude people who are being a bit provocative, the normal way of putting on Shakespeare is not by having people dress the way people normally dress, but by doing research and putting people in exotic clothing that clearly labels the characters as being From Another Time.

Shakespeare's plays are produced today because they speak today, in other words because they are timeless. Being timeless doesn't mean literally being unrelated to any specific historical context ("I went to the general store and they wouldn't sell me anything specific!"). It means that something appears in a particular context and in that context expresses human-ness richly and fully enough that that human fingerprint speaks beyond the initial context. It means that there is a human bond that can bridge the gap of time as beautifully as two people having a friendship that simultaneously embraces and reaches beyond the differences of culture that exist between their nations. And it reflects a center of gravity that the important thing about Shakespeare is not that his English was hard to understand even hundreds of years ago, nor that people dressed a certain way that is different from any country today, but a human, spiritual center of gravity that not only speaks powerfully in the West centuries later but speaks powerfully outside the West. Shakespeare's center of gravity is not in this or that detail, but in a human pulse.

Wind and Spirit

Let me look at something that appears to be unrelated.

The wind blows where it wills, and you hear the sound of it, but you do not know where it comes from or where it goes; so it is with every one who is born of the Spirit.	The wind blows where it wills, and you hear the sound of it, but you do not know where it comes from or where it goes; so it is every one who is born of the Wind.	The Spirit Spirits where it wills, and you hear the sound of it, but you do not know where it comes from or where it goes; so it is with every one who is born of the Spirit.

You don't need to study ancient languages to know the Bible well, but there are occasional points where a language issue cuts something out of the text.

In the text above (Jn 3.8), from Jesus' discussion of flesh and Spirit/spirit, the same word in Greek (ΠΝΕΥΜΑ) carries the meaning of "Spirit", "spirit", and "wind" in the broader passage. I was tempted to write that ΠΝΕΥΜΑ carries that range of meanings, but that's a little more deceptive than I'm comfortable with. It would be more accurate to say that neither "spirit" and "wind", nor "Spirit and spirit", represented sharply distinguished categories. In a way Jesus is punning but in a way he is making an observation about spirit/wind that does not rest on the distinction.

Let me quote the RSV for the longer passage (Jn 3.1-12):

> Now there was a man of the Pharisees, named Nicode'mus, a ruler of the Jews. This man came to Jesus by night and said to him, "Rabbi, we know that you are a teacher come from God; for no one can do these signs that you do, unless God is with him."
>
> Jesus answered him, "Truly, truly, I say to you, unless one is born anew, he cannot see the kingdom of God."

> Nicode'mus said to him, "How can a man be born when he is old? Can he enter a second time into his mother's womb and be born?"
>
> Jesus answered, "Truly, truly, I say to you, unless one is born of water and the Spirit, he cannot enter the kingdom of God. That which is born of the flesh is flesh, and that which is born of the Spirit is spirit. Do not marvel that I said to you, `You must be born anew.' The wind blows where it wills, and you hear the sound of it, but you do not know whence it comes or whither it goes; so it is with every one who is born of the Spirit."
>
> Nicode'mus said to him, "How can this be?"
>
> Jesus answered him, "Are you a teacher of Israel, and yet you do not understand this? Truly, truly, I say to you, we speak of what we know, and bear witness to what we have seen; but you do not receive our testimony. If I have told you earthly things and you do not believe, how can you believe if I tell you heavenly things?

This is a rather big passage to try to unravel, but let me point out one thing. Jesus is dealing with a spiritual leader, and that leader's question, "How can a man be born when he is old?" is probably not just a failure to recognize that Jesus was speaking figuratively (especially if "figuratively" means what it means today, i.e. "a consolation prize for something that is dismissed as not true, at least not literally"). Besides saying that Nicodemus might not be stupid, I might suggest that his failure to understand underscores that he was being told something that's difficult to understand.

I'm almost tempted to write ΠΝΕΥΜΑ instead of spirit or Spirit because that forces a distinction that isn't there at all in the Greek New Testament and often may not belong in good theology. With that noted, I'm going to write Spirit with the understanding that it is often not meant to be read as separated from spirit and often not distinguished.

A group of people misunderstood this and other Spirit/flesh texts to mean that we should live in the part of us that is spirit and the part of it that was flesh, and they made a number of theological errors, and unfortunately some Christians have since treated the Spirit/flesh texts as a "problem" that needs to be "handled" (and, one might infer, not quite something that was put in the Bible because it would help us). This reaction makes it harder to understand some passages that say something valuable.

We are to become all Spirit. This does not, as those Gnostics believed, mean that our bodies are evil, or that any part of God's Creation is created evil. To become Spirit is to begin to live the life of Heaven here on earth. That doesn't mean that what is not-God in our lives now is eliminated; it means that our whole lives are to become divine. It means that the whole cosmos has been in need of salvation, and Christ comes as Savior to his whole Creation and his whole Creation is to be drawn into him and made divine. If you buy a gift for a friend, let us say a watch, and delight in giving it, that watch is no longer merely a possession you can horde, not just something a machine spat out. It is part of your friendship with that friend and it has been drawn from the store aisle into that friendship. To use an ancient metaphor, it has been drawn into the body under the head of friendship. (And now it means something a factory could never put into it.) If you have begun to believe that things don't boil down to a materialist's bottom line, the watch has become more real. In the same sense, not just our "souls" or "spirits" misunderstood as opposite to our bodies, but all of us and all of our lives are to become Spirit, or in the more usual Orthodox terminology become deified or divinized.

To say that the here and now that God has placed us in is "the flesh of the Incarnation" is not intended as some kind of opposite to Spirit. That flesh *is* spiritual; it is the whole Creation as it becomes Spirit and as it has become Spirit.

That much is generic; it is legitimate to say about time, because it is legitimate to say about almost anything. I would now like to turn and say something more specific about time.

I don't like to put things in terms of "synchronicity." For those of you not familiar with synchronicity, it's an idea that there is more to causality and time than isolated particles moving along a linear timeline, which is well and good, but this is a body missing its head, the Spirit. It's kind of a strange way of being spiritual while not being fully connected to Spirit.

"That which is born of flesh is flesh; that which is born of Spirit is Spirit. The Spirit Spirits where it wills, and you hear the sound of it, but you do not know where it comes from or where it goes; *so it is with every one who is born of the Spirit*."

To live in the Spirit, and to become Spirit, is for one and the same reason the proper footing for synchronicity, synchronicity done right, and moving beyond "subjective time." Let me talk about subjective time before talking more about synchronicity.

Subjective time is what some people have observed when people have realized that a watch is a poor indicator of how we experience time. Time flies; it can drag; but whatever watches can do, they don't tell how fast it seems like time is moving. In other words, subjective time at least is not what a watch measures. Now this is good as an answer to the question "What can we call time besides 'what a watch measures'?" but doesn't go far enough. Subjective time is the subjective time of a "me, myself, and I". It is the time of an atom, that cannot be divided further. And that limits it.

Time in the Spirit is an orchestrated, community dance. Not that the specific person is annihilated, but the specific person is transfigured. And that means that what is merely part of the private inner world of a "me, myself, and I" is in fact something vibrant in a community. Liturgical time, which I will talk about later, is one instrument of this sharing. But it is not the only one. God is the Great Choreographer, and when his Spirit orders the dance, it is everything in synchronicity and everything in subjective time and more. What was eerie, a strange occult thing people try to mine out in Jungian synchronicity becomes a pile of gold out in the open. If Jungian synchronicity is a series of opportunities to shrewdly steal food, the Dance is an invitation to join the banquet table.

Dance, then, wherever you may be, for I am the Lord of the Dance, said he. (Old Shaker hymn)

Immortalists and Transhumanists

I was reading a novel by one of my favorite authors in which some troubled characters constantly waxed eloquent about a movement, the "Immortalists", which struck me as rather far-fetched, too preposterous a motivation for literature... until I found a group very much like them, the Transhumanist movement, on the web.

The idea of Transhumanism is that we have lived in biological bodies so far, but we are on the cusp of making progress, and "progress" is improving on the human race so that we humans (or transitional humans--"Transhumanism" abbreviates "transitional-human-ism", and transhumanists consider themselves transhuman) can be replaced by some "posthuman" (this is supposed to be a good thing) creatures of our own devising which are always as high as if they were on crack (or higher), can run and jump like superheroes, and in general represent the fulfillment of a certain class of fantasies. (It's like disturbing science fiction, only they're dead serious about replacing the human race with something they consider better.) It's the only time reading philosophy on the web has moved me to nausea, and that broad nexus of spiritual forces is something I tried to lampoon in Yonder.

Setting that obscure movement aside, it seems a lot like the progress of technology has been to achieve watered-down transhumanist goals while we live in the bodies God gave us. I read an interesting article describing how before electric lights even though there were candles most of society seemed to shut down at sundown. Now people tend to kind of sleep when it's dark and kind of sleep when it's light, but we have made ourselves independent of something most humans in history (let alone before history) were tightly attuned to. I can also buy pills to take to subdue pain, or slightly misuse my body and not feel as much of the natural pain. If I don't care either about my health or breaking laws that are there for our good, there are illicit pills that could make me colossally strong: I'm moderately strong now but I could become stronger than most professional athletes. As a member of my society I have space-conquering tools--a telling name--which mean that I can move around the world and I can email and talk with people without knowing and perhaps without caring if they are next door or a thousand miles away. I can also take other pills when I get much older and defeat the normal limits age puts on lust. There are a lot of limits humans have lived with time out of mind, but we've discovered how to push them aside.

I heard of a dialogue where one person said, "I don't have enough time," and received the answer, "*You have all the time there is.*" In many cultures people experience time more as something that surrounds them but they're not terribly aware of, like the air they breathe, than a sort of scant commodity one cannot have enough of. And that is a clue to something.

However much we've figured out mini-transhumanist ways to push back limitations, the limitation of "all the time there is" is one we can't eliminate. We can fudge a bit with coffee or buy into some time management system, but there is a specific significance to time in our culture that wouldn't be there in other cultures where people rise at sunrise and go to sleep at sunset. Compared to how much we can neutralize other limitations, the limitation of "all the time there is" is a limitation that resists most neutralization.

That sounds terrible, but I would draw your attention to what Transhumanism is really after. I heard one professor refer to a centuries-old Utopian vision of turning the sea into lemonade (among other things) as "*une Utopie des enfants gaspillés*" ("a Utopia of spoiled children"). The Transhumanist vision, which has already happened in miniature, is the ability to pursue "bigger better faster more" of what spoiled children want. What it is not is a way to grow into what a mature adult wants.

I'm not saying we should get rid of medicine, or anything like that. Medical knowledge has done some impressive things. But I would pointedly suggest that the kind of things technological advances give us give us much more what spoiled children want than what a mature adult would recognize as an aid to maturity. There are exceptions, and I would not argue any sort of straight Luddite position: I try to moderate my use of technology like I try to moderate a lot of other good things, but I am very glad for the opportunity to live in an age where webpages are possible, and to have gotten in at a good time. But the "all the time there is" limitation is in fact the kind of boundary that helps mature adults grow more mature, and if we are willing to take it there is an occasion for maturity because we can't take a pill to have all the time we want.

From the Fifth Gospel to Liturgical Time

The Gospel According to Thomas isn't the Fifth Gospel. (At least, in ancient times when Christians said "the Fifth Gospel" they didn't mean the Gospel According to Thomas. No comments from the peanut gallery about the Gospel According to Thomas being the Fifth Bird Cage Liner.)

If a couple of people meet, become acquainted, become friends, start dating, become engaged, and get married, when does the marriage begin? In one sense, the wedding is a formal threshold: before then they aren't married, afterwards they are. But in another sense the engagement becomes part of the marriage, as does the courtship, the friendship, the acquaintance, even the first meeting and possibly things in their lives that they would say prepared them for the meeting. The marriage moves forward from the wedding date but it also reaches backwards and creates something in the past. What may have been an improbable or forgettable first meeting is drawn into the marriage; the same thing is going on as with the watch which becomes not simply matter but part of a friendship.

John Behr has provocatively suggested that the worst thing that has happened to Christianity in the past 2000 years has been the canonization of the New Testament so it is placed as Scripture alongside the Old Testament, and becomes the second and final volume in a series. What he means by that may not be obvious.

The relationship between the Old and New Testament is misunderstood somewhat if the New Testament is simply the final chapter of the Old Testament. It would be better, if still imperfect, to say that the New Testament is Cliff's Notes on the Old Testament, or the Old Testament was a rich computer game and the New Testament was the strategy guide that we need to unlock it's secrets. It is no accident that the first people we know of to put the New Testament alongside the Old Testament, and make commentaries on both Testaments, were Gnostics who tried to unlock the New Testament when orthodox Christians let the New Testament unlock the Old.

Quick--which Christ-centered Gospel did Handel use in the Messiah to tell of the Messiah or Christ? The answer is the Fifth Gospel: Isaiah. The passages cited in the Messiah are not a few prophetic exceptions to a non-Christ-related Old Testament; they are part of the Old Testament unlocked, and that same reading is how the earliest Christians read the Old Testament Scriptures.

> Now it was Mary Mag'dalene and Jo-an'na and Mary the mother of James and the other women with them who told this to the apostles; but these words seemed to them an idle tale, and they did not believe them.
>
> That very day two of them were going to a village named Emma'us, about seven miles from Jerusalem, and talking with each other about all these things that had happened.
>
> While they were talking and discussing together, Jesus himself drew near and went with them.
>
> But their eyes were kept from recognizing him.

And he said to them, "What is this conversation which you are holding with each other as you walk?" And they stood still, looking sad.

Then one of them, named Cle'opas, answered him, "Are you the only visitor to Jerusalem who does not know the things that have happened there in these days?"

And he said to them, "What things?" And they said to him, "Concerning Jesus of Nazareth, who was a prophet mighty in deed and word before God and all the people, and how our chief priests and rulers delivered him up to be condemned to death, and crucified him. But we had hoped that he was the one to redeem Israel. Yes, and besides all this, it is now the third day since this happened. Moreover, some women of our company amazed us. They were at the tomb early in the morning and did not find his body; and they came back saying that they had even seen a vision of angels, who said that he was alive. Some of those who were with us went to the tomb, and found it just as the women had said; but him they did not see."

And he said to them, "O foolish men, and slow of heart to believe all that the prophets have spoken! Was it not necessary that the Christ should suffer these things and enter into his glory?"

And beginning with Moses and all the prophets, he interpreted to them in all the scriptures the things concerning himself. So they drew near to the village to which they were going. He appeared to be going further, but they constrained him, saying, "Stay with us, for it is toward evening and the day is now far spent." So he went in to stay with them.

When he was at table with them, he took the bread and blessed, and broke it, and gave it to them. And their eyes were opened and they recognized him; and he vanished out of their sight.

> They said to each other, "Did not our hearts burn within us while he talked to us on the road, while he opened to us the scriptures?"

There's a lot going on here; I'm not going to address why Mary Magdalene has been called the Apostle to the Apostles, but I would suggest that instead of saying today what a feminist would be tempted to say, that the men were sexist and wouldn't believe a woman when she bore the glad tidings, there was a veil over their minds, much like Paul describes in II Cor 3. If a woman's witness did not suffice, Jesus standing with them in person and talking with them still had no effect until the very end. And there is something going on here with a number of resonances in our lives. They couldn't see Christ in the Scriptures (which were then the Old Testament, because the Gospels and Epistles had never been written), and they couldn't see Christ appearing before them, even literally. And that is not because they are imperceptive and we are perceptive. The story is a crystallization of how we often meet Christ.

What is the point of all this? The most immediate reason is not to say that the Bible is 80% documents produced by Judaism before Christianity came around and 20% Christian documents, but transformed, transmuted if you will, into 100% Christian documents. When the book of Psalms opens with, "Blessed is the man who does not walk in the council of the wicked, nor stand in the way of sinners, nor sit in the seat of cynics," that refers first and foremost to Christ. I myself have not gotten very far in this way of reading the Scriptures, but I hope to, and I believe it will pay rich dividends.

And there is something going on here that is going on in when a marriage reaches backwards, or a watch becomes part of a friendship. It is connected with what is called "recapitulation", which I think is an unfortunate technical theological term because the metaphor comes across as in "Ok, let me try and recap what we've said so far," which is a wishy-washy metaphor for something deep. Orthodox talk about deification, and for us to be deified is a specific example of recapitulation in Christ. Recapitulation means "re-heading", and while in a sense very consistent with how recapitulation works, I've somewhat indistinguishably talked about how we can be Recapitulated or Re-headed in Christ, becoming body to his head and connected in the most intimate way, thereby becoming Christ (i.e. Recapitulation with a big 'R'), and how something can become part of the body of something that can itself be recapitulated in Christ (recapitulation with only a little 'R'). Perhaps that sentence should be dragged out into the street and shot, but when I talked about the gift of a watch becoming part of a friendship, the head of its reheading is something created, but both the watch and the friendship can be Recapitulated in Christ with the re-heading of the watch to be part of the friendship is itself part of what is Recapitulated in Christ, i.e. which is not merely brought under a head but connected to Christ as its head.

Let's move on to clearer language and a clearer example--one that has to do with our time. The head of the whole body of time we live is our time in worship, liturgical time. This both that there is a liturgical rhythm of day, week, and year, with different practices that help us connect with the different liturgical rhythms (by the way, the first major piece of advice my spiritual father gave me was to take 5-10 years to step into the liturgical rhythm), but that's not all. It means that our time in worshsip, which is not just time in a funnily decorated room with our particular club, sets the pace for life. It means that what is crystallized and visible in worship is perhaps hidden but if anything more powerfully manifest in a whole life of worship. It means that not just going to Church but working and playing are themselves worship, and they fulfill worship. It means, and I write this on the Sunday of the Last Judgment, that our worship is hollow and empty when we sing hymns to God on Sunday and then turn away in icy silence when someone asks our help--for it is not that someone we have icily turned away from, but Christ (see Matt 25:31-46). In the discourse at the Last Supper, Christ did not say that all would "know you are my disciples by this, that you have the most beautiful services," but that all would "know you are my disciples by this, that you love one another." (Jn 13.35) That is something that happens *outside* of Church first and foremost. Liturgical time is the basis for time in our lives.

Liturgical time is (or at least should be) the head of time in a life of worship (if "head" is used in the sense of "recapitulation" or "re-heading"), but it is not its own head. The head of time in worship is eternity in Heaven, and that means that just as life is the concrete manifestation of worship, in time but in other matters as well, but liturgical time is not people gathered in a room for an interval but people transported to Heaven in what is not exactly a time machine, or not *merely* a time machine, but an "eternity machine". The head of eternity in Heaven is the Eternal One whose glory shines through Heaven on earth.

What does this concretely mean for our experience of time? It means much the same as whether the material world was created good by God or evil by someone lesser. Pains and physical pleasures, to give a superficial example, will be there whether we believe the material world is good or evil. But it makes a difference whether you believe the sweetness of honey is a touch of love from God or a hatefully baited barb from Satan. Now part of really coming alive is being more than pleasure and pain and letting go of pleasures that they may be recapitulated or re-headed and drawn into what is Spirit. But even then, the Christian ascetic who lets go of a good is very different from a Gnostic ascetic who hatefully rejects it as evil. Pleasures and even pains, and joys and sorrows, are fuller depending on their basis.

Augustine has been accused of inadequate conversion--maybe he became Christian, but he continued being too much of a Manichee. I am sympathetic to that view, and it makes good sense of Augustine's sense that there is something violent to us about being in time, with our being stingily rationed out to us, infinitesimal bit by bit (some have said the present "barely exists" because it is an instantaneous boundary where the future rushes into the past without stopping to rest), while God has its being all at once. I was sympathetic to that view until not long ago; I thought of time as an evil thing we endure to get to the good of eternity--which is the wrong way of putting it.

Time is a moving image of eternity and is recapitulated in Christ. We miss something fundamental if we simply say that it is less than eternity; it participates in the glory. Furthermore, there is a case to be made that we misunderstand eternity if it is "frozen time" to us, if it is an instant in time which is prolonged, or even worse, is deprived of a moving timeline. Whatever eternity is, *that can't be it*. That is something fundamentally less than the time in which we grow and learn and breathe. Eternal life, which begins in this world, is God's own life, greater than created being but something that projects its glory into time. I once asked a friend if the difference between Maximus Confessor and Plato on Ideas was that for Plato there was one Idea that covered a bunch of material shadows (what we would think of as "real", but the Ideas were more real), and he waved that aside without really contradicting me. He said that the Ideas, or ΛΟΓΟΙ (*logoi*), were static in Plato but dynamic in Maximus Confessor. *Logoi* are ideas loved in the heart of God from all eternity, and you and I only exist because we each have a *logos* in the heart of God which is what we are trying to become. And I don't know how to reconcile what I know of dynamism with being outside of time, but eternity is not the deprivation of time, but something more time-like than time itself. Time becomes eternal when it is recapitulated in Christ.

Kairos and Chronos

Bishop K.T. Ware began one lecture/tape by saying that at the beginning of the Divine Liturgy, there is a line that is very easy to overlook: the deacon tells the bishop or his deputy the priest, "It's time to get started." Except that he doesn't say, "It's time to get started," but "It is time for the Lord to act."

He pointed out both that the liturgy is the Lord's work, even if both priest and faithful must participate for it to be valid (he said that the pop etymology of liturgy as "lit-urgy", "the people's work", may be bad etymology but it's good theology). But another point tightly tied to it is the exact Greek word that is translated "time."

There are two words that are both translated time, but their meanings are very different. Translating them both as time is like translating both genuine concern and hypocritical flattery as "politeness" because you are translating into a language that doesn't show the distinction. Perhaps the translators are not to be blamed, but there is something important going on in the original text that is flattened out in English. And when the deacon says "It's time to get started," it does *not* mean "My watch says 9:00 and that's when people expect us to start," but "This is the decisive moment." In the Gospels, when Jesus' own brothers and sisters failed to grasp who he was just as completely as the disciples on the road to Emmaus, he tells them, "My kairos has not yet come, but your kairos is always here." (Jn 7.6).

Orthodox do not have any kind of monopoly on this distinction, but we do have a distinction between what is called "chronos" and what is called "kairos." Chronos is ordinary if we take a harsh meaning to the word, instead of "everything is as it should be". Chronos at its worst is watching the clock while drudgery goes on and on. If chronos is meaningless time, kairos is meaningful time, dancing the Great Dance at a decisive moment. It is putting the case too strongly to say that the West is all about chronos and Eastern Christianity is all about kairos, but I do not believe it is putting the case too strongly to say that East and West place chronos and kairos differently, and kairos is less the air people breathe in the West than it should be.

I don't think that chronos needs as much explanation in the West; chronos is what a clock measures; the highbrow word for a stopwatch is "chronometer" and not "kairometer". The distinction between kairos and chronos is somewhat like the distinction between I-Thou and I-It relationship. But let me give "ingredients" to kairos, as if it were something cooked up in a recipe.

- Chronos.
- Eternity.
- Appointed time.
- Rhythmic circular time with interlocking wheels.
- Linear unfolding time.
- Moments when you are absorbed in what you are doing.
- Decisive moments when something is possible that was impossible a moment before and will be impossible a moment later.
- Dancing the serendipitous Great Dance.
- Total presence.

But kairos is not something cooked up in a recipe; chronos may be achievable that way, but kairos is a graced gift of God.

We Might All Be Alcoholics

A recovering alcoholic will tell you that alcoholism is Hell on earth. He would say that it is the worst suffering on earth, or that it is the kind of thing you wouldn't wish on your worst enemy.

And the point that healing and restoration begins is exquisitely painful. An alcoholic has a massive screen of denial that defeats reasoning. The only semi-effective way to defeat that denial is by a massive dose of even more painful reality that can break down that screen, some of the time. (An intervention.)

If alcoholism is Hell, why don't alcoholics step out of it? Some people in much less pain find out what they need to do to stop the pain and leave. They take off a pair of shoes that is too tight, or ask for an ambulance to treat their broken arm (and I believe someone who's been through both experiences would say that alcoholism is a much deeper kind of pain than a broken arm).

Surely alcoholics must have a sense that something is

wrong--and that's what they're trying to evade. That's what half an alcoholic's energy goes into evading, because stopping and saying "I'm an alcoholic." is the greatest terror an alcoholic can jump into. It may be a greater fear than the fear of death--or it *is* the fear of the death, a step into where nothing is guaranteed.

And that is where to become Orthodox might as well be recognizing you are an alcoholic. Not, perhaps, that every Orthodox has a problem with alcohol, but we all have a problem, a spiritual disease called sin that is not a crime, but is infinitely worse than mere criminality. And the experience an alcoholic says saying, "My name's Ashley, and I'm an alcoholic," for the first time, is foundational to Orthodox religion. "Here is trustworthy saying that deserves acceptance: Christ Jesus came into the world to save sinners, of whom I am the first."

There is a book, I have been told, among alcoholics called Not-God, because part of dealing with the cancer of alcoholism, as difficult as recognizing a terrible problem with alcohol, is recognizing that you have been trying to be God and not only are you not God, but your playing God has caused almost untold troubles.

Repentance is the most terrifying experience an Orthodox or an alcoholic can experience because when God really confronts you, he doesn't just say "Give me a little bit." He says, "Give me everything," and demands an unconditional surrender that you write a blank check. This is as terrifying as the fear of death--or perhaps it *is* the fear of death, because everything we are holding dear, and especially the one thing we hold most dear, must be absolutely surrendered to--the Great Physician never tells us what, because then it would not be the surrender we need. We are simply told, "Write a blank check to me. Now."

How does this square with becoming a little Christ?

> So if there is any encouragement in Christ, any incentive of love, any participation in the Spirit, any affection and sympathy, complete my joy by being of the same mind, having the same love, being in full

> accord and of one mind. Do nothing from selfishness or conceit, but in humility count others better than yourselves. Let each of you look not only to his own interests, but also to the interests of others.
>
> Have this mind among yourselves, which is yours in Christ Jesus, who, though he was in the form of God, did not count equality with God a thing to be grasped, but emptied himself, taking the form of a servant, being born in the likeness of men. And being found in human form he humbled himself and became obedient unto death, even death on a cross. Therefore God has highly exalted him and bestowed on him the name which is above every name, that at the name of Jesus every knee should bow, in heaven and on earth and under the earth, and every tongue confess that Jesus Christ is Lord, to the glory of God the Father.

The two paragraphs, as I have broken up Phil 2:1-11 (RSV), are complementary. What the last paragraph says is that the equal Son of God emptied himself and kept on emptying himself further and suffering further until there is nothing left to give. And this is not a sinner, a mere creature, but the spotless and sinless Son of God showing what it means to be divine. It is not in Heaven that Christ shows the full force of divinity, but by emptying himself, willingly, to death on a cross and a descent into the realm of the dead. That is the moment when death itself began to work backwards--and humbling and emptying ourselves before God is the sigil of being exalted and filled with God's goodness. But the other side of the coin is that if we think we can become divine, or even be human, while not being emptied, we are asking to be above Christ and expecting to have something that is utterly incoherent.

When we recognize that we are not God, then we become christs. When we empty ourselves, and let go of that one thing we are most afraid of giving to God, then we discover, along with the recovering alcoholic, that what we were most afraid to give up was a piece of Hell. We discover, with the alcoholic, that what we were fighting God about, and offering him consolation prizes in place of, was not something God needed, but something we needed to be freed from.

This emptying, this blank check and unconditional surrender, is what makes divinization possible. I was tempted in writing this to say that it is the ultimate kairos, but that's exaggerating: the ultimate kairos is the Eucharist, but if we refuse this kairos, we befoul what we could experience in the Eucharist. If we are talking about a decisive moment that is not our saying "I want to make myself holier" so much as us hearing God say "You need to listen to me NOW," then however painful it may be it is a step into kairos and a step further into kairos. And only after the surrender do we discover that what we were fighting against was an opportunity to step one step further into Heaven.

Repentance is appointed time. Repentance is *the* decisive moment, one we enter into again. Repentance is simultaneously death and transfiguration, the death that is transfiguration and the transfiguration that recapitulates death. Repentance is eternity breaking into time. Repentance is one eternal moment, and the moment we cycle back to, and the steps of climbing into Heaven. Repentance is being pulled out of the mud and painfully scrubbed clean. Repentance is fighting your way into the Great Peace. Repentance is the moment when we step out of unreality and unreal time into reality and the deepest time. Repentance is not the only moment in kairos, but it is among the most powerful and the most deeply transforming, decisive moments that appointed kairos has to offer.

Miscellanea

I do not have time to write, and perhaps you do not have time to read, separate sections about some things I will briefly summarize:

- Life neither begins at 18 nor ends at 30. Every age is to be part of a kaleidoscope. Contrary to popular opinion in America, not only is it not a sin to grow old, but each age has its own beauty, like the seasons in turn and like the colors in a kaleidoscope. And that is why I do not guiltily talk about having "hit 30" any more than I would guiltily talk about having "hit 18" or "hit 5", because in the end feeling guilty about approaching a ripe age is as strange as feeling guilty about being born: not that there is anything wrong with being a child in the womb, but the purpose of that special age is not to remain perennially in the womb but to grow in maturity and stature until our life is complete and God, who has numbered the hairs on our heads and without whom not even a sparrow can die, come to the thing we fear in age and discover that this, "death", is not the end of a Christian's life but the portal to the fulness of Heaven where we will see in full what we can now merely glimpse.

- When we reach Heaven or Hell, they will have reached back so completely that our whole lives will have been the beginning of Heaven or the beginning of Hell.
- People make a dichotomy between linear and cyclical time. The two can be combined in spiral (or maybe helical) time, and the movement of time forwards in growth combined with the liturgical cycles makes a rhythmic but never-repeating helix or spiral. (If that is embedded in what Maximus Confessor said about linear, circular, and spiral motion.)
- One step away from saying that time is a line is saying that time is a pole on which a living vine grows, making a richer kind of connection than a materialist would see. That is a little bit of why we are contemporaries of Christ.

The Horn of Joy

> ...Sandy called after [Meg], "And also in 1865 Rudyard Kipling was born, and Verlaine wrote *Poèmes saturniens*, and John Stuart Mill wrote *Auguste Comte and Positivism*, and Purdue, Cornell, and the universities of Maine were founded."
>
> She waved back at him, then paused as he continued, "And Matthew Maddox's first novel, *Once More United*, was published."
>
> She turned back, asking in a carefully controlled voice, "Maddox? I don't think I've ever heard of that author."
>
> "You stuck to math in school."
>
> "Yeah, Calvin always helped me with my English papers. Did this Matthew Maddox write anything else?"
>
> Sandy flipped through the pages. "Let's see. Nothing in 1866, 1867. 1868, here we are, *The Horn of Joy*."
>
> "Oh, that," Dennys said. "I remember him now. I had to take a lit course my sophomore year in college, and I took nineteenth-century American literature. We read that, Matthew Maddox's second and last book, *The Horn of Joy*. My prof said if he hadn't died he'd have been right up there with Hawthorne and James. It was a strange book, passionately anti-war, I remember, and it went way back into the past, and there was some weird theory of the future influencing the past--not my kind of book at all." (Madeleine l'Engle, A Swiftly Tilting Planet.)

Madeleine l'Engle's A Swiftly Tilting Planet immediately follows my favorite children's book, A Wind in the Door. I wished I could visit Patagonia, and tried to find a book she mentions in Walking on Water: Reflections on Faith and Art as seminal to the Welsh legend in A Swiftly Tilting Planet. I also looked for *The Horn of Joy* and was disappointed, if not necessarily surprised, to learn that this was the one fictional addition to an otherwise historical list.

It would be not only strange but presumptuous to suggest that this piece I am writing is what she was referring to. Perhaps it is presumptuous to use that title, although it may seem less presumptuous if one understands how special and even formative Madeleine l'Engle's work has been to me. But what does not seem strange to suggest is that this work may affect the meaning of A Swiftly Tilting Planet. That would only be determined by other people's judgment and is not my call to make, but I don't think Madeleine l'Engle would be offended if someone said that this enhanced the value of her work, or added another layer to what she said about time. Her own words not only in that work but in Walking on Water: Reflections on Faith and Art about how a work can be enhanced by future insights would suggest the possible. It is quite possible that my work is not good enough or not relevant enough to serve as such a key, but the suggestion is not that strange to make.

But let us move on to one closing remark.

Extraordinary and Utterly Ordinary

The Enlightenment has left us with a lot of wreckage, and one of this is great difficulty seeing what causality could be besides "one domino mechanically toppling others."

Aristotle listed four causes: the material cause, formal cause, efficient cause, and final cause. The material and formal cause are interesting to me as something the Enlightenment would not think to include in causality: Aristotle's Physics portrays the bronze in a statue as a material cause to the statue. If we listen to the hint, this could suggest that causality for Aristotle is something besides just dominoes falling. He does deal with mechanical, domino-like causation when he describes the efficient cause, but I remember being taken with the "final cause", the goal something is progressing towards, because I thought it was domino causation that had the effect before the cause.

The best response I can give now to what I believed then was, "Um, kind of." Aristotle's four causes address a broader and more human kind of causation that looks at questions like why something happened and not just how it was produced. It is in fact an utterly ordinary way of looking at things. It's not the *only* serious way of describing causality (my favorite physics teacher said in class, "If Aristotle said it, it was wrong," and I think he was right about much more than physics), but it's one kind of richer view. And if you think it's something exotic, you misunderstand it. It is an utterly ordinary, even commonsense way of looking at why things happen.

And an Aristotle's-four-causes kind of time is better than an Enlightenment-domino-causation kind of time, for a number of reasons. The best essay about time, which I cannot write, would encompass the better parts of what I have said above while remaining "normal" even when it underscored something extraordinary. Or at least would do better at that than I have.

Orthodoxy is not something absolutely unique; I have said things here which I hope resonate with some sense of home whether or not you are Orthodox. When I moved from being an Evangelical to becoming Orthodox, I did not move from absolute error into absolute truth but from something partial to its full expression. (And there are other clarifications I haven't made, like how much of this essay is owed to Irenaeus and to John Behr helping Irenaeus come alive.) But let me close.

In Orthodoxy, here and now, there is an ordinary way to do what alchemy aimed at: be transfigured in a transfiguration that embraces the material world--and, as we have seen, time. Time is to be transmuted, or rather transfigured, until it becomes eternity.

The Sign of the Grail

George had finally gotten through the first week at Calix College, and the chaos was subsiding. Bored for a minute, and too exhausted from the busy work to start researching something, he sat down, tried to remember something strange that he meant to investigate, and tried some more.

When he finally gave up and tried to think about what else he could do, he remembered a book he had seen in his closet, perhaps left over by a previous resident. He pulled out a fan and a lamp that were placed on it, and pulled out a large book. The entire leather cover had only eleven letters, and the dark leather showed signs of wear but seemed to be in remarkably good condition. The golden calligraphy formed a single word: *Brocéliande*. All across the front lay dark, intricate leather scrollwork.

What was "*Brocéliande*?" After looking at the leather and goldwork a short while, George opened *Brocéliande* and read:

> The knight and the hermit wept and kissed together, and the hermit did ask, "Sir knight, wete thou what the Sign of the Grail be?"
>
> The knight said, "Is that one of the Secrets of the Grail?"
>
> "If it be one of the Secrets of the Grail, that is neither for thee to ask nor to know. The Secrets of the Grail are

very different from what thou mightest imagine in thine heart, and no man will get them by looking for secrets. But knowest thou what the Sign of the Grail is?"

"I never heard of it, nor do I know it."

"Thou wete it better than thou knowest, though thou wouldst wete better still if thou knewest that thou wete."

"That be perplexed, and travail sore to understand."

The hermit said, "Knowest thou the Sign of the Cross?"

"I am a Christian and I know it. It is no secret amongst Christians."

"Then know well that the sacred kiss, the kiss of the mass, even if it be given and received but once per year, is the Sign of the Grail."

"How is that? What makes it such as I have never heard?"

"I know that not in its fullness. Nor could I count reasons even knew I the fullness of truth. But makest thou the Sign of the Cross when thou art alone?"

"Often, good hermit; what Christian does not?"

"Canst thou make the Sign of the Grail upon another Christian when thou art alone?"

George's cell phone rang, and he closed the book and ran to hear the call better. When he came back, though he spent an hour searching, he could not find his place in the heavy book. He turned outside.

There were a lot of people, but what he saw was the castle-like stonework of the campus, the timeworn statues, and finally the great wood with its paths, streams, and meadows. He got lost several times, but not truly *lost*, as he was exploring and finding interesting places no less when he lost his sense of direction. The next time he found his way, he went to the cafeteria and sat down at a table, part listening and part sifting through thoughts.

When he got home, his mind was hungry again, and he opened *Brocéliande* to the middle:

Merlin howled.

"Lord of Heaven and Earth, I have everything I want, or rather everything I fled to. I have left the city and the company of men, and am become as a wild beast, living on grass and nuts.

"Is this because of whose son I am? Some say I have powers from my father, serving the Light only because the prayers spoken when some learned of that dread project. Yet here outside of castle and city I have learned things hidden from most men. I can conjure up a castle from the air, but not enter and live in one: I live in the wood as a man quite mad."

Then he looked around. The trees were a verdant green, yet he found apples. Presently he came to the fountain of Brocéliande; he rang not the bell but drew deep and drank a draught. The forest were his labyrinth and his lair.

A hawk came and set him on the branch close up.

Merlin said to it, "Yet I can speak with thee: no element is a stranger to me."

A sound of footsteps sounded, and Merlin ran not away.

Merlin his sister Ganeida laid a hand on Merlin his arm. "Come, Merlin. This is unworthy. I have brought thee food for a journey: King Arthur summoneth thee to his court."

Merlin beheld the wood called Brocéliande. He beheld its holly, its ivy, its trees shaken by storm and wind. He thought of the animals. And there was something about this forest that drew him: it seemed larger on the inside than the outside, and there was something alway that seemed shining through it, like faint and haunting music which he had by struggles learned to catch as he withdrew from castles and the world of men.

Then Ganieda did start to sing a different song, a

> plain and simple folk tune, and Merlin his heart settled, and he did walk with his sister.

George slowly closed the book.

He imagined the scene; there was something about Merlin that haunted and eluded him. There was--

There was a knock on the door.

He opened it. It was one of the people from dinner.

"Do you want to see a movie?"

"What movie?"

"We're still deciding. But there are a few of us going to the theater."

George thought for a moment. Up until that point he thought he didn't want to read more of the book for now. When he declined the invitation, there was a fleeting insight which he forgot the next moment.

The next day in class, the figure of Merlin had a stronger grip on his imagination.

If George had less energy, his classes might have suffered more. As it was, he was getting by, and he slowly began to realize that there was something more that gripped him than horses, swords, and armor. He kept opening more to see the beautiful fantasy, so different from his world. At one point he turned the page:

> Then Queen Guinevere did sigh and wept sore.
>
> A lady asked, "Milady, what is it?"
>
> "This Grail cometh even now. Is it accursed?
>
> "The Round Table shattered sore hard and knights return with strange tales. Such a holy thing this Grail is called, yet when it cometh the rich Grail yet burneth like fire. Already King Arthur his work is unraveling.
>
> "Will it even take from me my Sir Lancelot? Or can I take even my Lancelot from the Holy Grail?"

There was something in the back of George's mind. He sat

back, thinking, and then closed the book to make a brief visit to the unspoilt beauty of the wood.

When he went in, he noticed a great beech tree, lying, weeping. It seemed that there was something trying to get out of the verdure. There were ferns and moss around, and he walked and walked. The path took many turns, and George began to realize several things. First, it was dark. Second, he was lost. Third, a chill was setting in. Fourth, he could not see even the stars.

Before long he was running in heavy, icy rain, branches lashing, until a branch hitting his chest winded him. He sat down in stinging pain and regained his breath, then felt around and crawled beneath an outcropping. Here the rain at least would not get to him any more. He spent the night in waking shock at what this great pristine nature, unsullied by human contamination, was really like: the forest seemed to be without reason or order right down to the awkward surface of the rock that he was painfully lying on. Long-forgotten fears returned: when a little light broke through the clouds, were those things he saw rocks, fallen trees, or goblins? He spent a long time shivering, and when the sun rose, he thirsted for light, and got up, only half awake, and followed it until he came to the edge of the forest and saw the castle-inspired buildings of the college. A short while later he was warming up with a welcome blanket and the welcome sound of voices in conversation.

Something was eating away at the back of George's mind.

Perhaps because of his weariness, his attention in class was chiefly on the flicker of the fluorescent light and how the buildings, which on the outside were so evocative of castles, were so modern on the inside. The one thing that caught his mind was a set of comments about either how we must be individuals and do our own thing or else we are all community and individuality is an illusion. He wanted to be haunted and meet hints of a larger world, and others' passionately held opinions seemed like they were taken from *Newsweek* and *USA Today.*

What was on TV? He stopped in the lobby and saw a show

with a medieval set, very carefully done to convey a medieval flavor, and watched until a heroine looked at a magical apparition in a full-length mirror and said, "I am having... a biochemical reaction!" He could not explain what failed to confront him, but he walked out. It was Freya's Day, commonly shortened to "Friday." When he learned how the days of the week were named, for Norse gods or celestial bodies--namely, Sun's Day, Moon's Day, Tiw's Day, Wotan's Day, Thor's Day, Freya's Day, and Saturn's Day--something seemingly pedestrian met him with a touch of a larger world. Now, it seemed, things that looked like they could tell of a larger world confronted him with the utterly pedestrian?

His homework did not take long.

Then, amidst Bon Jovi blaring through the hall, George began read. What he was reading seemed to affect him more like a song would than a story: a lullabye almost. He read of Arthur walking into battle, carrying an icon of the Virgin above him. There were mighty blows, armies with their mounted shock troops, great knights clothed in chainmail hauberks astride elephantine destriers, and in the center Arthur holding what seemed to be a story within a story, an icon that opened out onto something larger, and yet something he could not see in his mind's eye.

Then at another place he read as Arthur crossed land and sea and placed his sword on the ground and claimed a second Britain, and then gave of his knights, his brothers, and his substance to make a place like Great Britain, with forests and orchards, fields and towns, until he had given what he could of his spirit to make a Little Britain.

George looked through and began to see things weaving in and out: an intensity, a concentration, and not just that he was entering another time but he was entering another *time*, though he could not tell how it was different: he only sensed that time moved differently, and that his watch told something very different.

Then all of this seemed to crystallize as a grievously

wounded Sir Lancelot came to an hospitable knight and Elaine his daughter spent endless time healing his wounds. Love so overwhelmed her that she poured herself out with such intensity that when Lancelot left for the only woman he could love, her body emptied of spirit and life floated on a bier in a boat until Arthur's court wept at the most piteous tale of her love. George found himself wishing he could weep.

> --over hill, over dale until the night was black, and neither candle nor star pierced it. The great knight his destrier shook the earth. The great knight was clad in a double coat of mail and the shaft of his greater spear was as a weaver's beam. Then he did stop to dismount and his own steps shook the earth.
>
> Before him was a chalice of purest gold, radiant with light--radiant as the day. He walked before it, his steps shook the earth, and he stood taller than ever he did stand, until his hand grasped it.
>
> The light blazed brighter and a voice in the air spake, "Lancelot, Lancelot, why mockest thou me?" The light blazed, and Sir Lancelot fell against the ground in tremors, and his horse fled far away in terror.
>
> Then Sir Lancelot spake a question which I will not tell you.
>
> The voice answered with words not lawful for man to write, and the pure gold chalice vanished and the light with it.
>
> The knight wist not why he ran, and later he awoke him in a strange place where there were neither man nor beast in sight.

George closed the book. He had been reading for a long time, he told himself. What was there to do?

He looked around the school website for clubs and organizations, and none of the many things people were doing caught his eye. He walked around the campus, looking at the buildings. He went to the library and wandered around the bookshelves, and picked up a few items but set them down. Then he returned to his room and sat down for a while.

He was bored for the rest of the day.

That night, as he dreamed, he saw a castle, and walked into it. Whenever he looked at his body, he saw what looked like his ordinary clothing, and yet he believed he was wearing armor. He walked through hallways, chambers, the great hall, even dungeons, trying to see what he was searching for. At last he was in a room where he heard people, and smelt something ineffable. He caught a glimpse of a chalice that he could not see, yet he sensed its silhouette, bathed in indescribable light on either side, and he saw light rising above its core. But he never succeeded in seeing it.

He awoke from the strain to see it. He heard birdsong, and the fingers of the light of the dawn were brushing against his face.

Something crystallized in George's mind, and he did not need to tell himself, "I am on a quest."

The next day he went into the city to look around in the medieval institute, and tried to see what was there. He managed to walk at a brisk pace, almost run, through the museum, and was nervous over whether he would get out by the time he had to leave to catch dinner. Nothing caught his eye; nothing seemed interesting; everything seemed good only for a glimpse.

There was something eating at him.

During the next week, George discovered online reproduction sword dealers and looked at the perfectly machined character of the many closeup images available online. He didn't buy anything, but after the week thinking and failing to find other places, George returned to the museum. Maybe there was something he had missed.

He stopped at the first sword.

The sword, or what was left of it, looked like it had been eaten by worms, if that were possible. The deeply pitted surface intrigued him; it had all the surface of the complexity of a rock, and he thought that if he could take a magnifying glass or a zoomed-in camera lens to this or that part, it could pass for the intricate surface of a volcanic rock.

The handle didn't look right at all. It was a thin square rod connecting a thick blade and a thicker pommel, and seemed the very definition of "ergonomically incorrect," as if it had been designed to gouge the wearer's hand or generate blisters. It held for George something of the fascination of a car wreck. Why on earth had the museum put such a poor-quality specimen on display?

Then he read the rather large plaque.

The plaque read:

> This sword was excavated in what is now Cornwall in Great Britain and dates to the 5th or 6th century AD. It is considered to be remarkably well-preserved, being one of few such finds to be straight and in one solid piece, the metal part lacking only a handguard, and is one of this museum's prized holdings and one of the most valuable gifts from an anonymous donor. The handle, of which only the metal tang remains, was probably wood or possibly other organic materials.
>
> Think for a moment about the time and place this sword would have come from. Everything was made by hand, and there was little wealth: owning a sword would have been like owning a car today. Microscopic examination suggests that this sword was made for someone wealthy, as there are tiny fragments of gold embedded in the blade.
>
> What was life like when nothing was made by machines or mass-produced and therefore things were more expensive and there was less you could buy? What was life when you could not travel faster than a horse and what we today call information could not travel faster than people? What would your life have been like when you would have probably been born, lived, and died within a few miles of the same spot? Life was hard.

> But then look at the other side of the coin: can you think of anything people then would have had that you do not have today?

George looked at the sword, and tried to imagine it whole. At least he could tell what shape it suggested. And he tried to think about what the placard said, with none of the technologies he was used to. What would one do? Practice at swordplay? Wander in the forest?

George saw in his mind's eye Sir Lancelot kneeling on one knee, his sword point in earth, his sword pointing down, taking an oath. Then George looked over the sword again and it looked like Lancelot's sword: he imagined Sir Lancelot--or was it George?--laying his right hand on the sword and taking a mighty oath, and for a moment the sword in the museum took its full cruciform shape. And then as his eyes traced over the contours of the sword, it looked almost a relic, and he saw now one thing, now another: one scene from *Brocéliande* gave way to another, and something tugged at his heart.

He tried to imagine a great feast given by King Arthur to his nobles. There was something of that feast right in front of him, and it seemed to suggest an unfolding pageant. Knights and ladies dined with uproarious laughter, while minstrels sung enchanting ballads, and--

George realized someone was tapping on his shoulder. "Sir? Excuse me, but it's time for you to leave."

George turned and saw a security guard, and in puzzlement asked her, "Why? Have I done something wrong?"

She smiled and said, "You haven't done anything wrong, but I'm sorry, the museum is now closing. Come back another day!"

George looked out a window and saw that the daylight had completely fled. He realized he was very hungry.

He left after briefly saying, "Thank-you."

When he arrived home he was even hungrier, but even before he began eating he began looking through the same sites, selling swords.

None of them looked real to him.

After eating part of his meal, George opened *Brocéliande*, flipping from place to place until an illustration caught his eye. He read:

> Merlin walked about in the clearing on the Isle of Avalon. To his right was the castle, and to his left was the forest. Amidst the birdsong a brook babbled, and a faint fragrance of frankincense flowed.
>
> Sir Galahad walked out of the castle portal, and he bore a basket of bread.
>
> Then Galahad asked Merlin about his secrets and ways, of what he could do and his lore, of his calling forth from the wood what a man anchored in the castle could never call forth. And Galahad enquired, and Merlin answered, and Galahad enquired of Merlin if Merlin knew words that were more words than our words and more mystically real than the British tongue, and then the High Latin tongue, and then the tongue of Old Atlantis. And then Galahad asked after anything beyond Atlantis, and Merlin's inexhaustible fount ran dry.
>
> Then Sir Galahad asked Merlin of his wood, of the stones and herbs, and the trees and birds, and the adder and the dragon, the gryphon and the lion, and the unicorn whom only a virgin may touch. And Merlin spake to him him of the pelican, piercing her bosom that her young may feed, and the wonders, virtues, and interpretation of each creature, until Galahad asked of the dragon's head for which Uther had been called Uther Pendragon, and every Pendragon after him bore the title of King and Pendragon. Merlin wot the virtue of the dragon's body, but of the dragon's head he wot nothing, and Sir Galahad spake that it was better that Merlin wist not.
>
> Then Sir Galahad did ask Merlin after things of which he knew him nothing, of what was the weight of fire, and of what is the end of natural philosophy without magic art, and

what is a man if he enters not in the castle, and "Whom doth the Grail serve?", and of how many layers the Grail hath. And Merlin did avow that of these he wist not none.

Then Merlin asked, "How is it that you are wise to ask after these all?"

Then Galahad spake of a soft voice in Merlin his ear and anon Merlin ran into the wood, bearing bread from the castle.

George was tired, and he wished he could read more. But he absently closed the book, threw away what was left of his hamburgers and fries, and crawled into bed. It seemed but a moment that he was dreaming.

George found himself on the enchanted Isle of Avalon, and it seemed that the Grail Castle was not far off.

George was in the castle, and explored room after room, entranced. Then he opened a heavy wooden door and found himself facing the museum exhibit, and he knew he was seeing the same 5th-6th century sword from the Celtic lands, only it looked exactly like a wall hanger sword he had seen online, a replica of a 13th century Provençale longsword that was mass produced, bore no artisan's fingerprints, and would split if it struck a bale of hay. He tried to make it look like the real surface, ever so real, that he had seen, but machined steel never changed.

Then George looked at the plaque, and every letter, every word, every sentence was something he could read but the whole thing made no sense. Then the plaque grew larger and larger, until the words and even letters grew undecipherable, and he heard what he knew were a dragon's footprints and smelled the stench of acrid smoke. George went through room and passage until the noises grew louder, and chanced to glance at a pool and see his reflection.

He could never remember what his body looked like, but his head was unmistakably the head of a dragon.

George sat bolt upright on his bunk, awake in a cold sweat, and hit his head on the ceiling.

The next day, George went to the medieval history library that was almost at the center of the campus, housed in a white limestone tower with one timeworn spire, and intricately woven with passages like rabbit holes. The librarian was nowhere in sight, and owing to his eccentricities the library still had only a paper card catalog, emanating a strange, musty aroma. George started to walk towards it, before deciding to wander around the shelves and get a feel for things medieval. The medieval history librarian was rumored to be somewhat eccentric, and insisted on a paper card catalog with no computers provided, which many of the students said might as well have been medieval.

His first read traced the development of symbol from something that could not give rise to science to something that apparently paved the way in that a symbol and what it refers to were no longer seen as connected. It seemed hard to follow, some where the argument was obscure and even more when he followed the reasoning: he grasped it and grasped it not. As he read, he read of the cultivation of cabbages and tales of kings, and whether grotesques could let pigs have wings. He read of boys doing the work of men and men who acted like boys, of children who asked for bread and their fathers would give them stones *in* their bread, of careful historians ages before the great discovery of history and classicists preserving the ancient life after the ancient life met its demise, of strange things that turned familiar and yet familiar things turned strange, of time becoming something a clock could measure, of those who forged, those who plagiarized, and arguments today why no medieval author should be accused of plagiarism for what he copied, and yet he read of a world where few died of old age and minor cuts and illnesses could kill. He read of the problem of underpopulation, the challenge of having enough births, and untold suffering when there were not enough people.

Yet to speak this way is deceptive, because all these wonders and more were made pedestrian. The more he studied, the fewer wonders he met, or at least the fewer wonders he could find, and the more he met a catalog of details. He read the chronicles of kings and those seeking what could be recovered through them, and however much he read King Arthur was not mentioned once. Though he spent weeks searching in the library, the haunting beauty of Brocéliande had been rare to begin with and now he wot of it not none.

And the fruitless search for the history of Arthur led him to knock on the librarian's door.

"I'm in a bad mood. Leave me alone!"

"Please."

"You can come in if you must, but you would be better off leaving."

"I've looked all over and found neither hide nor hair of a book on King Arthur. Does this library have *nothing* on him?"

"King Arthur? No, not this part of the library; look in the appropriate sections on the electronic card catalog in the regular library."

"But I want to know the history of Arthur."

"The history of King Arthur?!? What can you *possibly* mean?"

"I had been reading about King Arthur outside the library."

"The general library has a number of the original sources, along with more literary criticism than one person can possibly read, and what little the history of literature knows about more and less obscure authors. And our literature department has several renowned scholars on Arthurian literature. But why are you trying to find King Arthur in a medieval *history* library? That's as silly as looking for the history of the animals in Aesop's fables."

"You don't believe in Arthur?"

"No, I don't. Though I could be wrong. A lot of scholars, *wrong* as they may be, believe there was an Arthur around the 6th century, a warrior owning a horse, though the consensus is that he was not a king. These--"

"So Arthur was a knight and not a king?!?"

"No, he wasn't a knight. He couldn't have been. If there ever was such a person."

"But you said he had a horse and--"

"You're making a basic historical mistake if you're imagining a warrior then, even one with a horse, as a '*knight*'. It would like a historian five or six centuries from now studying our technology, and knowing that Saint Thomas Aquinas was an author, imagining him doing Google searches and composing, in *Latin* of course, on his computer's word processor.

"Warriors owned horses, but stirrups hadn't reached Arthur's supposed land, and without a stirrup it is almost impossible to fight while mounted. A horse was a taxi to get a warrior to battle to fight on foot like everybody else, and nothing more. A warrior with a horse was a warrior with a better taxi to get to the scene of battle. A knight, on the most material level, is an almost invincible mounted shock troop compared to the defenseless-as-children so-called 'infantry.' And then you have the ideal, almost the mythos, of chivalry that developed about these mighty brutal warriors.

"The Arthurian legends were never even close to history to begin with, even if they hadn't grown barnacles on top of barnacles, like... a bestseller with too many spinoffs. All the versions have their own anachronisms, or rather the earlier versions are nothing like anachronisms, projecting a legendary past for the kind of knight that was then becoming fashionable. You have a late medieval Sir Thomas Mallory fitting knights with plate armor that would have been as anachronous for an Arthur of the 5th or 6th century to wear as it would have been for a knight of Mallory's day to be equipped with today's Kevlar version of a bulletproof vest.

"I don't think it's a particularly big deal for there to be anachronisms; the idea that anachronism is a problem is a complete anachronism in evaluating medieval literature; saying that Chrétien de Troyes built an anachronous social ideal is as silly as complaining that the accounts of animals in a medieval bestiary are not doing the same job in the same way as a scientific biology textbook. Of course they aren't, but you're being equally silly to read a medieval bestiary as something that should be empirical scientific biology.

"Of course, getting back to anachronism, Mallory has guns which--"

"Guns?!? Machine guns? Handguns? Rifles?" George said.

"Nothing fancy, just early cannon, not a modern assault rifle. But there are none the less guns in the pivotal late medieval version of the story, which had Arthur's son and nephew, Mordred, besieging--"

"Which one was Mordred, and what was the other one's name?" George said.

"'Which one'? What do you mean..." The librarian said, pausing. "Aah, you get it. For that matter, the stories tend to include endless nobles whose family tree is, like a good nobility family tree, more of a family braid, and--"

It was around then that the conversation became something that George remembered with the confused memory of a dream. He knew that the librarian had explained something, but the closest he could come to remembering it was a discussion of how networked computers as the next generation of computing contributed to a unique medieval synthesis, or what actually seemed to make more sense of the shape of that "memory," the sound of an elephant repeatedly ramming stone walls.

What he remembered next was walking--walking through the library, walking around campus, walking through the forest, and then...

Had he been asked, he might have been collected enough to say that this was the first time in a long while he was not on a quest.

What was he doing now?

Was he doing anything?

Where was George?

He was lost, although that didn't register on his mind. Or perhaps he wasn't lost, if "lost" means not only that you don't know where you are, but that you wish you knew.

George was in the city somewhere, if that was where he was. A great forest of steel, glass, and brick. Some was adorned by graffiti, other bits by ugly paint. This was definitely not the castle to him, but the wild wood, much more the wild wood than what was merely a place with many trees and few buildings. What made the wood a wood and not like a castle, anyway?

George looked around. In front of him was a boarded-up restaurant. The sign said, "Closed for minor renovations. REOPENING SOON." Its paint looked chipped and timeworn, and from what he could see looking in the dirty windows, it was dusty inside. What, exactly, did the menu say? George could see the menu, and some pictures of what was probably supposed to be food, but even though he was on the edge of hunger, the hazy blurs did nothing to make his mouth water.

George walked a good distance further, and saw the bright colors of a store, and heard music playing. He wandered in.

Inside, the store was bustling with activity. Just inside, there was a demonstration of electronic puppies: an employee was showing the puppy off. On a whim, George walked over.

The young woman was saying words commands which the puppy sometimes did not respond to. She handed it to children to pet, who responded with exuberant warmth. But the more George watched the scene, the more the whole scene seemed off-kilter.

The puppies were cute, but there seemed to be something much less cute when they moved. What was it? The puppy's animation seemed neither like a cute stuffed animal nor like a toy robot. It seemed like a robot in a puppy costume, but the effect was... almost vampiric.

Then George looked at the employee again. She was quite attractive, but her smile and the exaggerated energy for her role... reminded George of makeup almost covering dark circles under someone's eyes.

He ducked into an aisle. Below were not only unflavored dental floss and mint floss, but many different kinds of floss in all different colors, thicknesses, and several different flavors. But the choices in the actual floss were dwarfed by the choices in the cases: purple-and-pink containers of floss for preteen girls, larger rough-looking containers made of dark stonelike plastic for a man's man, and sundry groups--including trainers for babies who were still teething. George saw a sign above a display that said, "We bring you the freedom *TO CHOOSE*!"

He tried not to think about sledgehammers. He tried.

George was looking for a reason to stay in the store. There was eye-catching color everywhere, and he saw a section of posters, and started flipping through art posters, looking for something to buy, until he saw the sign above the posters. It said, "Priceless masterpieces from the greatest museums of the world, conveniently made available to you in American standard poster size and format, for only $4.99 each."

Somehow the store's showmanlike displays seemed a bit hollow. George left.

George wandered out, something not quite clicking in his mind. He knocked on the building next door, and a voice said, "Just a minute; come in." He opened the door and saw a sight in shadows. A man was heading out a door. "As soon as I've finished taking out the trash and washed my hands, I can help you."

A short while later, the man emerged. "Hi. I'm Fr. Elijah." He extended his hand, his head and hands standing out against the darkness and his dark robe, and shook George's hand. George said, "I'm George."

"What can I do for you?"

George stopped, and thought. He said, "I was just looking around while I was waiting for my thoughts to clear."

Fr. Elijah said, "Are you a student?"

George said, "Yes."

Fr. Elijah said nothing, but it did not seem he needed to say anything just then. George was growing calm.

"May I offer you something to drink? I was just going to make tea, and I don't have a full range of soft drinks, but there should be something worth drinking. There's a pitcher of ice-cold water if you don't care for an old man's coffee or tea."

George said "Yes."

"Wonderful. Come with me." The two began walking, and they sat down.

George looked at him.

Fr. Elijah said, "Please sit down," motioning to an armchair. "Did you want coffee, water, or tea? I have cookies. Oh, and there's milk too."

George smiled. "Could I have a chalice of milk?"

Fr. Elijah turned to get the cookies, a cup and some milk.

George said, "I meant to say a cup of milk. Sorry, I was trying to be a little more serious."

Fr. Elijah said, "You can explain, or not explain. It's your choice. But I think you *were* being serious. Just not the way you expected. But we can change the subject. Do you have a favorite book? Or has anything interesting happened to you lately? I can at least listen to you."

George said, "I was just at the store nearby."

Fr. Elijah asked, "What do you think of it?"

George said, "Are you sure you won't be offended?"

Fr. Elijah said, "One of the things I have found in my work is that people can be very considerate about not being offensive, but sometimes I have something valuable to learn with things people think might offend me."

"Ever wonder about the direction our society has headed? Or see something that left you wishing you could still wonder about that?"

"A lot of people do."

"I was already having a bad day when I wandered into a store, and just when I thought things couldn't get any more crass, they got more crass. I've just been invited to buy an identity with the help of a market-segment dental floss container."

"You're a man after my own heart. I've heard that the store manager has some pretty impressive connections. I've heard that if none of the dental floss containers in the store suit the identity you want to have, and you ask the manager, he can get your choice of floss in a custom container made by a sculptor to meet your whims!"

"But isn't there more to life than that?"

"I certainly hope so! Oh, and did I mention that I've found that store an excellent place for important shopping for April

Fools' Day? I'm hoping to get my godson horribly artificial sugary-sweet tasting lacy pink floss in a container covered by red and white hearts and words like 'Oochie-pooh.' He'll hit the roof! On second thought, he'll be expecting such a gift... I should probably give it to him on what you'd consider August 12."

"Why? What's special about August 12?"

"That's a bit of a labyrinth to sort out. Some Orthodox keep the old Julian calendar, while some keep the 'new' civil calendar, which means that those who preserve the old calendar, even if we manage not to go off in right field, are thirteen days 'late' for saints' days, celebrating July 30, the Feast of Saint Valentine, on what you'd consider August 12. What you call Valentine's Day is the Western celebration of the saint we celebrate on another day, and it's a bit of a Western borrowing to use it for pseudo-romantic purposes to pick on my godson, as that saint's feast did not pick up all the Western romantic connotations; Saint Valentine's story is a typical story of a bishop who strengthened people against paganism and was martyred eventually. Every day is a feast of some sort, and every feast--that is, every day--has several saints to celebrate... but I'm going on and on. Have I confused you yet?"

"Um, 'right field'? What does that mean?"

"Oops, sorry, personal expression. In the West people go out in left field and go loony liberal. In Orthodoxy, people go out in right field and go loony conservative. Some of the stuff I've been told would make me at least laugh if I didn't want to cry so badly. Sorry, I'm rambling, and I was trying to hear you out when it looked like you've had a rough day, right up to a store telling you there was nothing more to hope for in life than things like dental floss with a container designed for your market segment. Let me let you change the subject."

"Um, you're probably wondering why I said, 'chalice of milk.'"

"I would be interested in hearing that, but only if you want to tell. I have a guess, but I really don't want you to feel obligated to say something you'd rather not."

"What is your guess?"

"That you said 'chalice of milk' for an interesting reason that probably has an interesting connection to what, in life, you hope goes beyond the trivialities you were pushed into at that store. A chalice, whatever that means to you, is something deeper and richer."

George opened his mouth, then closed it for a moment, and said, "Does a chalice mean anything to you?"

"Oh, yes. A chalice means quite a lot to me."

"What does it mean to you?"

"George, have you ever seen a chalice?"

"No, but it's pretty important in something I've read."

"Would you like to see a chalice?"

"The chalice I've read about was made of purest gold. I'd imagine that if you have a fancy wine glass, maybe lead crystal, it would look poorer than what I'd imagine, and there are some things that are big enough that I'd rather not imagine."

"Well, there are some things that are bigger than can be seen, and that includes a chalice. But the chalice I have--I can't show it to you now--has the glint of gold, which has more layers than I can explain or know."

"Is there a time you can show it to me?"

"Yes, come during the Divine Liturgy, and you can see the chalice from which I serve the Eucharist. I can't explain--I know this offends some people, and I will understand if you are offended--that it would not be good for me to give you the Eucharist if you are not Orthodox. But you can see the chalice as it holds a treasure infinitely more valuable than its goldwork."

"What is that?"

"The Eucharist."

"Isn't that just a symbol?"

"Hmm, there are six hundred ways to respond to that. I can get into some of the intricacies later. If you want. Or we need never talk about it. But...

"Saying the Eucharist is 'just a symbol' is as silly as saying that the Eucharist is 'just the body and blood of Christ'. What else do you want it to be--a designer container of dental floss?"

George's laugh was interrupted by a knock at a door. Fr. Elijah looked at his watch, and his face fell. He said, "Just when the conversation was getting interesting! I'm sorry; I have an appointment."

George said, "Well, I won't take any more of your time; I'll come on Sunday. What time?"

"The Divine Liturgy starts at 9:00 Sunday morning; I'm sorry, that isn't a very good time for college students. Arriving five minutes late isn't a big deal. Most of the professors of campus can give you directions to my parish, the Church of the Holy Trinity. And bother that I have to end our talk!"

"That's OK. Do you have some literature that you want to give me? Where are your pamphlets?"

"Hmm, that would take some time to explain, and I can explain later if you want. But I don't have any pamphlets. If you want a book I can go to the library and you can borrow one. But Orthodox people don't usually feel obligated to stuff your pockets with as much paper as we can and leave you walking away feeling guilty that you dread the prospect of reading it. Come back; I enjoyed talking with you, and if you want I can get something from the library. But only if you want. Please excuse me." Fr. Elijah stood up and bowed slightly, but reverently, to George as they shook hands.

"Coming!" Fr. Elijah said. "I'm sorry; I was just trying to wrap up a conversation. Please come in. It's been a long time since I've seen you, and I've been looking forward to it."

George stepped out, and walked out. He stopped by a window to look into the Church building again.

He could tell nothing that looked to him like a chalice, but everywhere was the glint of gold.

George wandered back with a spring in his step.

He returned home and opened *Brocéliande*, and read:

> Blaise turned at a slow step. "Why callest thou thyself empty? Hast thou none, my son?"
>
> Merlin answered him. "Forgive me, my master, my

lord."

The wind was deadly still.

Blaise turned even more fully. "What is it, my pupil?"

Merlin reached out his hand. A mighty wind blew, such as openeth doors that be closed and closeth doors that be open.

An apple tree shook of a violence and apples met their place on the humble earth, all apples did so which fell, save one which Merlin his hand did close upon it.

The wind blew and blew, stronger and stronger it blew, and Blaise looked upon Merlin, and spake: "Flyest thou now, my hawk?"

Merlin his chaste teeth closed in on the apple, and the great and mighty wind closed a door against the stone and hushed to become a soft murmuring breeze, as a still small voice.

Merlin looked upon his master. "Though the Grail remain a secret and a secret remain the Grail, men shall know it even under its cloak of samite most red. When a man shall grasp the secret of the Grail then shall he grasp the mystery of the Trinity."

Blaise looked upon his servant. "And who shall be in that grasp?"

Merlin spake softly. "My lord, I wit me not."

Blaise said, "My lord, it is well with thee."

Merlin abode in a quiet still spirit.

The hours and days passed quickly, until it was Sunday and George left a little early and arrived at the Church of the Holy Trinity early, looked at his watch and saw 8:53 AM.

He stepped inside and found things suddenly cool. There was a dazzling darkness, with pure candlelight and lamplight glittering off of gold, with fragrances of smoke and beeswax and incense. There was a soft chanting, and the funny thing was that it was hard to say whether the Church seemed full or empty. He saw few people, even for the small space, but he had rather a sense that the place was full of worshipers, mostly unseen. He could feel glory, almost as a weight.

There seemed to be a continuous faint commotion as people entered, went to the front, doing something he could not tell, and walked around. He stood as most people were standing, although some were sitting and people seemed to bow or move their hands. It is not exactly that George did not feel conspicuous as to how he was standing out, as that that was not quite the greatest way he felt conspicuous.

How did he feel conspicuous? George found no answer he liked. The whole situation seemed foreign to him, and for the first time it did not seem so much that he was examining something but that something, or someone, was examining him and judging him.

Something happened. Or rather, this time the something that happened meant that people were sitting down, in pews around the edges or on the floor, and the chant had become ordinary speech. Fr. Elijah said,

> In the Name of the Father, of the Son, and of the Holy Ghost. Amen.
>
> Last week after Liturgy, little John came up to me and said, "Fr. Elijah, I have a question." "What, I asked." "I saw *Indiana Jones and the Raiders of the Lost Ark* Friday and it was really, really cool! Could you tell me all about the Ark?" So I paused in thought, and exercised a spiritual father's prerogative. I said, "You know what? That's a good question. Let me think a bit and I'll answer that question in my homily." And when his father said, "But weren't you going to--" I said, "Don't worry about *that*. I'll blame the homily on him, and if people find it duller than a worn-out butter knife, they can call you at work and complain." And *finally* I got him to crack a faint smile.
>
> So this is the homily I'm blaming on him. First of all, the Ark of the Covenant is a spiritual treasure, and is spiritually understood. It is not lost, but it is found in a

> much deeper way than some expect. For it is both a *what* and, more deeply, a *who*. You can look up in fact where it is, and the amazing thing is that it is still guarded as a relic rather than treated simply as something that merely belongs in a museum, and the hidden Ark is in fact greater than if it were displayed in a showcase. It is one of many treasures the Church guards, and it is at the Church of our Lady Mary of Zion in the Ethiopian city of Axum. I've been there, even if I could not see the Ark. But the Ark which holds the bread from Heaven and the tablets on which the Ten Commandments were inscribed is in the shadow of the Ark to whom we sing, "Rejoice, O Volume wherein the Word was inscribed" and whose womb is a garden of spiritual treasures, "more spacious than the Heavens" as we say, by whom we are given the greater and in fact greatest Bread from Heaven. When we read of the Ark coming to King David and of the Theotokos or Mother of God coming to Lady Elizabeth, there are some surprising parallels which seem stunning until we recognize that that is just how Luke might be telling us that the Theotokos is someone to whom the Ark hints. There is a profound connection to the Arthurian legends, in which the Sir Galahad is granted to see into the Holy Grail and beholds a wonder beyond the power of words to tell. And it is in fact a misunderstanding on a number of levels to think that that rich Grail is confined to--

If George were sitting on a chair, he might have fallen off it. He was, fortunately, sitting on the floor. When he caught himself enough to follow the words, he listened closely:

> ...these other images. It was from the virgin earth that the first Adam, by whom we all live natural life, was taken. It was from the parched earth of the Virgin Theotokos that the last Adam, by whom we are called to the divine life, was given. And still this is not to tell how the first Adam,

wanting to become God, lost his divinity, until God became the Last Adam, raising up Adam that all of us who bear Adam's likeness might become divine, bearing the likeness of God. Death entered when we took and ate the fruit from the Tree of the Knowledge of Good and Evil, and now everlasting begins when we obey the summons to take and eat the Fruit from the Tree of Life.

Is it possible to call Mary Magdalene the Holy Grail? Yes and amen. We can call Mary Magdalene the Holy Grail in a very deep sense. She spoke before the Emperor, and that incident is why after all these years Christians still color Easter eggs, red eggs for the Orthodox Church as the were for Mary Magdalene, when she presented a red egg to the Emperor, perhaps miraculously. There are only a few dozen people the Church has ever honored more. She bears the rank of "Equal to the Apostles," and an angel told her the mysterious news of the Resurrection, and it was she who told the Apostles who in turn would be sent ("Apostle" means "Sent One") to the uttermost ends of the earth.

The Holy Grail is that vessel which first held the blood of Christ, and it is the shadow of that symbol in which the body and blood of Christ become real so that they can transform us. The Eucharist is misunderstood through the question of just what happens when the priest consecrates the gift, because the entire point of the transformation of the gifts is the transformation of the faithful so that we can be the Body of Christ and have the divine blood, the royal bloodline, the divine life coursing through our veins. God the Father the Father for whom every fatherhood in Heaven and earth is named. Father, Son, and Holy Spirit are each the King for whom every kingdom is named, so that the Kingdom of Heaven is more, not less, of a Kingdom than the kingdoms we can study on earth.

In the third prayer before communion, we are invited to pray, "O Thou Who by the coming of the Comforter, the

Spirit, didst make thy sacred disciples precious vessels, declare me also to be a receptacle of his coming." Mary Magdalene bears powerful witness to what a disciple can be if she becomes a humble earthen vessel in which there is another coming of Christ. She became the Holy Grail, as does every one of us transformed by the power of Christ's body and blood. If you only ask questions about the transformation of bread and wine, the Holy Grail is merely a *what*... but if you recognize the larger transformation that has the smaller transformation as a microcosm, the Holy Grail can also be a *who*: you and I.

It would take much longer to even begin to speak of that nobility of which you will only find the trace and shadow if you study royalty and their bloodlines. I have spoken enough.

In the Name of the Father, and of the Son, and of the Holy Ghost. Amen.

George was at once attracted, entranced, repulsed, and terrified. It seemed like more than he had dared to dream was proclaimed as truth, but that this meant he was no longer dealing with his choice of fantasy, but perhaps with reality itself. The chanting resumed. There was a procession, and what was in it? Ornate candles, a golden spoon and something that looked like a miniature golden lance, something covered with a cloth but that from its base might have been an intricately worked golden goblet, a cross that seemed to be glory itself, and other things he could not name. It was not long before George heard, "The holy things are for those who are holy," and the reply--was it a correction?--immediately followed: "One is holy. One is Lord, Jesus Christ, to the glory of God the Father. Amen."

George wanted to squirm when he heard the former, and when he heard the latter, he headed for the door. The spiritual weight he had been feeling seemed more intense; or rather, it seemed something he couldn't bear even though he hoped it would continue. He felt, just for a moment that this was more than him having an experience, but he failed to put his finger on what more it might be.

Once outside, he tried to calmly walk home, but found himself running.

George found himself walking, but in completely unfamiliar surroundings. He spent a good deal of time wandering until he recognized a major road, and walked alongside it until he returned home, hungry and parched.

He opened *Brocéliande* for a moment, but did not feel much like reading it. George went to check his email, began looking through his spam folder--to see if anything important got through, he told himself--and found himself wandering around the seedier side of the net.

In the days that followed, people seemed to be getting in his way, his homework was more of a waste of time, and somehow *Brocéliande* no longer seemed interesting.

Friday, George missed dinner and went, hungry, to a crowded store where a white-haired man stood right between him and the food he wanted... not only blocking the aisle with his cart, but adding a third 12-pack of soda to the bottom of his cart... and seeming to take forever to perform such a simple task.

After waiting what seemed too long, George refrained from saying "Gramps," but found himself hissing through his teeth, "Do you need help getting that onto your cart?"

The white-haired man turned around in surprise, and then said, "Certainly, George, how are you?"

George stopped.

It was Fr. Elijah.

"Can, um, I help you get that in your cart?"

"Thank you, George, and I would appreciate if you would help me choose another one. Do you have a favorite soda?"

"This may sound silly, but Grape Crush. Why?"

"Help me find a 12-pack of it. I realized after you came that it was kind of silly for me to inviting people like you inside and not having any soda for them, and I've been procrastinating ever since. Aah, I think I see them over there. Could you put that under your cart?"

George began walking over to the Grape Crush.

Fr. Elijah asked, less perfunctorily, "How are you, George?" and reached out his hand. At least George thought Fr. Elijah was reaching out his hand, but it was as if Fr. Elijah was standing on the other side of an abyss of defilement, and holding out a live coal.

Fr. Elijah shook George's hand.

George tried to find his footing on shifting ground, and managed to ask, "Fr. Elijah, how are you going to get that soda out to your car?"

"Usually someone from the store helps me put things in my trunk or something; I've never found a grocery store to be a place where nothing is provided."

The chasm yawned; George felt as if he were clothed in filthy rags.

"Um, and at home?"

"The Lord always provides something. Sorry, that sounded super spiritual. Usually it's not too long before someone strong comes by and can carry things."

George tried to smile. "I'm fine. How are you?"

Fr. Elijah made no answer with words. He smiled a welcoming smile, and somehow the store began to remind him of Fr. Elijah's office.

George kept waiting for Fr. Elijah to say something more, to answer, but Fr. Elijah remained silent. There seemed to be a warmth about him, as well as something he feared would burn his defilement, but Fr. Elijah remained silent, and pushed his cart, which had a small armload of groceries and a heavy weight of soda cases, to the register.

"I can help you load things into your car, Fr. Elijah."

Fr. Elijah turned with warmth. Gratitude was almost visible in his features, but he remained strangely silent.

George momentarily remembered to grab a sandwich, then returned to Fr. Elijah in line.

George began to wonder why Fr. Elijah was not speaking to

him. Or rather, that was the wrong way to put it. George could not accuse Fr. Elijah of being inattentive, but why was he silent?

George began to think about what he had been doing, and trying not to, to think of something else, to think of something else to talk about. But images returned to his mind, and a desire to--he certainly couldn't mention *that*.

Where were they? Fr. Elijah had just pushed the cart to his car, and slowly fumbled with his keys to unlock his trunk. George thought with a shudder about what it would be like to an old man to load cases of soda, even 12-packs.

"I can help you unload the soda at your house."

Fr. Elijah turned and made the slightest bow.

Once inside the car, George made a few nervous remarks about the weather. Fr. Elijah simply turned with what must have been a fatherly smile, but said nothing.

George did not consider himself strong, but it was only a few minutes for him to get the handful of cases of soda tucked into a slightly messy closet.

Once back in the car, Fr. Elijah seemed to arrive almost immediately at the dorm.

George said, "Now I remember. I wouldn't ask for another ride back, but I should have asked to borrow a book from your library."

Fr. Elijah turned. "*Should* you?"

George said, "What do you mean, should I? Are you mad at me? Didn't you tell me that I could borrow any book in your library if you wanted?"

Fr. Elijah said, "For all I am concerned now, you may borrow the whole library, if you want to. Or keep it, if you want."

"Then why don't you want me borrowing a book now?"

"I have many good books you could read, but right now, you don't really want one of my books."

"What do you mean?"

"If you genuinely want to borrow a book, I will gladly talk with you and suggest what I think would be your deepest joy. But why are you asking me for a book now?"

"I thought it would be polite to..."

Fr. Elijah waited an interminable moment and said, "Something is eating you."

George said, "You have no right to--"

Fr. Elijah said, "I have no right to this discussion, and neither do you. Thinking in terms of rights is a way to miss the glory we were made for. But let us stop looking at rights and start looking at what is beneficial. You don't have to answer, but are you happy now?"

George waited, and waited, and waited for an escape route to open up. Then he said, and the saying seemed like he was passing through white-hot ice, "I've been looking at--"

Fr. Elijah said, "Stop, You've said enough."

George said, "But how did you know?"

Fr. Elijah sighed, and for a moment looked like he wanted to weep. "George, I would like to say something deep and mysterious about some special insight I have into people's souls, but that is not it. I am a father, a confessor, and one of the biggest sins I hear in confession--'biggest' not because it is unforgivable; Jesus was always ready, more than ready, to forgive this kind of sin, but 'biggest' because it keeps coming up and causing misery, is the sort of sin you've been struggling with. I count myself very fortunate that I grew up in an age when you could have all the basic utilities without getting all sorts of vile invitations coming whether you want them or not, and I am glad that I do not feel obligated to purchase some nasty pills because I'm not a real man unless I have the same drives I had at the age of eighteen. What a miserably small and constricted caricature of manhood! I count myself a real man, much more because I have not suffered what tends to become such a *dreary* dissipation and deflation of any real manhood."

George said, "You're not mad?"

Fr. Elijah raised his hand, moved it up and down and side to side, and said, "I am blessing you, priceless son."

George said, "How can I be free of this?"

Fr. Elijah said, "Come with me. Get back in the car."

They drove for a few more minutes, neither one needing to say anything, until George noticed with alarm the shape of the hospital.

George said, "Where are we going?"

Fr. Elijah said, "To the emergency room."

George looked around in panic. "I don't have money for--"

"Relax. None of the treatment you will be receiving will generate bills."

"What on earth are you--"

"I'm not telling you. Just come with me."

They walked through a side door, George's heart pounding, and George noticed two people approaching immediately.

Fr. Elijah turned momentarily, saying, "*Buenos noches, Señoras,*" and motioned with his hand for them to follow him.

As they and George followed, Fr. Elijah said, "Because of the triage in an emergency room, and because mere seconds are a matter of life and death in treating really severe injuries, people with relatively 'minor' injuries that still need medical attention can wait for an interminable amount of time."

Fr. Elijah suddenly stopped. George saw a boy with skinned knees, whose mother was slowly working through paperwork. Fr. Elijah said, "Take away his pain."

George looked at him, halfway to being dumbfounded. "What?"

Fr. Elijah said, "You heard me." Then he turned and left, so that George saw only Fr. Elijah's back and heard from him only broken Spanish.

George felt grateful that at least he wasn't too easily grossed out. He could look at lacerated flesh and eat if he needed to. George sat next to the boy, smelled an overwhelming odor from his blood, and suddenly felt sick to his stomach.

George tried to refrain from swearing about what Fr. Elijah could possibly have meant. Badger the hospital into giving anaesthesia sooner? Kiss it and make it better? Use some psychic power he didn't have? Find a switch on the back of the kid's neck and reboot him?

For a while, nothing happened, until the boy stopped sobbing, and looked at him, a little bit puzzled.

George said, "Hi, I'm George."

The boy said, "Mr. George."

George tried to think of something to say. He said, "What do you get when you cross an elephant with a kangaroo?"

"What?"

"Really big holes all over Australia."

The boy looked at him, but showed no hint of a smile.

"Do you not get it?" George asked.

The boy said, very quietly, "No."

"An elephant has a lot of weight, and a kangaroo bounces up and down. If you put 'weight' and 'bouncy' together, then you get something that, when it bounces, is so heavy it makes big holes in the ground."

The boy said nothing until George added, "That's what makes it funny."

The boy made himself laugh loudly, and just as soon winced in pain.

George tried to think of what to do. After a while, he asked, "What's your favorite color?"

When the boy said nothing, George looked at his face and was surprised at the pain he saw.

"What is your name?"

"My name is Tommy."

George thought about what to say. He began to tell a story. He told of things he had done as a boy, and funny things that had happened (the boy didn't laugh), and asked questions which met with incomprehension. And this went on and on and on.

George wondered why he was having so much fun.

Then George looked at Tommy.

When was the last time George had even *begun* to do something for someone else?

George realized three things. First, he had stopped talking. Second, a hand was holding tightly to his sleeve. Third, there was something he was trying very hard not to think about.

George looked, and Tommy asked, "Mister, are you a knight? I want to be a knight when I grow up."

George had never before felt such shame that he wished the earth would swallow him up.

"Mister?"

"No, I am not a knight."

"You seem like a knight."

"Why?"

"You just do. Do you know anything about knights?"

"I've been reading a book."

"What's it called?"

"*Brocéliande*."

"Tell me the story of Brookie-Land."

"I can't."

"Why?"

"Because I haven't read all of it."

"What have you read?"

George closed his eyes. All he could remember now was a flurry of images, but when he tried to put them together nothing worked.

George was interrupted. "Do you have a suit of armor?"

Immediately, and without thought, George said, "What kind of armor? I mean, is it chain mail, like a steel, I mean iron, sweater, or is it the later plate armor that gets into the later depictions? Because if there were a King Arthur, he would--"

"Did King Arthur know powerful Merlin? Because Merlin could--"

"I've read a lot about Merlin--he could build a castle just with his magic. And it apparently matters whose son he is, but I couldn't--"

"I want you to show me--"

A voice cut in. "Tommy!"

"Yes?" the boy said.

"The doctor is ready to see you... Sir, I'm sorry to interrupt, but--"

"Why does the doctor want to see me?"

"Because she wants to stitch up your knees, Silly Sweetie. Let the nurses roll you away. I'm glad--"

Tommy looked in puzzlement at his knees, saw how badly lacerated they were, and began screaming in pain.

There was a minor commotion as the nurses took Tommy in to be stitched up, or so George would later guess; he could never remember the moment. He only remembered walking around the emergency room, dazed.

Truth be told, though, George felt wonderful. He faintly noticed hearing Fr. Elijah's voice, saying something in Spanish, and joined a group of people among whom he felt immediate welcome. Then the woman who was on the bed was taken in, and Fr. Elijah, and to his own surprise, George, bid farewell to the other members of the group.

George and Fr. Elijah were both silent for a long time in the car.

Fr. Elijah broke the silence.

"Would it be helpful to talk with me about anything?"

"I have to choose just one?"

"No, you can ask as many questions as you want."

"Besides what I started to tell you--"

"Yes?"

"When I was talking with that boy, I mean Tommy, the boy you introduced me to, I--I'm not sure I would have said exactly this, but I've been spending a lot of time reading *Brocéliande* and no time choosing to be with other people... would you keep that book for me, at least for a time?"

"I certainly could, but let's look at our option. You sound less than fully convinced."

"I don't want to give it up."

"Well, yes, I wouldn't want to give it up either. But is that it?"

"No... I'm really puzzled. Just when I thought I had managed to stop thinking about never-never land and start thinking about Tommy, the kid asked me about never--I mean, he said that he wanted to grow up to be a knight, and he asked me if

I was a knight. Which I am *not*."

"That's very mature of you..."

"And?"

"What would you imagine yourself doing as the right thing?"

"Getting away from that silly desire and be with other people instead."

"Hmm."

"Hmm what?"

"Have you ever read C.S. Lewis's 'The Weight of Glory'?"

"No."

"Ok, I want to stop by my office before I drop you off at home, because I'm going to go against my word and give you literature to read. Although I only want you to read a few pages' essay out of the book, unless you want to read more essays--is this OK?--"

"I suppose."

"Because C.S. Lewis talked about the idea of unselfishness as a virtue, and said that there's something pitiable about letting unselfishness be the center of goodness instead of the divine love. Or something like that. And the reason I remembered that is that somewhere connected with this is this terrible fear that people have that their desires are too strong, and maybe their desires are too much in need of being deepened and layered, except I think he only said, 'too weak.' Today I would add: in a much deeper way that you can remedy by dangerous pills in your spam.

"Maybe you don't need to get rid of that book at all... maybe you should lend it to me for a time, and let me enjoy it, but maybe not even that is necessary."

"Why?"

"My guess is that if you read enough in that book--or at least the ones I've read--you may notice a pattern. The knight goes to the company of the castle and then plunges into the woodland for adventure and quests, and you need a rhythm of both to make a good story. Or a good knight."

"I fail to see how I could become a knight, or how

knighthood applies to me."

"Hmm..."

"Hmm what?"

"Maybe that's a can of worms we can open another time... For now, I will say that the reason the stories have knights doing that is not because the knights wore armor and rode horses, but because the people telling the stories were telling the stories of men. Who need both castle and wood. Keep reading *Brocéliande*, and push it further. Push it to the point that your college and your city are to you what the castle was to the knight. Or even so that you don't see the difference. And alongside your trek into the enchanted wood, meet people. I would suggest that you find a way to connect with people, and work with it over time. If I may offer a prescription--"

"Prescription?"

"A priest is meant to be a spiritual physician, or at least that is what Orthodox understand. And part of the priest's job is to prescribe something. If you're willing."

"I'll at least listen."

"First, I want you to spend *some* of your time with other people. Not all."

"Doing what?"

"That's something you need to decide, and even if I can offer feedback to you, I would not make that decision for you. You need to have a think about it.

"Second, something for you to at least consider... Come to me for confession. I cannot give the sacrament I give to Orthodox, but I can bless you. Which isn't the immediate reason I mention it. Even if I were not to bless you, and even if Christ were not listening to your confession, there would still be power in owning up to what you have done. It gives power in the struggle.

"Third, do you access the Internet through a cable or through wireless?"

"An ethernet cable. I don't have a laptop, and I've heard that the wireless network on campus is worth its weight in drool."

"Do you have a USB key?"

"Yes."

"Then give me your Ethernet cable."

"What kind of Luddite--"

"I'm not being a Luddite. I'm offering a prescription for you... There are different prescriptions offered for the needs of different people."

"So for some people it is beneficial to visit--"

"For me it has been. When I was trying to figure out what was going on, I went to a couple's house, and with their permission started looking through the pictures in their spam folder until I'd had more than enough. And I wept for a long time; I suddenly understood something I didn't understand about what I was hearing in confession. I still pray for the people photographed and those looking at the photograph, and some of the women's faces still haunt me--"

"The *faces* haunt you?"

"Yes. Understand that at my age, *some* temptations are weaker... but I looked at those faces and saw that each one was somebody's daughter, or maybe somebody's son, and my understanding is that it's nothing pleasant to pose for those pictures. At least the faces I saw reminded me of an airline stewardess trying really hard to smile peacefully to someone who is being abrasive and offensive. But as I was saying, I count my hour of looking to be of the greatest spiritual benefit. But it would not benefit you, and it is my judgment that in *your* case a little of what programmers call a 'net vacation'--though I invite you to use lab and library computers--could help you in--"

"Do you know what it's like to give up the convenience of computers in your room?"

"Do you know what it's like to ride a horse instead of a car for a short time? I do..."

"But riding a horse is at least... like... um... it's more like Arthur's world, isn't it?"

"If you want to look at it that way, you're welcome to..." Fr. Elijah stopped the car and stepped out, saying, "Please excuse me for a moment." The shuffling seemed to drag on, and Fr. Elijah stepped out with a book and got back in the car. "Oh, and I almost forgot. Please don't make this a matter of 'I won't do such-and-such or even think about it,' because trying not to think about a temptation is a losing game. I am inviting you to a trek from castle to wood, and wood to castle, with both feeding into a balance. Here is the book with 'The Weight of Glory' and other essays. Now..."

Calix College was in sight almost immediately, and Fr. Elijah waited outside George's dorm for what became a surprisingly long time... he wondered if he should go up and see if George had changed his mind, and--

George walked out and handed him a cable in the dark. It was thick and stiff.

"I thought Ethernet cables weren't this thick and stiff."

"It's my power cable. I put stuff I need on my USB key."

"Good man."

"Goodbye."

"Goodbye, and George, one other thing..."

"Yes?"

"There is no better time to be in a Church than when you know how unworthy you are."

"Um..."

"What?"

"I appreciate how much you're stretching, but..."

"George, I want to ask you something."

"I've been serving the Divine Liturgy for thirty-eight years now. How long have I been worthy to do so?"

"Is this a trick question? All thirty-eight?"

"It is indeed a trick question, but the answer is not 'thirty-eight.' I have *never* been worthy to serve the Divine Liturgy, nor have I ever been worthy to receive communion, nor have I ever been worthy to pray at Church, or anywhere else. We can talk about this if you like, but am not just being polite when I say that there is no better time to enter the Church than when you know yourself unworthy. Maybe we can talk later about what trumps unworthiness. For now, I wish you good night, and I would be delighted to see you join and adorn our company on Sunday."

George climbed up in his room and sat in his armchair, and it felt like a throne. He was exhausted--and on the other side of shame. He began dutifully opening the C.S. Lewis book, glanced at the title, then tossed it aside. It was not what he really wanted. He picked up *Brocéliande*, wiped the dust off the cover with his hand, and opened to its middle, to its heart. George read:

> rode until he saw a river, and in the river a boat, and in the boat a man.
>
> The man was clad all in black, and exceeding simple he appeared. At his side was a spear, and was a basket full of oysters filled.
>
> "I ask your pardon that I cannot stand. For the same cause I can not hunt, for I am wounded through the thighs. I do what I might, and fish to share with others."
>
> The knight rode on, Sir Perceval he hyght, until he came upon a castle. And in that castle he met a welcome rich, before a King all in sable clad round, and a sash of purple royal girt about his head, and full majestic he looked.
>
> Then in walked a youth, bearing a sword full straight, for it were not falchion neither scimitar, but a naked sword with a blade of gold, bright as light, straight as light, light as light. The very base of that sword were gem work, of ivory made and with sapphires encrusted. And the boy was girt tightly with a baldric and put the sword in its place. In utmost decorum the sword hung at his side.
>
> The boy placed what he shouldered at the feet of the King.
>
> Spake the King: "I ask your forgiveness that I do not rise. Partake of my feast."
>
> Simpler fare was never adorned by such wealth of wisdom. The body was nourished, and ever more spirit in the fare that was read.
>
> Anon processed one man holding a candelabra of

purest gold with seven candles, anon another, anon a maiden mother holding a Grail, it was such a holy thing! Anon a lance that ever bore three drops of blood. And ever Perceval wondered, and never Perceval spake, though it passed many a time. With a war inside him Sir Perceval kept him his peace. Anon the King spake, "See thou mine only food," and anon came the Grail holding not a stone neither a snake but a single wheaten host, afloat as a pearl in a sea of wine, red as blood. And never the King ate he none else.

Here a page was ripped out from *Brocéliande*, with yellowed marks where once tape failed to mend what was torn.

The damsel arose from her weeping. "Perceval! Perceval! Why askedst thou not thine enquiry?"

George soon fell into a deep and dreamless sleep.
Saturday he rested him all the day long: barely he stirred.
In his dream, George heard a song.
All was in darkness.

The song it came out of a mist, like as a mist, melodic, mysterious, piercing, like as a prayer, mighty, haunting, subtle, token of home and a trace of a deep place. How long this continued he wot not.

The one high, lilting voice, tinged with starlight, became two, three, many, woven in and out as a braid of three strands, or five, or ten, as a Celtic knot ever turning in and out. And as it wove in and out, it was as the waters of a lake, of an ocean, of a sea, and George swam in them. George was ever thirsty, and ever he swam. He swam in an ever-rippling reflection of the Heavens at midnight, a sea of unending midnight blue and living sapphire.

George's feet sunk and he walked on the noiseless loam. Up about him sprung blades of grass and he walked into a forest growing of emerald and jade atop pillars of sculpted earth. Anon he walked slowly and slowly he saw a farm with the green grass of wheat growing of the fertile fecund field.

Upon a ruins he came, a soft, silent place where a castle still lingered and the verdant moss grew. Then through a city he walked, a city alive and vibrant in its stones, though its streets were a for a moment at a rest from its men. And in that city, he walked into the Church his heart, and found a tome opened upon a wooden stand entwined by vines.

George looked for a moment at the volume, and for a moment he saw letters of sable inscribed in a field argent. Then the words shifted, grew older, deepened into the depth of a root and the play of quicksilver. The script changed, the words spoke from afar, and became one word whose letters were hidden as behind a veil, one word inscribed at once in ciphers of luminous gold and congealed light that filled the book and shone all around it until--

George was awake, bright awake, wide awake, looking at a window the color of sunrise.

He arose to greet the coming of the dawn.

George went to Church and arrived almost an hour earlier than the 9:00 Fr. Elijah had given, and found to his surprise that although there were few other people, things had already begun. The fragrance of frankincense flowed and gold glittered, and he caught a word here and a phrase there--"Volume wherein the Word was inscribed," "Holy God, Holy Mighty, Holy Immortal," "Blessed is the Kingdom," "Lord have mercy." Then he heard a phrase he had heard innumerable times in other contexts. A shibboleth later taken from the New Testament, "The just shall live by faith," completely broke the illusion. George had had plenty of time to get sick of words he knew too well, or so it appeared to George. Yes, he was glad people understood them, but wasn't there more to understand than that? Even if they were both straightforward and important...

The homily began.

In the Name of the Father, and of the Son, and of the Holy Ghost. Amen.

One of the surprises in the Divine Comedy--to a few people at least--is that the Pope is in Hell. Or at least it's a surprise to people who know Dante was a devoted Catholic but don't recognize how good Patriarch John Paul and Patriarch Benedict have been; there have been some moments Catholics aren't proud of, and while Luther doesn't speak for Catholics today, he did put his finger on a lot of things that bothered people then. Now I remember an exasperated Catholic friend asking, "Don't some Protestants know anything *else* about the Catholic Church *besides* the problems we had in the sixteenth century?" And when Luther made a centerpiece out of what the Bible said about those who are righteous or just, "The just shall live by faith," which was in the Bible's readings today, he changed it, chiefly by using it as a battle axe to attack his opponents and even things he didn't like in Scripture.

It's a little hard to see how Luther changed Paul, since in Paul the words are also a battle axe against legalistic opponents. Or at least it's hard to see directly. Paul, too, is quoting, and I'd like to say exactly *what* Paul is quoting.

In one of the minor prophets, Habakkuk, the prophet calls out to the Lord and decries the wickedness of those who should be worshiping the Lord. The Lord's response is to say that he's sending in the Babylonians to conquer, and if you want to see some really gruesome archaeological findings, look up what it meant for the Babylonians or Chaldeans to conquer a people. I'm not saying what they did to the people they conquered because I don't want to leave you trying to get disturbing images out of your minds, but this was a terrible doomsday prophecy.

The prophet answered the Lord in anguish and asked how a God whose eyes were too pure to look on evil could possibly punish his wicked people by the much more wicked Babylonians. And the Lord's response is very mysterious: "The just shall live by faith."

Let me ask you a question: How is this an answer to

what the prophet asked the Lord? Answer: It isn't. It's a refusal to answer. The same thing could have been said by saying, "I AM the Lord, and my thoughts are not your thoughts, nor are my ways your ways. I AM WHO I AM and *I will do what I will do*, and I am sovereign in this. I choose not to tell you how, in my righteousness, I choose to let my wicked children be punished by the gruesomely wicked Babylonians. Only know this: even in these conditions, the just shall live by faith."

The words "The just shall live by faith" are an enigma, a shroud, and a protecting veil. To use them as Paul did is a legitimate use of authority, an authority that can only be understood from the inside, but these words remain a protecting veil even as they take on a more active role in the New Testament. The New Testament assumes the Old Testament even as the New Testament unlocks the Old Testament.

Paul does not say, "The just shall live by sight," even as he invokes the words, "The just shall live by faith."

Here's something to ponder: The righteous shall walk by faith even in their understanding of the words, "The just shall live by faith."

In the Name of the Father, and of the Son, and of the Holy Ghost. Amen.

George was awash and realized with a start that he was not knocked off his feet, gasping for air. He felt a light, joyful fluidity and wondered what was coming next. This time he realized he was sure he saw a chalice; the liturgy seemed to go a little more smoothly and quickly.

As soon as he was free, Fr. Elijah came up to him. "Good to see you, George. How are you?"

George said, "Delighted... but I'm sorry, I haven't read 'The Weight of Glory' for you yet."

Fr. Elijah said, "Good man... no, I'm not being sarcastic. Put first things first, and read it when you have leisure. How did you find the homily?"

George said, "It was excellent... by the way, it was really for me that you preached last week's homily, right? You seemed to be going a good bit out of your way."

"It was really for you, as it was also really for others for reasons you do not know."

"But weren't you getting off track?"

"George, I have a great deal of responsibility, concerns, and duties as a priest. But I have a great deal of freedom, too. I can, if you want, draw on King Arthur and his court every service I preach at from now until Christmas."

"How much do you mean, I mean literally? One or two? Four or five?"

"Huh? 'Literally'? Um, there is a temptation in the West to devote entirely too much time to what is literal. I *was* exaggerating when I said every service from now until Chrismas... *but*, if you want, I'd be perfectly happy to do that literally, for every service you're here." Fr. Elijah extended his had. "Deal?"

George paused in thought a moment. "Um, you've said that I could take all the books in your library and keep them if I want. I know you were exaggerating, but..."

"Yes, I was. But I am not exaggerating when I say that you can take them if you want."

"Don't you love books?"

"Immensely, but not as much as I want to love people! They're just possessions, and there are much greater treasures in my life than a good book, even though books can be quite good. Can we agree that I'll preach on something in Arthurian literature every liturgy I preach at until Christmas?"

"What if I'm not here?"

"We can make it part of the deal that I'll only preach on that topic if you're here."

George hesitated, and then shook his hand. "Deal."

Fr. Elijah smiled. "Some people have said my best homilies and best surprises have come from this kind of rash vow."

George started to walk away, and then stopped.

Fr. Elijah said, "Is something on your mind?"

George said, "What if other people don't like you preaching on something so odd? What will you do if people complain?"

Fr. Elijah said, "Then I can give them your cell phone number and have them call you at all hours of the day and night to grouse at you for foisting such a terrible proposal on me. Now get some coffee. Go! Shoo!"

After getting home, George did his laundry, looked to see if anyone was hanging out in the lounge (everybody was gone), and played games in the computer lab. It was a nice break.

The next day in math class, the teacher drew a grid on the board, drew dots where the lines crossed, erased everything but the dots, and set the chalk down. "Today I'd like to show a game. I'm handing out graph paper; draw dots where the lines cross. We're going to have two people taking turns drawing lines between dots that are next to each other. If you draw a line that completes a little square, you get a point. I'd like a couple of students to come up and play on the board." After a game, there was a momentary shuffle, and George found himself playing against the kid next to him. This continued for longer than he expected, and George began to piece together patterns of what would let his opponent score points, then what laid the groundwork for scoring points...

The teacher said, "Have any of you noticed things you want to avoid in this game? Why do these things lead to you giving points to your opponent when you don't want to, or scoring points yourself? This kind of observation is at the heart of a branch of mathematics called 'combinatorics.' And almost any kind of game a computer can play--I'm not talking about tennis--is something that computers can only play through combinatorics. I'd like to show you some more 'mathematical' examples of problems with things we call 'graphs' where a lot of those same kinds of things are--"

She continued giving problems and showing the kinds of thought in those problems.

George felt a spark of recognition--the same thing that attracted him to puzzles. Or was it something deeper? Many "twenty questions" puzzles only depended on identifying an unusual usage of common words, "53 bicycles" referring to "Bicycle" brand playing cards rather than any kind of vehicle, and so on and so forth. Some of what the teacher was showing seemed deeper...

...and for the first time in his life, the ring of a buzzer left George realizing he was spellbound in a math class. It set his mind thinking.

In English class, he winced, as just as before-class chatter seemed about to end, one of the other students said, "A man gets up in the morning, looks out his window, and sees the sun rising in the West. Why?"

George was not in particular looking forward to a discussion of literature he wasn't interested in, but he wanted even less to hear people blundering about another "twenty questions" problem, and cut in, "Because the earth's magnetic poles, we suppose, were fluctuating, and so the direction the sun was rising from was momentarily the magnetic West."

The teacher laughed. "That isn't the answer, is it?"

The student who had posed the question said, "Um... it is..."

The professor said, "So we are to imagine someone going to a gas station, saying, 'Which way is East?', and the attendant responding with, 'Just a sec, lemme check... I know usually this way is East, but with the Earth's magnetic fluctuations, who knows?' You know that in a lot of literature, East and West are less like numbers than like colors?"

"Um... How could a direction be like a number *or* a color?"

"There's colorful difference and colorless difference. If I tell you there are 57 pens in my desk, I haven't said anything very colorful that tells much about pens, or about my desk. But if I tell you a rose is a delicate pink, I've told you something about what it's like, what it's *like*, to experience a rose."

"So what color is East, then? Camouflage green?"

"East isn't a color, but it's *like* a color where camouflage green and fiery red are different. In both Greek and Russian, people use the same word for 'East' and 'sunrise'... and if you're really into etymology, English does this too, only we don't realize it any more. 'East' in English originally *means* 'sunrise,' as 'Easter' comes from the Anglo-Saxon name of a goddess of light and spring. Such terrible things the Orthodox miss out on by their quaint use of 'Pascha.' For us, the 'big' direction, the one which has the longest arrow or the biggest letter, the one all other directions are arranged around, is North; in Hebrew, it's East. There is a reason many churches are arranged East-West and we often worship towards the East, and that has meant something for the U.S... Would you agree that we are part of the West?"

"So our land is the worst land?" George said.

"Well, if you read enough Orthodox nut jobs, yes... particularly if this land is their home. But U.S. land, or part of it at least, is called utter East... the one U.S. state where Orthodoxy isn't edgy, exotic, fruitcake or 'other,' is Alaska, where there has been a native Orthodox presence, strong today, for over two hundred years. You know how, in *The Voyage of the Dawn Treader*, C.S. Lewis has a wood nymph speak an oracle that has drawn Sir Reepicheep all his life?

"Where sky and water meet,
Where the waves grow sweet,
Doubt not, Reepicheep,
To find all you seek,
There is the utter East.

"There's something big you'll miss about the holy land of Alaska if you just think of it as fully a state, but just one more state, just like every other state. It's the only state, if 'state' is an adequate term, with a still-working mechanical clock on the outside of a public building that was made by an Orthodox saint. Among other things.

"And the idea of holy land that you would want you to travel to feeds into things, even in Protestant literature like

Pilgrim's Progress, which you will misunderstand if you treat the pilgrimage as just there as a metaphor for spiritual process. I have found it very interesting to look at what people classify as 'just part of the allegory,' even though we will read no simpler allegory among the readings for this class. Now in reading for today, have any of you had an experience like Pilgrim's wakeup call at the beginning of Bunyan?"

George's head was swimming.

Why were his classes so dull before this week? He remembered previous math lessons which, in various ways, failed to give him puzzle solving, and in annoyance, turned to previous English lessons, when--

--why hadn't he paid attention? Or, more accurately, when George had paid attention, why hadn't he let it be interesting?

Philosophy also turned out to be interesting; the professor began the unit on medieval philosophy by asking, "How many angels can dance on the head of a pin?", eliciting various forms of derision, then asking people *what* they were deriding, began asking "How many of you can touch the head of the same pin at once?", produced a pin, and after students made various jostling efforts, asked whether a pin could accommodate a finite or infinite number of angels.

This was used to a class discussion about the nature of matter and spirit and whether angels dancing on the head of a pin would push each other away the way human bodies would... and at the end of class the professor began asking if people wanted to talk about how unfortunate it was that medieval philosophers *had* to use the poetic image of angels dancing on the head of a pin where others would have used the colorless language of analytic philosophy.

In chemistry, the professor did nothing in particular to make things interesting. George still enjoyed the lecture as it built to a discussion of isotope distributions as used to compute average molecular weights.

George was quite surprised when the weekend approached, spent the weekend playing card games, and wondered at how quickly Sunday came.

On Sunday, George entered the strange world of the Church building. It seemed more, not less, strange, but things began to make sense. "In the Name of the Father, and of the Son, and of the Holy Ghost. Amen." was something he noticed often, and he, if not understanding, was at least comfortable with the continual hubbub as people seemed to be moving about, sometimes to the front.

As the service passed, he found his eyes returning to, and then fixed on, an icon that showed three ?angels? sitting around a stone table. In the back was a mountain, a tree, and a building, a faroff building that George somehow seemed to be seeing from the inside...

The perspective in the picture was wrong. Wait, the perspective wouldn't be *that* wrong by accident... the picture looked very distorted, and George wanted to reach out and--

George looked. The perspective vanished, not at some faroff place on the other side of the picture, but behind him, and the picture seemed at once faroff and something seen from inside.

And what was it, almost at the heart of the icon, or somewhere beneath it, that the three peaceful, radiant, great ?angels? almost seemed clustered around? It looked like a chalice of gold.

George was looking, trying to see into the picture, wishing he could go closer, and seeing one person after another come closer in the dance of song and incense. George instinctively found himself backing up, and then realized people were sitting down and Fr. Elijah began:

> In the Name of the Father, and of the Son, and of the Holy Ghost. Amen.
>
> Sir Thomas Mallory in *Le Morte d'Arthur* has any number of characters, and I want to describe one of them, Sir Griflet, who is completely forgettable if you don't know French: he appears briefly, never stays in the narrative for very long, never does anything really striking at all. His

lone claim to fame, if you can call it that, is that Mallory refers to him as "Sir Griflet *le fils de Dieu*." For those of you who don't know French, we've just been cued in, in passing, that by the way, Sir Griflet is the Son of God.

Now why would this be? There some pretty striking things you can do if you are a character in that work. Sir Griflet is not a singular character who has the kind of energy of Sir Galahad, or in a different but highly significant way, Merlin. For that matter, he does not have even a more routine memorability like Sir Balin who wielded two swords at the same time. He's just forgettable, so why is he called *le fils de Dieu*, I mean the Son of God?

In Chretien de Troyes, who is a pivotal author before Mallory, a character with a name that would become "Griflet" is equally pedestrian and is named "fis de Do", son of Do, which has a root spelling of D-O where the word for God in that form of French is D-E-U. So a starkly pedestrian character, by an equally pedestrian language error, seems to have his father's name mixed up with how you spell the word for God. How pedestrian, disappointing, and appropriate.

There is a somewhat more interesting case in the story of a monk who believed that Melchizedek was the Son of God, and this is not due to a language error. If you were listening when the readings were chanted from the Bible, you would have heard that Melchizedek was "Without father, without mother, without descent, having neither beginning of days nor end of life: but made like unto the Son of God, abideth a priest continually." This may be surprising to us today, but that's because most of us have lost certain ways of reading Scripture, and it was a holy monk who thought this. He made a theological error, not a mere language error, and when his bishop asked his assistance in praying over whether Melchizedek or Christ was the Son of God, he arrived at the correct answer.

Now let me ask you who is really the Son of God. Do

you have an answer now?

I'm *positive* you're wrong. It's a forgettable person like Sir Griflet or Melchizedek.

When the Son of God returns in glory, he will say, "Depart from me, you who are damned, into the eternal fire prepared for the Devil and his angels. For I was hungry and you gave me nothing to eat; I was thirsty and you gave me nothing to drink; I was a stranger, and you showed me no hospitality; naked, and you did not clothe me; sick or in prison, and you did not visit me." And when the damned are confounded and ask when they could have possibly failed to do that, he will answer them, "I swear to you, just as you did not do it to one of the least of these, you did not do it for me."

We, in our very nature, are symbols of the Trinity, and this does not mean a sort of miniature copy that stands on its own in detachment. The Orthodox understanding of symbol is very difficult to grasp in the West, even if you haven't heard people trying to be rigorous or, worse, clever by saying "The word is not the thing it represents." And talking about symbols doesn't just mean that you can show reverence to a saint through an icon. It means that everything you fail to do to your forgettable neighbor, to that person who does absolutely nothing that draws your attention, you fail to do to Christ.

And if you are going to say, "But my neighbor is not Christ," are you not straining out a gnat and swallowing a camel in what you are being careful about? Your neighbor as such is not Christ as such. True, but this is really beside the point. It betrays a fundamental confusion if any of the damned answer their Judge and say, "But I wasn't unkind to *you.* I was just unkind to other people." We are so formed by the image of Christ that there is no way to do something to another person without doing that to Christ, or as this parable specifically says, fail to do. And I'd like you to stop for a second. The last time you were at an unexpected funeral, did you regret more the unkind thing you said, or the kind word you failed say, the kind action you failed to take? Perhaps it may be the latter.

Christ hides in each of us, and in every person you meet. There is a mystery: the divine became human that the human might become divine. The Son of God became a man that men might become the Sons of God. God and the Son of God became man that men might become gods and the Sons of God. Christ took on our nature so that by grace we might become what he is by nature, and that does not just mean something for what we should do in our own spiritual practices. It means that Christ hides in each person, and to each person we owe infinite respect, whether they're boring, annoying, mean, lovely, offensive, fascinating, confusing, predictable, pedestrian, or just plain forgettable like old Sir Griflet.

You owe infinite respect.

In the Name of the Father, and of the Son, and of the Holy Ghost. Amen.

Did George want to go up to the icon? He went up, feeling terribly awkward, but hearing only chant and the same shuffle of people in motion. He went up, awkwardly kissed the three figures someplace low, started to walk away in inner turmoil, turned back to the image, bowed as he had seen people see, and kissed the chalice of wine.

It was not long before he saw Fr. Elijah come out with a chalice, and draw from it with a golden spoon. This time he noticed people kissing the base of the chalice. There was nothing awkward about them, and there seemed to be something majestic that he began to catch a glimmer of in each of those present.

George later realized that he had never experienced worship "stopping" and coffee hour "beginning." The same majestic people went from one activity into another, where there was neither chanting nor incense nor the surrounding icons of a cloud of witnesses, but seemed to be a continuation of worship rather than a second activity begun after worship. He was with the same people.

It didn't occur until much later to George to wonder why the picture had a chalice... and then he could not stop wondering. He picked up *Brocéliande* and read:

> The knight and the hermit wept and kissed together, and the hermit did ask, "Sir knight, wete thou what the Sign of the Grail be?"
>
> The knight said, "Is that one of the Secrets of the Grail?"
>
> "If it be one of the Secrets of the Grail, that is neither for thee to ask nor to know. The Secrets of the Grail are very different from what thou mightest imagine in thine heart, and no man will get them by looking for secrets. But knowest thou what the Sign of the Grail is?"
>
> "I never heard of it, nor do I know it."
>
> "Thou wote it better than thou knowest, though thou wouldst wete better still if thou knewest that thou wote."
>
> "That is perplexing and hard to understand."
>
> The hermit said, "Knowest thou the Sign of the Cross?"
>
> "I am a Christian and I know it. It is no secret amongst Christians."
>
> "Then know well that the sacred kiss, the kiss of the mass, even if it be given and received but once per year, is the Sign of the Grail."
>
> "How is that? What makes it such as I have never heard?"
>
> "I know that not in its fullness. Nor could I count reasons even knew I the fullness of truth. But makest thou the Sign of the Cross when thou art alone?"
>
> "Often, good hermit; what Christian does not?"
>
> "Canst thou make the Sign of the Grail upon another Christian when thou art alone?"
>
> "What madness askest thou?"

> "Callest thou it madness? Such it is. But methinks thou wete not all that may be told."
>
> "Of a certainty speakest thou."
>
> "When thou dwellest in the darkness that doth compass round about the Trinity round about that none mayeth compass, then wilt thou dwell in the light of the Sign of the Grail with thy fellow man and thy brother Christian, for the darkness of the Trinity is the light of the Grail."

George got up, closed the book, and slowly put it away. He wondered, but he had read enough.

George dreamed again of a chalice whose silhouette was Light and held Light inside. Then the Light took shape and became three figures. George almost awoke when he recognized the figures from the icon. George dreamed much more, but he could never remember the rest of his dream.

That week, Fr. Elijah's homily was in George's mind. He passed the check-in counter as he walked into the cafeteria, began to wonder where he might apply Fr. Elijah's words... and stopped.

The line was moving slowly; he had come in late after wandering somewhat. Sheepishly, he stopped, looked at the woman who had scanned his ID, and extended his hand. "Hi, I'm George."

The woman pushed back a strand of silver hair. "Hi. It's good to meet you, George. I'm Georgina."

George stood, trying to think of something to say.

Georgina said, "What are you majoring in?"

"I haven't decided. I like reading... um... it's really obscure, but some stuff about Arthur."

"King Arthur and the Round Table?"

"Yes."

"Wonderful, son. Can you tell me about it sometime? I always love hearing about things."

George said, "Ok. What do you... um..."

"I been working at this for a long time. It's nice seeing all you students, and I get some good chats. You remind me of my grandson a little. But you're probably pretty hungry now, and the lines are closing in a few minutes. Stop by another day!"

George ate his food, thoughtfully, and walked out of the cafeteria wishing he had said hi to more of the support staff.

That week, the halls seemed to be filled with more treasure than he had guessed. He did not work up the courage to introduce himself to too many people, but he had the sense that there was something interesting in even the people he hadn't met.

On Wednesday, George went to register for his classes next semester, and realized his passwords were... on his computer, the one without a power cord.

After a while, thinking what to do, he knocked on a floormates' door. "Um, Ivan?"

"Come in, George. What do you want?"

George hesitated and said, "Could I borrow a power cord? Just for a minute? I'll give it right back."

Ivan turned around and dragged a medium-sized box from under his bed. It was full of cables.

"Here, and don't worry about returning it. Take a cord. Take twenty, I don't care. I have them coming out of my ears."

George grabbed one cord, then remembered he did not have the cord for his monitor. He took another. "I'll have these back in a minute."

"George, you're being silly. Is there any reason you need *not* to have a power cord?"

"Um..." George opened his mouth and closed it. Then he hesitated. "No."

George left, registered online, shut his computer down, left the room, did some work at the library, and went to bed.

Thursday he was distracted.

Friday, it was raining heavily, and after getting soaked in icy rain running to and from his classes, George decided he would check his email from his room... and found himself wandering through the spam folder, and threw the cords out in the dumpster.

Sunday he walked into church with hesitation, and Fr.

Elijah almost immediately came over. "Yes, George?"

George hesitated.

Then he told Fr. Elijah what was going on.

Fr. Elijah paused, and said, "George, do you know about the Desert Fathers?"

"No."

"A group of people a bit like the hermits in Arthurian legend. Some people think that Merlin was originally based on such monks... but aside from that speculation, they were much holier than either of us. And there was one time when someone asked them, 'What do you do?' And what do you think the Desert Father said?"

"Pray? Worship? Live a good life?"

"'We fall and get up, fall and get up, fall and get up.' That is the motion of Orthodox life, and if you see prostrations, you will literally see us fall and get up. I'm not sure if you think that if you repent of a sin once, the hard part's over and it's all behind you. In my sins, I have to keep repenting again and again. You have fallen, now get up. And get up again. And again. And again. And keep getting up.

"The Lord bless you, in the Name of the Father, and of the Son, and of the Holy Spirit. Amen."

George walked away still feeling unworthy, and everywhere saw a grandeur that seemed to be for others more worthy than him. Everything around him seemed royal, and Fr. Elijah preached:

> In the Name of the Father, and of the Son, and of the Holy Ghost. Amen.
>
> In our commemorations, we commemorate "Orthodox kings and queens, faithful princes and princesses," before we commemorate various grades of bishops. The bishop is in fact royalty; instead of calling him "Your Majesty," we call him "Your Grace," "Your Eminence," "Your Holiness," "Your All Holiness." If you do research, you will find that the bishop is more than a king: the bishop is the Emperor,

and wears the full regalia of the Roman Emperor.

One question that has been asked is, "The king for the kingdom, or the kingdom for the king:" is the king made king for the benefit of the kingdom, or is the kingdom a privilege for the benefit of the king? The Orthodox choice of now requiring bishops to be monks is not because married persons are unfit, or rather necessarily more unfit, to serve. Most of the apostles in whose shadows the monastic bishops stand were married, and the monk bishops I have met consider themselves infinitely less than the married apostles. But a monk is given to be a whole burnt offering where nothing is kept back and everything is offered to God to be consumed by the holy sacrificial fire. (Or at least that's what's supposed to happen, but even if this is also what's supposed to happen in a marriage, it's more explicit in monasticism.) And it is this whole burnt offering, unworthy though he may be, who makes a bishop: Orthodoxy answers "the king for the kingdom:" the king is made king for the benefit of the kingdom, the bishop serves as a whole burnt offering for the benefit of the diocese.

Now let me ask: Which of us is royalty? And I want you to listen very carefully. All of us bear the royal bloodline of Lord Adam and Lady Eve. It's not just the bishops. I will not go into this in detail now, but the essence of priesthood is not what I have that "ordinary" Orthodox don't have. It's what I have that Orthodox faithful *do* have. And without you I can celebrate the liturgy. And the essence of royalty is not what a king or bishop has that a "commoner" or faithful does not have; it's what king and bishop share with the ordinary faithful. The Greek Fathers have no sense that "real" royal rule is humans ruling other humans; that's a bit of an aberration; the real royal rule is humans ruling over what God has given them and over themselves, and doing that rightly is a much bigger deal than being one of the handful of kings and bishops.

And each of us is called to be what a bishop is: a

whole burnt offering in humble service to the kingdom--large or small is not really the point--over which the Lord has appointed us king. It may mean showing conscience by cleaning up your room--and if you have a first world abundance of property, it is a very small way of offering them back to the Lord to keep them in good order. It means carefully stewarding precious moments with other people, maybe saying, "I hope you have a wonderful day," and saying it like you mean it, to support staff. And it means humbly ruling your kingdom within, in which both Heaven and Hell may be found. It is when you serve as king, the king made for the kingdom, that your kingdom will be your crown and glory.

In the Name of the Father, and of the Son, and of the Holy Ghost. Amen.

After Church, a young woman stormed up to Fr. Elijah. She had, at as far arm's length from her body as she could hold it, a clear trash bag holding a pink heart-shaped piece of artisan paper that appeared to have writing on it. She stopped opposite Fr. Elijah and said, "Do *you* know anything about this note?"

Fr. Elijah smiled gently. "It appears someone has sent you some sort of love note. How sweet!"

"Were *you* involved?"

"What, you think I would do something like that? I'm hurt!"

The young woman stood up straight and put her hand on her hip. Fr. Elijah turned to George and said, "Would you like to know what's going on?"

The young woman said, "Yes, I'd love to hear you explain *this*."

Fr. Elijah said, "George, the elephant population in Sri Lanka is in some peril. They're not being hunted for their ivory, let alone for their meat, but there is a limited amount of land, and farmers and elephants are both trying to use an area of land that makes it difficult for them to both support themselves. So some people tried to think about whether there was a way to make a win-win situation, and make the elephants an economic asset. They asked themselves whether elephants produce anything. And it turns out that something that eats the enormous amount of food an elephant eats does, in fact, produce a *lot* of something."

George said, "I don't see the connection. Have I just missed that you're changing the subject?"

The young woman said, "He *hasn't* changed the subject."

Fr. Elijah said, "They're using it to make hand-crafted artisan paper, colored and available in a heart shape, which you can buy online at MrElliePooh.com if you're interested."

George looked at Fr. Elijah in shock and awe.

The woman said, "Grandpappy, you are *such* a pest!"

Fr. Elijah lightly placed an arm around her shoulder and said, "George, I'd like to introduce you to my granddaughter Abigail. She has a face as white as alabaster, raven-black hair, and lips are red as blood. And she has many merits besides being fun to pick on."

Abigail stuck out her tongue at her grandfather and then shifted to his side. "And my grandfather does many fine things besides be obnoxious... Can't live with him, can't shoot him... You should get to know him, if you haven't." She gave him a gentle squeeze. "There are brownies today, George, and they're great! Can I get you some?"

George read in *Brocéliande*, and wandered in the wood, and the castle of Calix College, and the surrounding city. Fr. Elijah began to introduce fasting, and George found something new in his struggles... and began to make progress. Nor was that the only thing in George's life. He began to find the Middle Ages not too different from his own... and he was puzzled when he read in *Brocéliande*:

> And in that wood anon saw Sir Yvain a lion fighting against a primeval serpent, and the serpent breathed fire against the lion his heel, and a baleful cry did the lion wail. Then Lord Yvain thought in his heart of which animal he should aid, and in his heart spake, "The lion is the more

natural of the twain." And anon he put his resources on the side of the lion, and with his sword he cleft the ancient serpent in twain and hew the serpent his head in seven, and warred against the wicked wyrm until he were reduced to many small bits. And he cleaned his sword of the serpent his venomous filth, and anon the lion kept him at his side.

And anon Sir Yvain slept and an advision saw: an old woman, whose colour was full of life and whose strength intact and yet who were wizened, riding upon a serpent and clothed in a robe black as coal, and spake and said, "Sir Yvain, why have ye offended me? Betake ye as my companion." Then Sir Yvain refused her and there was a stench as brimstone aflame. Then a woman clad in white, riding astride a lion, new as white snow did courtesy and said, "Sir Yvain, I salute thee." And about her was a fragrance of myrrh.

Anon Sir Yvain awoke, and sore amazed was he, and none could interpret his advision.

George spoke with Fr. Elijah, and asked him what the passage meant. Fr. Elijah said, "What does this passage *mean*? You know, that isn't as big a question in Orthodoxy as you think... but I'll try to answer. In fact, I think I'll answer in a homily."

"It had better be impressive."

"Fine. I'll preach it as impressive as you want."

"When?"

"On Christmas."

That evening, George called Fr. Elijah to say that he was going home for Christmas... and then, later in the week, said, "Fr. Elijah? Do you know anybody who could keep me? My parents were going to buy me a ticket home with frequent flier mileage on an airline, but my grandfather is ill and my mother used up those miles getting a ticket... and money is tight... I don't know what I'm going to do."

"Well, you could talk with your College and try to get special permission to stay over break... but I'd prefer if you stayed with me. Because we agreed that I would only preach on the Arthurian legends, including your Old Law and New Law, if you were there... and I was *so* looking forward to preaching a Christmas homily on the Arthurian legends."

"Can't you preach it without me?"

"We agreed and shook hands. I have that homily for Christmas, but only if you're there."

"Um... I would be an intruding--"

"George, I am a priest because I love God and I love people. And I do meet people quite a lot, but my house is empty now. It would be nice to have some young energy and someone to share more than a Christmas dinner with?"

"Are you sure?"

"You know how to get to my place. I'll see you whenever you want to come over."

On Christmas, Fr. Elijah preached,

> In the Name of the Father, and of the Son, and of the Holy Ghost. Amen.
>
> Christ is born! Glorify him!
>
> In the Arthurian legends, there is a story of a knight who sees a serpent fighting a lion, kills the serpent, and wins a kind response from the lion. In some versions the knight has a vision in which one woman appears on the serpent and another on the lion, and we learn that these women represent the Old Law and the New Law.
>
> What are the Old Law and the New Law? One can say the Torah or Law of Moses, and the Gospel, and that is true up to a point, but the "Old Law" is not just a take on Judaism. Sir Palomides, a Saracen, described with profound confusion between Islam and paganism (and the problem with Islam is not that it is pagan but that it is not pagan enough--it is more emphatic about there being one God, even more than the one God is), becomes a Christian and is asked to renounce the Old Law and embrace the New Law. Even if Sir Palomides is in no sense a Jew.

In the ancient world, it is not enough to say that the Orthodox Church understood itself as the fulfillment of Judaism, politically incorrect as that may be. The Orthodox Church was even more fully the fulfillment of paganism, and if you understand what was going on in Plato, you understand that paganism was deepening. The Orthodox Church is the place where that final deepening of paganism took place. And I would like to explain for a moment why Orthodoxy is pagan and neo-"pagan" forms like Druidry aren't.

The popular stereotype is that paganism was merry and free until Christianity's grim hand came down, and that's like saying that difficult toil was carefree until someone came along and with a grim hand invited people to a feast. Pagan virtues--courage, justice, wisdom, moderation--are retained in Christianity, but they are not the virtues of joy by themselves. C.S. Lewis said that if you're not going to be a Christian, the next best thing is to be a Norseman, because the Norse pagans sided with the good gods, not because they were going to win, but because they were going to lose. The Norse decision was to meet the Day of Doom, called Ragnarok, and go down fighting on the right side. And so the Norse have a tale of the war-god Tyr who took and kept an oath even at the price of letting a wolf bite off his right hand, and there is something very much like ancient paganism in keeping an oath though it cost your right hand.

What Orthodoxy offered paganism in the ancient world was precisely not a grim hand flattening everything, but retaining the virtue already recognized in paganism while deepening them with faith, hope, and love that live the life of Heaven here on earth. The Christian virtues of faith, hope, and love are the virtues that can see beauty, that bring Heaven down to earth, that can call for the whole Creation to worship God: as we sing at the Eucharist, joining the Song that summons the host of angels, sun, moon and stars, heavens and waters above the heavens, sea monsters and all deeps, fire and hail, snow and frost, stormy wind fulfilling his command, mountains and hills, fruit trees and cedars, beasts and all cattle, creeping things and flying fowl, kings and all people, princes and rulers, young men and maidens, old men and children--all called in the Psalmist's summons to praise the Lord.

If you want to know how today's "neo-paganism" can fail to be pagan, I would recall to you the Medieval Collectibles website which offers a medieval toilet cover so you can have a real medieval coat of arms on your, um, "throne." The website's marketing slogan is "Own a piece of history," but you're not owning a piece of history... or think of the interior decorator who was told, "I want an authentic colonial American bathroom," to which the decorator replied, "Ok, so exactly how far from the house do you want it?"

Some have noted that the majority of books written by Orthodox today are by Western converts, and there is a reason for that. The Reformation almost created literate culture, but the opposite of literate is not illiterate, but oral, in a way that neo-paganism may want to create but is awfully hard to recreate. Even in its spiritual *reading* the Orthodox Church remains an oral culture in its core while it uses writing: many of its most devout would never write a book, and even now, sensible Orthodox will answer the question, "What should I read to understand Orthodoxy?" by saying "Don't read, at least not at first, and don't *ever* let reading be the center of how you understand Orthodoxy. Come and join the life of our community in liturgy." Orthodoxy is not better than classical paganism in this regard, but it is like classical paganism and it keeps alive elements of classical paganism that neo-paganism has trouble duplicating. (A neo-"pagan" restoration of oral culture bears a hint of... I'm not sure how to describe it... an oxymoron like "committee to revitalize" comes close.) After years of the West tearing itself away from nature, people in the West are trying to reconnect with nature, and some neo-"pagans" are spearheading that. But look at Orthodoxy. Come and see the flowers, the water and oil, the beeswax candles and herbs, the bread and wine that are at the heart of Orthodox worship: the Orthodox Church has not lost its connection with the natural world even as it uses technology, and it may even have a fuller connection with the natural world than paganism had; classical Rome could sow salt in the soil of Carthage and go out of their way to pollute out of spite, which even environmentally irresponsible companies rarely do today. Which isn't getting into the full depth of a spiritually disciplined connection to nature like that of St. Symeon the New Theologian--in the Orthodox Church we call him "new" even though he's from the fourteenth century--but it's missing the point to ask if Orthodoxy is pagan because of the role of the saints in worshiping God. If you want the deep structure, the culture, the way of life, of paganism, the place where you will find it most alive is precisely Orthodoxy.

The Arthurian author Charles Williams makes a very obscure figure, the bard Taliesin, the pilgrim who comes to Byzantium sent to bring a treasure and returns with the Pearl of Great Price, the New Law. In Stephen Lawhead, it is Merlin who appears as the culmination of the Druidic Order and the apex of the Old Law: the old learned brotherhood is disbanded and Merlin proclaims the New Law, and this is really not just a story. The Evangelical Orthodox Church was formed when a group of Protestants tried to do something very Protestant, reconstruct the original Christian Church through studying old documents. *Very* Protestant. And they came to a certain point, that when they quizzed an Orthodox priest, they realized something. And the Evangelical Orthodox Church entered the Orthodox Church because they realized that the Old Law of Protestant searching to reconstruct the ancient Church needed to be fulfilled in what they realized was the New Law. The Holy Order of MANS--MANS is an acronym, but not in English; it stands for *Mysterion*, *Agape*, *Nous*, *Sophia*, some terms from Greek that are deep enough to be hard to translate, but something like "profound mystery, divine love, spiritual eye, wisdom." Do these mean something Christian? Do they mean something esoteric? In fact the Holy Order of MANS was something of both, and they pushed their tradition deeper and deeper... until the Holy Order of MANS was dissolved and many of its people followed their leader's sense that their Old Law led to this New Law. If you know the story of the Aleut religion in Alaska, the shamans--and it is difficult to explain their "shamans" in contemporary terms; perhaps I should refer to them as people who had tasted spiritual realities--said that certain people were coming and to listen to the people who were to come. And the people the shamans foretold were Orthodox monks who had in turn tasted of spiritual realities, such as St. Herman of Alaska. Not, necessarily, that moving from paganism to Orthodoxy was that big of a change for them. It wasn't. But the Aleuts recognized in these monks something that was very close to their way of life, but something that could deepen it, and it was because of their depth in their Old Law as pagans that they were ready for an Orthodox New Law. Stephen Lawhead has a lot of carefully researched history--at times I wished for a little less meticulous research and a little more riveting story--but whether or not anything like this can be confirmed archaeologically in the Celtic lands, the same kind of thing can be confirmed, even as having happened very recently.

But when I say "Merlin," many of you do not think of the herald of the New Law, and for that matter many of the older sources do not do this either. If a boy today is enchanted by just one character from the Arthuriad, it is ordinarily not King Arthur, Pendragon though he may be, nor Sir Galahad, who achieved the Holy Grail in some versions, nor Sir Lancelot, who is proven to be the greatest knight in the world, nor the Fisher-King, nor the fairy enchantress Morgana le Fay, nor King Arthur's peerless Queen Guinevere, whose name has become our "Jennifer." It is the figure of Merlin.

Today, if you ask *what* Merlin was--and I intentionally say, "what," not "who," for reasons I will detail--the usual answer is, "a wizard." But if you look at the stories that were spread from the Celtic lands, the answer is, "a prophet." In the Old Testament, one of the prophets protests, "I am neither a prophet, nor a prophet's son," and another prophet says something to the Lord that somehow never gets rendered clearly in English Bible translations never choose to get right: "You violated my trust, and I was utterly betrayed." The Hebrew word for prophet, '*nabi*', means "called one," and one never gets the sense in reading the Old Testament prophets that the prophets, when they were children, said, "I want to grow up to be a prophet" the way people today say, "I want to be the President of the United States."

And this idea of Merlin as *prophet* is not just a different or a more Christianly correct word. The Arthurian legends may be thought of today as "something like fiction;" even when people in the Middle Ages questioned their historical accuracy, those people were throwing a wet blanket on something a great many people took as literal fact. There is a book called *The Prophecies of Merlin*, which was taken extremely seriously for centuries, as the word of a prophet. And one gets the sense that in modern terms Merlin's identity was not a self-definition that he chose, not in modern terms, but something that was thrust upon him.

It may sound strange to some if I say that the earlier attempt to build a castle on Merlin's blood, and Merlin's later calling a castle out of the wind, relate to Christ. But if you think I am pounding a square peg into a round hole, consider this: Sir Galahad, whom some consider a painfully obvious Christ-figure, whose strength is as the strength of ten because his heart is pure and who is always strong in the face of temptation, enters the world after Sir Lancelot, the greatest knight in the world and a man who goes above and beyond the call of duty of faithfulness in his devotion to another man's wife, goes to a castle, is given the Arthurian equivalent of a date-rape pill in the form of a potion that makes him think his hostess is the woman he's been carrying on with, and that night sires Galahad. You may call this a magical birth story if you like, but it doesn't give us much advance notice that the son born will turn out to be the Arthurian icon of purity who will achieve the Grail.

So how is Merlin, who reeks of magic, introduced? In the oldest surviving work that flourished outside of Celtic circles, in fact written by a Celtic bishop, Merlin appears when King Vortigern searches for a boy without a father, and hears Merlin being teased for being without a father. And let me be clear, this is not because his father has passed away. We learn that the Devil wished to be incarnate, could only come into the world of a virgin, found a virgin who was spiritually pure, having only slipped in her prayers once, and thus the person meant to be the anti-Christ was conceived. The Church, just in time, said powerful prayers and the boy, born of a virgin without a sire, commanded all the power over the natural world he was meant to, but would serve the good. Now is anyone going to say that that's not a reference to Christ? Merlin is most interesting because of how the story itself places him in the shadow of Christ.

One thing that's very easy to overlook is that in the story where there's a terrible storm and Christ is sleeping in the front of the boat while his disciples are asking if he doesn't care that they were going to die, is not just that the disciples were right: in that part of the world there were storms that could very quickly flood a boat and kill people when the boat sank. Christ stands up, and says something to the storm before rebuking the disciples for their lack of faith. And that's when the disciples *really* began to be afraid. Mark's Gospel is the one Gospel with the simplest, "I don't speak Greek very well" Greek, and at this point he uses the King James- or Shakespeare-style Greek Old Testament language to say that when Jesus commands the storm to be still and it actually obeys him, *that* is when they are most terrified.

Before Jesus stopped the storm, they were afraid enough; they knew the storm they saw was easily enough to kill them. But this was nothing compared to the fear out of which they asked, "Who is this, that even the wind and the waves obey him?" This person who had been teaching them had just displayed a command over nature that left them wondering who or what he was, a "what" that goes beyond today's concern about "who am I?" and has something that cannot be reached by angst-ridden wrestling with who you are.

Something like that question is at the heart of debates that people argued for centuries and are trying to reopen. What, exactly, was Jesus? Was he an ancient sage and teacher? Was he a prophet? A healer or a worker of wonders? Someone who had drunk of deeper spiritual realities and wanted to initiate others into the same? Was he something more than a man, the bridge between God and his world?

The answer taken as final was the maximum possible. It was "Every one of these and more." It pushed the envelope on these even as it pushed into a claim for the maximum in every respect: Christ was maximally divine, maximally human, maximally united, and maximally preserved the divine and human while being the final image both for our understanding of what it is to be God and what it is to be human.

And what, finally, would we have if we deepened Merlin? What if he were the son, not of the worst finite creature, but of the best and infinite Creator? What if he had not simply power over nature but were the one through whom the world was created and in whom all things consist? What if we were dealing with, not the one who prophesied that a few would find the Holy Grail, but the one who gave the Holy Grail and its gifts that are still with us? What if Merlin were made to be like the pattern he is compared to? When Merlin is deepened far enough, he becomes Christ.

The Christian lord of Cyprus was out hawking when his dearly beloved hawk--I don't know if the hawk was a merlin, but I can say that a merlin is a type of hawk--became entangled in the brush in the wood. Loving the hawk dearly, he ordered that the branches be cut away so that he would still have this hawk, and when that was done, not only was his hawk found, but an icon showing the Queen and Mother of God on a throne, and the Divine Child enthroned upon her lap and an angel on either side. They found what they were looking for, but they also found a singularly majestic icon of the Incarnation.

The Christ Mass, the Nativity, is an invasion in the dead of winter. It is the feast of the Incarnation, or more properly one of the feasts of the Incarnation, which is not something that stopped happening once after the Annunciation when the Mother of God bore the God-man in her womb.

Everything that the Christ Mass stands for will eventually be made plain, but the Christ Mass is a day of veiled glory. When God became man, he was born in a stable. When Christ returns, he will appear riding on the clouds. When he came, a choir of angels proclaimed the news to shepherds and a few knees bowed. When he returns, rank upon rank of angels will come in eternal radiant glory and every knee will bow and every tongue will confess that Jesus Christ is Lord, to the manifest glory of God the Father. When he came once, a star heralded the hour of his birth. When he returns, the stars will fall as ripe figs from a tree and the sky itself will recede as a vanishing scroll. Every thing that is a secret not will be made plain, but he first came in secret...

...and he comes today in secret, hidden in us. For the Incarnation was not finished after the Annunciation, but unfolds still as Christ is incarnate in the Church, in the saints like St. Herman of Alaska, a wonderworker who was seen carrying logs weighing much more than himself, stopped a forest fire, calmed a stormy sea, and left behind a body preserved from corruption as it was on display for a month at room temperature, and left behind much of the Aleut Orthodox community that remains to this day--and also in us. And the Incarnation is still unfolding today. The castle of the Arthurian world is more than stone walls and a porticullis; the castle is almost everything we mean by city, or society, or community. And it is the castle writ large that we find in the Church, not only a fortress waging war against the Devil but a people ruled by her Lord. This Castle is at once founded upon a fluid more precious than ichor, not the blood of a boy without a father but the blood of a God-man, without father on the side of his mother and without mother on the side of his Father. It is the Castle still being built by the wind of his Spirit still blowing--and remember that the world behind the Medieval West did not always stow "spirit" and "wind" in sealed watertight compartments: the wind blows where it will and the Spirit inspires where it will, so this Castle has a Spirit blowing through it that is more windlike than wind itself.

And until the Last Judgment, when every eye will see him, even those that pierced him, it is his will to be incarnate where he is hidden behind a veil to those who cannot see him: incarnate in the Church and in each of us, called to be his saints, and called to become Christ.

Christ is born! Glorify him!

In the Name of the Father, and of the Son, and of the Holy Ghost. Amen.

Fr. Elijah turned around, stopped, bent his head a moment, and at last turned back. "Oh, and one more thing... George's number is in the parish directory, and these homilies that talk about King Arthur and his court have been all his fault. If there's *anything at all* that you don't like about them, I invite you to call him at all hours of the day and night to grouse at him for foisting such terrible ideas on me."

That evening, George came, and after some hesitancies, said, "When can I become Orthodox?"

"At Pascha. We can continue working, and you will be received in the Church."

George thanked him, and began to walk out.

"Um, Fr. Elijah, aren't you somewhat surprised?"

"George, I was waiting for you to see that you wanted to become Orthodox. Go back to your reading."

The Christmas break passed quickly, and the first class after break was the introduction to computer science. The professor said, "Most of my students call me Dr. Blaise, although you can use my last name if you're comfortable. I wanted to offer a few remarks.

"Many of your professors think their class is your most important class, and that entitles them to be your number one priority in homework and demands outside the classroom. I don't. I believe this class is a puzzle piece that fits into a larger puzzle. Exactly how it fits in will differ, depending on whether you become a major--which I invite you to consider--or whether you choose an allied major but focus on something other than computer science, or whether your interests lie elsewhere and I am broadening your horizons even if your main interests lie somewhere else. I will try to help give you a good puzzle piece, and in office hours especially I want to support you in helping fit this piece of the puzzle into the broader picture.

"My best student was a mechanic; car and airplane mechanics, for instance, are solving a problem with a system, and I have never been so stunned at how quickly a student learned to debug well as with this mechanic. I've found that people who know something about physics, mathematics, or engineering pick up computer work more quickly even if you don't see a single physics equation in this class: learn physics and programming is a little easier to learn. And it goes the other way too: one of my colleagues in the math department explained that students who know the process of taking something and writing a computer program to reach the desired results, correctly, are prepared to do something similar in mathematics, and take something and write a correct proof to reach the desired results. Learn something in one hard science and you have an advantage in others."

One student raised her hand. "Yes?" Dr. Blaise asked.

"What about those of us interested in philosophy or religion? What if we're doing something computers won't help us with? Are you going to teach us how to use word processors?"

"Well, I'd point out that there is a long tradition of studying mathematics--geometry--as a sort of mental weightlifting before studying philosophy or theology. Or some of my poet friends say that it's a way of poisoning the mind, and I'll respect them if they want to say that. But for many of you, it is useful, even if we don't teach word processing--ask the lab tech for sessions that will teach you how to use computer software. Computer *science* is about something else; computer science isn't any more about how to use computers than astronomy is about how to use telescopes."

The student raised her hand again, slightly, and then put it down.

Dr. Blaise said, "I'd like to hear your thought. If you aren't convinced, other people probably aren't convinced either, and it will do everybody good to have it out in the open."

"Um... But why does..." She paused, and Dr. Blaise smiled. "I want to study English."

"Good stuff. So does my daughter. It's a bit of a cross-cultural encounter, and I think it can benefit English students for the same reason my majors benefit from taking English classes. But never mind programming specifically; I want to talk about how the disciplines can integrate. Programming won't help you the same way as some of the humanities will, but I'd like to talk about how things might fit together.

"I saw one of your English professors, a lovely medievalist who knows the Arthurian legends well. She was talking with one of the campus ethicists, who has interests in the history of moral theology. The topic of discussion? One that you might wince at, on the short list of positions the Catholic Church is unpopular for: contraception. And the ethicist said he'd found something he thought the medievalist literature professor might find interesting.

"The history of contraception, like almost any other big question, involves a lot of other things. And one of those things involves a suggestion by John Noonan, not for one of several proposed answers for a question, but of an answer to a puzzle that has no other answers, at least as of the time Noonan wrote.

"The vision of courtly love, and what is celebrated in that love between a man and a woman--probably another man's wife, for what it's worth--is an ideal that was all about celebrating 'love', and in this celebration of 'love,' there was a big idea of 'Play all you want; we will encourage and celebrate play, whether or not you're in marriage; just be sure that you do it in a way that won't generate a child.'

"Scholars do have difficulty keeping a straight face in the idea that the courtly romances are coded messages about secret Cathar teachings. They aren't. But they flourished as nowhere before in a land where something of Catharism was in the air, and, like contraception, the idea of celebrating 'love' and encouraging people, 'Play, but do it in a way that don't generate a child' is not exactly Cathar, but is the sort of thing that could come if Catharism was in the air.

"And, the ethicist went further, the Arthurian romances are done in such a way that it is very difficult to demonstrate any clear and conscious authorial understanding of Cathar teachings, let alone coded messages sent to those 'in the know'... but that doesn't mean that Catharism had nothing to do with it. And not just because strict Cathars would have taken a dim view of *this* way of taking their ball and running with it. A *very* dim view, for that matter.

"Catharism, called Gnosticism as it appeared in the ancient world and various other things as it resurfaces today, has various things about it, and not just wanting to celebrate love to high Heaven while understanding this wonderful 'love' as something which one should be able to do without generating children. That's not the only thing, and it is one point of including Cathar elements without doing them very well.

"Catharism, or Gnosticism or whatever the day's version of it is called, is deeply connected with magic, and this occult element has a lot of ideas, or something like ideas, if you get very deep into it. And in the Arthurian legends, there is an occult element, but it isn't done very well. There are dweomers all over the place, and Merlin and almost every woman work enchantments, not to mention that all sorts of items have magical 'virtues', but the English professor had almost no sense that the authors were really involved with the occult themselves. It was kind of a surface impression that never had any of the deeper and darker features, or the deeper secret doctrines of one in the know. It kind of portrays magic the way a poorly researched TV show portrays a faroff land--there may be a sense of interest and enchantment untainted by actual *understanding* of what is being portrayed.

"And besides that surface impression, there is something of self-centered pride. The only people who really have a pulse are nobles living in large measure for themselves, knights who are trying to do something impressive. Commerce never seems to really taint the screen of luxury; furthermore there is a sense that being in fights for one's glory is no great sin, and it doesn't really matter what those fights do to the others. It's a very different view of fighting from 'just war.'

"The Arthurian legends are undoubtedly classics of world literature, and it is terribly reductive to say that they're simply a bad version of Cathar doctrine. That denigration of their literary qualities is not justified, just as dismissing Star Wars as just a bit of violent Gnosticism or Catharism or whatever is out of line. Star Wars would never succeed if it were just dressed up Gnosticism.

"But it does raise the question of whether the literature of courtly love, so foundational to how people can understand 'love' today and understand what it means to celebrate 'love' and say that the Catholic Church hates love between men and women if it will not recognize that contraception will help that love be celebrated with less unwelcome 'consequences'... It raises the question, not of whether the literature is bad literature and not worth study, but whether it is very good literature that contains something fatal."

There was one more question, and Dr. Blaise began discussing computer science. At least George believed later that the professor had been discussing computer science, and trusted others' reports on that score.

But George did not hear a word more of what Dr. Blaise said that day.

The computer science class was a night class, and when it was finished, George found himself surprised when he entered the parsonage.

Fr. Elijah was sitting, his back to the door, staring into the fireplace. A large volume, looking like an encyclopedia volume, was sitting open on Fr. Elijah's sparsely appointed desk. Fr. Elijah, his back still to the door, said, "Come in, George. What is the matter?"

George said, "I hope I didn't interrupt--"

Fr. Elijah said, "I was just resting a bit after reading something. St. Maximus's language gives me such trouble."

George rushed over to the desk. "Maybe I can help." He looked, and looked again, until he realized the volume had columns of Latin and Greek. The volume was printed, but it looked old, and there were worm holes.

"Come in and sit down, George. You don't need to be reading St. Maximus the Confessor quite yet, even if your Greek is better than mine, or you find the Latin easier. Now sit down. You didn't come here so you could help me understand the Greek, even if I wouldn't be surprised if, bright lad as you are, you know Greek a good deal better than I do."

"It's Greek to me," George said, forcing a smile, and then shaking. Fr. Elijah rose, turned around, and said, "Sit down in my chair, George, and enjoy the fire. I'll step out into the kitchen, make some hot cocoa, and then we can talk. I wish my cat were still around; she was a real sweetheart, and she would sit in your lap and purr. Even if it was the first time she met you." Fr. Elijah left, silently, and went about making hot cocoa. He returned, holding two mugs, and gave one mug to George. "I put extra marshmallows in yours."

Then Fr. Elijah sat down in a smaller chair, in the corner, and sat, listening.

George blurted out, after some silence, "I think the Arthurian stuff I read may be Gnostic."

Fr. Elijah took a sip.

"One of the people in my class said that Arthurian literature arose because of the Cathars."

Fr. Elijah took another sip.

"Or something like that. It seems that a lot of what people do as glorious things in courtly literature is Gnostic."

Fr. Elijah took a slow sip, and asked, "Like what?"

"Well, the ideal of love is big on celebrating love, only it's better if children don't get in the way, and you're careful to keep children out of the way. And there's magic all over the place, and nobles are superior."

Fr. Elijah took another sip.

"At least that's how I remember it, only I'm probably wrong."

Fr. Elijah stroked his beard for a moment and said, "Well, that's a big enough question that we should respect the matter by not trying to sort it out all at once. Let's not assume that because it is so big a question, we are obligated to rush things. If it is a big question, we are more obligated *not* to rush things."

"*Why*?"

"Ever hear of Arius or Arianism?"

"You mean racism?"

"No, not that spelling. A-R-I-U-S and A-R-I-A-N-I-S-M. The race-related bit is spelled with a 'Y'."

"Ok."

"Arius was a deacon who was really worried that his bishop was saying something wrong. So he rushed to correct his bishop, and in his rush to correct the Orthodox Church founded a heresy. He gets it worse in the Orthodox liturgy than even Judas; various other heretics are accused of being taught by Arius.

"There were two mistakes he made. The biggest and worst mistake was fighting the Orthodox Church when they said he was wrong, and that was the real problem with Arius. But another mistake was trying to rush and fix the problem of heresy he thought his bishop was guilty of.

"Holier men than either of us have rushed and said something heretical in their rush job. I'm not sure either of us are going to go warring against the Church and trying to fix it has thought about our correction and said 'No,' but if you've raised a big question, or your class has, that's all the more reason *not* to rush."

George said, "So what should we do?"

Fr. Elijah said, "Take a deep breath and a sip of cocoa," and waited. Then he said, "Now what is it that has you so wound up?"

"I thought there was really something in what I was reading."

"There probably is."

"But the idea of love, and all the magic, are some sort of second-rate Cathar stuff."

"Why do you think that?"

"Well, I'm not sure... um... well, they're big on the experience of love."

Fr. Elijah sank a little into his chair. "In other forms of Gnosticism, there is an idea of some things as experience... and they are understood as experiences, significant as experiences, and not as significant for other reasons... and I can see some pretty Gnostic assumptions feeding into that ideal of love. You may be right..."

"But isn't love to be celebrated? How else could it be celebrated?"

"In the New Testament times, celibacy was encouraged despite the fact that it was giving up something big. But the something big is not the obvious 'something big' people would be worried about giving up today... it's having children to carry on one's name. There is a good deal more.... People, even with hormones, were interested in some other things *besides* pleasurable experiences. There is more I could explain about what else *besides* 'being in love' could make a happy marriage between happy people, but... Sorry, I'm ranting, and you're not happy."

"Fr. Elijah, if what I'm saying makes sense, then why on earth did you preach those homilies? Were you lying... um, I mean..."

"Don't look for a nicer word; if you think I might have been lying, I would really rather have you bring it out into the open than have it smouldering and damaging other things. No, I'm not angry with you, and no, I wasn't lying."

"Then why--"

"George, allow me to state the very obvious. Something was going on in you. And still is. It seemed, and seems to me, that you were coming alive in reading the Arthurian legends. As a pastor or priest or spiritual father or whatever you want to call me, I made an appropriate response and preached homilies that blessed not just you, but also several other people as well. Now, maybe, you are shattered, or maybe you are ready to begin hungering for something more. You know how, in classic Gnosticism, there's a distinction the Gnostics hold between the so-called 'hylic' people who don't have much of any spiritual life, meaning people who aren't Christian in any sense, and the 'psychic,' meaning soulish, not ESP people, of Christians who have a sort of half-baked spiritual awakening, and the 'pneumatic,' meaning spiritual, Gnostics who are the real spiritual elite?"

George said, "It doesn't surprise me. It's absolute bosh from beginning to end. It has nothing to do with the truth."

Fr. Elijah closed his eyes for a moment. "George, I am not quite sure I would say that."

"What, you're going to tell me the Gnostics had it right?"

"They had more right than you think; they're *seductively* similar to Christianity. They wouldn't have anywhere near the effect they're having if it were any other way.

"You know how Orthodox Christianity is patted on the head as a sort of lesser outer revelation that is permissible for those who have reached the outer courts but are not ready to enter the inner sanctum of the Gnostics' secret knowledge? That's *backwards*. The Gnostic 'knowledge' might be excusable for people who have not reached the inner reaches of Orthodoxy. It is the Gnostic that is the light-weight spiritual reality. And it is the light-weight spiritual reality that is the Old Law which the New Law fulfills more than the Old Law can fulfill itself. You reacted to something in the Arthurian legends because there is something there, and if you now know that they are not the New Law, I will ask you to excuse me if I still hold those legends to be an Old Law that finds its completion in the New Law. The highest does not stand without the lowest, and part of the New Law is that it makes a place for the Old Law. Including that spark of life you saw in the Arthurian legends."

"But why *preach* as if you found so much in them? I were to ask you to do something silly, like preach a sermon on how things have been censored out of the Bible, would you do that too?" George took a breath. "I'm sorry; you can change the subject if you want."

Fr. Elias said, slowly, "I have a question for you, and I want you to think carefully. Are you ready for the question?"

George said, "Yes."

"Can we know, better than God, what the Bible should say?"

"No."

"But quite a lot of people do think that. A lot of people seem to be trying to help the Bible doing a better job of what it's trying so hard to say, but can't quite manage. Or something like that."

"I've read some liberals doing that."

"It's not just liberals. Let me give one example. George, have you been big in Creation and evolution debates?"

"Not really."

"Christians have several options, but for the *Newsweek* crowd, there are only two options. Either you're a young earther, or you're an evolutionist, and the new 'intelligent design' is just the old creationism with a more euphemistic name. Rather depressing for a set of options, but let's pretend those are the only two options.

"Now are you familiar with what this means for dinosaurs?"

"Um..."

"The connection isn't obvious. We've seen, or at least I have, cartoons in magazines that have cave men running from T. rexes or hunting a brontosaurus. Which is, to an evolutionist, over a hundred times worse than having cave men whining loudly about the World Wide Wait. There's a *long* time between the last dinosaurs of any kind, and the first humans of any kind, were around. As in hundreds of millions of years longer than humans have been around in any form. On that timeline, it's a rather big mistake to have humans interacting with dinosaurs.

"But if you have a young earth timeline, with the whole world created in six days, then it's not such a ludicrous idea that humans might have interacted with dinosaurs... and your English Bible offers an interesting reason to believe that humans have seen living dinosaurs. Have you read the book of Job?"

George said, "Um, no. It's one of a lot of..."

Fr. Elijah interrupted. "There's a lot in the Bible to read, and even people who read the Bible a lot don't read it quickly unless they're speed-reading, and then it still takes them a couple of weeks. If you can call that 'reading the Bible;' I've tried it and I think it's one of the sillier things I've tried--a sort of spiritual 'get rich quick' scheme. I was smart enough to stop. But if you check your English Bible, you will see in Job a creature called the 'behemoth,' perhaps because the translators on the King James Version didn't know how to translate it, and the 'behemoth,' whatever that may be, is a mighty impressive creature. We are told that it is not afraid though the river rushes against it, suggesting that whatever the behemoth is, it is a big beast. And we are told that it stiffens or swings its tail like a cedar, the cedar being a magnificent, and quite enormous, tree which reaches heights of something like one hundred fifty to two hundred feet. And regardless of where you stand on Creation and evolution, the only creature that has ever walked the earth with a tail that big, or anywhere *near* that big, is one of the bigger dinosaurs. So the Bible offers what seems to be excellent evidence that people have seen dinosaurs--alive.

"Which is all very lovely, of course given to the English Bible. But first, the 'behemoth' is in fact an overgrown relative of the pig, the hippopotamus, and second, it isn't really talking about his *tail.* The same image basic is translated unclearly in the Song of Songs, amongst--"

George spit out a mouthful of soda and took a moment to compose himself. "I'm sorry. Did I--"

Fr. Elijah looked around. "I'm sorry. I shouldn't have said that as you were taking a sip. Let me get you a napkin. Here."

George said, "Ok, so maybe there are some other vivid images that have been, bowlderized--you know, edited for television. Anything more? Were any ideas censored?"

Fr. Elijah said, " A bit murky, but I'm tempted to say 'yes.' One idea has been made less clear; there may be other tidbits here and there. A couple of forceful passages that may be interpreted as implying things about contraception don't come across as clearly. But that may not be censorship; there is a double meaning that is hard to translate correctly in English. I don't find the English translation strange. But there's one story in the Old Testament, where the future King David is running from King Saul, who is leading a manhunt and trying to kill David. There are a couple of points that David could have killed Saul, and at one of these points, David's assistant either encourages David to kill Saul or offers to kill Saul himself, and David says what your English Bible puts as, 'I will not lay my hand on the Lord's anointed,' or something like that. Would you like to know what it says in Hebrew or Greek, or in Latin translation?"

George said, "Um..."

Fr. Elijah got up. "I wasn't expecting that you would; it's really not that important or even as impressive as some people think. If you don't know those languages, it may be easiest to see in the Latin. Aah! Here's my Latin Bible. Just a minute. Let me get my magnifying glass." After almost dropping a dark green Bible with golden letters on the cover, and an interminable amount of flipping, he said, "What is this word here?"

"I don't know Latin."

"Never mind that. What does that word look like?"

"It's a lowercase version of 'Christ,' with an 'um' added."

"Yes indeed. And at the top it says the name of an Old Testament book, in Latin 'Liber Samuhelis.' What do you think the word you pointed out means?"

"I told you that I don't know Latin."

"What's an obvious guess?"

"Um..." George paused. "Christ."

"Yes indeed."

"What does the lowercase 'c' mean?"

"It means nothing. As a matter of language-loving curiosity, the text is in Latin; either in the manuscripts or in this printed Bible, capitalizations follow a different rule, and 'christus'/'christum'/... isn't automatically capitalized. Now why is the Old Testament book of Samuel using the equivalent of the 'Christ'?"

"Because the Latin is messed up?"

"Ernk. Sorry. Bzzt. Thank you for playing, but no. The Latin is *fine*. It's the *English* that's messed up. The Latin correctly translates, 'I will not lay my hand on,' meaning violently strike, 'the Lord's Christ.' Didn't you know that the word 'Christ' means 'anointed'?"

"Yes, but..."

"The Bible, Old Testament and New, uses 'Christ' for those who are anointed--the Son of God, prophets, priests, kings, and ultimately the people of God. The whole point of becoming Christian is to become by grace what Christ is by nature, and even if we can never be perfect in Christ, there is something real that happens. If you ever become Orthodox, you will be 'Christed,' or in the related and standard term, 'chrismated,' meaning, 'anointed with holy oil.' And, at a deeper level, the anointing is about anointing with the Holy Spirit, as Christ was. And the New Testament in particular says a lot about Christ, but the Bible calls Christ or Christs others who are anointed. But the Bible translations, coincidentally by people who have much less room for this in their theology, introduce a division that isn't in Hebrew, Greek, or the Catholic Church's Latin, and translate the Hebrew 'moshiah' or the Greek 'christos' one way when it refers to the one they think is 'really' Christ, and another way when it refers to other Christs even if what the text says is, quite literally, 'Christ.' They introduce a very clear divide where none exists in the text, using a language shenanigan not entirely different from some mistranslations translating 'God' with a big 'G' when the Bible talks about the Father, and a 'god' with a little 'g' when the Bible refers to Christ. Perhaps your Bible's translators still say 'anointed one,' but there is some degree of censorship. The reader is saved the shock of too many correctly translated and explicit statements that we are to be little Christs, Sons of God, living the divine life--there's a word for the divine life in Greek that is different from the word for mere created life, and that dimension doesn't seem to come through. It's not all censorship, but there's something not quite right about the translators who refuse to either consistently say 'Christ,' or else consistently say 'Anointed One,' so that the readers never get the something important in the Bible that Western Christianity does not always get. But there is enough mystery in the Bible. Sacred Scripture is unfathomable even apart from relatively few areas where the translators try to make sure that the reader does *not* get the full force of the what the text is saying. God exceeds our grasp; he is and ever shall be

Light, but whenever we try to shine a light to search him out, its beam falls off in darkness, and the God who is Light meets us beyond the cloud of darkness enshrouding him.

"I say this to answer your question, which I know was purely rhetorical. I'd prefer not to scandalize people and have to clean up the pieces later, but even the tough old women you see in our parish aren't so prissy as you might think. But I want to more directly speak to your intent, and the deep question behind your asking if, because you had hypothetically asked me, I would preach a sermon about the Bible and censorship. I wasn't crossing my fingers or simply saying what I thought would please you, when I preached about the Arthurian legends, and there is nothing I wish to take back. I really was preaching in good faith."

"Then I don't want *Brocéliande* for now."

George said, "You may like the book. I don't. I don't want it any more."

"Then may I take a look at it? I would like to have it, to look at. If you don't want it any more, that's fine, but you can have it back any time."

"Fine. Maybe it will be better for you than for me."

"By the way, what are you doing for Spring Break?"

"Dunno. Do you have any suggestions?"

"There are some truly beautiful places where you could get blasted out of your mind, acquire a couple of new diseases, and if you time it right, come back still in possession of a rather impressive hangover."

"Um..."

"Yes?"

"Why don't we just cut to the chase and get to your real suggestion?"

"Aah, yes. It turns out that there's a finishing school which is offering a week-long intensive course in the gentle art of polite conversation, but--oh, wait, I was going to suggest that to my granddaughter Abigail. I would never make such a suggestion to you. Finishing school--what was I thinking? What I was really wondering was whether you have considered one of the alternative spring breaks."

"Like Habitat for Humanity? But I have no skill in construction."

"That's not really the point. Last I checked, Habitat for Humanity had nothing on their website about how only seasoned construction workers can be of any use."

"But aren't there a lot of things that could go wrong?"

"Like what?"

"I might hit myself on the thumb with a hammer."

"If you're worried about being at a loss for words, last April Fool's Day my godson gave me a book listing bad words in something like a thousand languages, and you can borrow it. There are worse things in life than hitting your thumb with a hammer, and if it's that big of an issue, I'd be happy to ask the head of Habitat for Humanity to refund your wasted time. If you're worried about getting sunburned, the store next door has an impressive collection of sunscreen containers, giving you options that rival those for dental floss. I personally recommend the SPF 30 in your choice of soft pastel-hued plastic bottles with a delicate floral scent created through a carefully blended confection of unnatural chemicals. I don't think that Habitat is going anywhere where you'd be in real danger of snakebite, but I can help find a kit you can use to bite the snake back. Have I left something out?"

A week later, and (though he did not tell Fr. Elijah) realizing that Abigail was also a student at Calix College, George returned. Fr. Elijah said, "Why the long face, George? Just a minute while I make some tea."

"Um, I'm not signed up for the alternative spring break."

"George, I only asked you to consider... tell me what's on your mind... *if* you want to."

"I was in line, and I just missed signing up."

Fr. Elijah sat in silence.

"I could have gone, but there was a girl in line after me, and she really wanted to go. I let her have the last slot."

"Excellent. Some would call it sexist, but I'd call it one of the finer points of chivalry."

Fr. Elijah paused and then said, "Could you come with me to the house for a second?"

George gulped.

Fr. Elijah led George out to the house and rummaged on a shelf before pulling out a CD. "George, could you put this in the CD player and hit play? I've figured out how to use the CD player several times, but I keep forgetting, and I don't want to keep you waiting." He handed the CD to George and said, "I'll be right out. I need to make a phone call." He stepped into another room and closed the door.

George looked at the CD, did a double take, and looked at the player. He began to hear a rap beat.

As I walk through the valley where I harvest my grain,
I take a look at my wife and realize she's very plain.
But that's just perfect for an Amish like me.
You know, I shun fancy things like electricity.
At 4:30 in the morning I'm milkin' cows.
Jebediah feeds the chickens and Jacob plows... Fool!
And I've been milkin' and plowin' so long that
Even Ezekiel thinks that my mind is gone.
I'm a man of the land! I'm into discipline!
Got a Bible in my hand and a beard on my chin.
But if I finish all my chores and you finish thine,
Then tonight we're gonna party like it's 1699!

We been spending most our lives, living in an Amish paradise.
I've churned butter once or twice, living in an Amish paradise.
It's hard work and sacrifice, living in an Amish paradise.
We sell quilts at discount price, living in an Amish paradise.

A local boy kicked me in the butt last week.
I just smiled at him and turned the other cheek!

I really don't care; in fact, I wish him well.
'Cause I'll be laughing my head off when he's burning in
Hell!
But I ain't never punched a tourist even if he deserved it
An Amish with a 'tude? You know that's unheard of!
I never wear buttons but I got a cool hat.
And my homies agree, I really look good in black... Fool!
If you'll come to visit, you'll be bored to tears.
We haven't even paid the phone bill in 300 years
But we ain't really quaint, so please don't point and stare;
We're just technologically impaired!

There's no phone, no lights, no motorcar,
Not a single luxury,
Like Robinson Caruso,
It's as primitive as can be!

We been spending most our lives, living in an Amish
paradise.
We're just plain and simple guys, living in an Amish
paradise.
There's no time for sin and vice, living in an Amish
paradise.
We don't fight. We all play nice, living in an Amish
paradise.

Hitchin' up the buggy, churnin' lots of butter,
Raised a barn on Monday, soon I'll raise another!
Think you're really righteous? Think you're pure in heart?
Well, I know I'm a million times as humble as thou art!
I'm the pious guy the little Amlettes wanna be like,
On my knees day and night, scorin' points for the afterlife,
So don't be vain and don't be whiny,
Or else, my brother, I might have to get medieval on your
heinie!

We been spending most our lives, living in an Amish
paradise.
We're all crazy Mennonites, living in an Amish paradise.
There's no cops or traffic lights, living in an Amish
paradise.
But you'd probably think it bites, living in an Amish
paradise.

Fr. Elijah walked back into the room and served the tea, smiling gently.

George said, "Um..."

Fr. Elijah said, "Yes?"

"I'm not sure how to put this delicately."

"Then put it indelicately. Bluntly, if you wish."

"I hadn't picked you out for a Weird Al fan."

"It was a present."

"Who would buy you a Weird Al CD?"

"A loved one."

"Um... do you ever do something less spectacular, like play chess?"

"I'm not a big fan of chess, and besides, I've visited the chess club at the Episcopalian church, and it seems the Anglican Communion isn't going to produce that many more good chess players."

"Why?"

Fr. Elijah sipped his tea. "Can't tell a bishop from a queen."

George coughed, sputtered, tried to keep a straight face, and then tried to steer the conversation back. "When were you given the Weird Al CD?"

"For April Fools' Day. The present is much appreciated."

"I like Weird Al, but why did you play that?"

"Because I was just on the phone."

"And?"

"I've just arranged for you to spend your Spring Break at an Amish paradise."

"Um..."

"Yes?"

"Are you joking?"

"No."

"Are you being *serious*?"

"Yes."

"Are you being sadistic again?"

"Yes, I'm being very sadistic."

"*Why?*"

"I'm not saying."

"I'll be bored to tears."

"Perhaps. But boredom can be good, and not just because it can build character."

"Um... Never mind. I've grown rather fond of computers. I've found out the hard way that I rather need them."

"If it's *that* hard for you to spend a few days without spam, you can use your cell phone to read all the insulting messages telling you that you can't handle money, or that you need snake oil diets, or some part of your body is too small, or you're not man enough for a relationship with a real woman and must content yourself with pixels on a screen. And if you forget leave your cell phone at home, you might be able to borrow one of theirs."

"Amish don't use phones or the Internet. They're 'just technologically impaired;' didn't the song say that?"

"You can ask them; I'm sure one of them would be willing to lend you his cell phone."

"Um..."

"Let's forget about *that*; we can talk about it later if you want. Anyway, after school gets out, come over here with your bag. Someone else is doing some running, and will give you a ride. He's a bit hard of hearing, so he's not much good for chatting in the car, but he's a great guy. But you can gripe to him about how backwards the Amish are.

"Oh, and one more thing... I'm not exactly sending you into bear country, but if one of the workmen were attacked by a bear, I'd be very worried."

"Um..."

"Yes?"

"*That* seems obvious."

"But not for the reason you think. I'll explain why after you return."

There was a knock on the door, and Fr. Elijah opened it.

"George, I'd like to introduce you to Jehu. Jehu, this is George. Oh, George, I'm sorry for being a pest, but could you open your bag and pull out everything inside?"

George looked at Fr. Elijah, rolled his eyes, and began unpacking.

"Which of these items mean anything at all to you? Which have a story, or were expensive, or were a gift?"

George looked at Fr. Elijah, who stood in silence.

"You can put anything that means anything to you in this closet; it will be here when you get back. I'm not sending you to a den of thieves, but..."

George began shuffling and sorting while Fr. Elijah waited. When he was finished, Fr. Elijah said, "How much does your windbreaker mean to you?"

"It's new, but I want to have it with me on the trip."

"Take it off. You have an old sweatshirt or two."

"Sorry, I insist on this one. It doesn't mean that much to me."

Fr. Elijah said, "If you must..."

George said, "I've taken enough out. Have a good evening." He stiffly shook Fr. Elijah's hand. "You better have a good reason for your odd behavior."

Fr. Elijah said, "I can explain later, if you need me to."

George repacked the remaining half of his luggage into the duffle bag, and left with Jehu.

Some days later, Fr. Elijah heard a knock and opened the door. "George, George! How are you? I must hear about your trip. That's a lovely jeans jacket you have there. Is there a story behind it?"

George gave Fr. Elijah a look that could have been poured on a waffle, and then began quickly taking his coat off.

Fr. Elijah said, "You wouldn't throw a coat at an old man who doesn't have the reflexes to block it... I must hear the story about the coat, though."

George closed his mouth for a second, and then said, "Filthy sadist!"

Fr. Elijah said, "It sounded like you had an interesting trip."

"Did you call and *ask* them to be obnoxious?"

"I did no such thing."

"Honest?"

"I called and asked them to go easy on you."

"You called and asked them to go *easy* on me?"

"Well, you seem to have gotten through the matter without getting any black eyes."

"You call that going *easy*? These guys are pacifists, right?"

"That depends on your idea of a 'pacifist'. If you mean that they don't believe you should use violence to solve conflicts, then yes, they are pacifists."

George said, "*And...*"

"But does that make them wimps? In any sense at all?"

"You *did* say that you would be worried if one of them were attacked by a bear... *Why*?"

"I'd be worried for the bear."

George sunk down into his chair.

"You must have some stories to tell."

"They wanted help raising a barn, and they wouldn't let me do any of the stunts they were doing *without a harness*, but when I went to the outhouse, things shook, and when I opened the door, I was over ten feet in the air."

"Earthquake?"

"Forklift. I don't know why they had one."

"Did you ever think you would sit on such a high throne? I have a suspicion that's higher than even my bishop's throne."

"We are *not* amused."

"You are using the royal 'We,' Your Majesty. Excellent."

"The first day, I didn't take off my shirt at work, but I did take off my windbreaker, and when I left, they nailed it to the beams!"

"Excellent. Is that why Your Majesty has a new, handmade jeans jacket?"

George gave Fr. Elijah another look that could have been poured on a waffle.

"I should maybe have told you... They don't think anything of nailing down any clothing that's taken off as a practical joke. Did you ever get an opportunity to nail down some clothing or something of theirs?"

"Yes, but like a gentleman, I did not."

"That was rude of you."

"You mean they're *offended* at what I didn't do?"

"No; I just said it was rude. They wouldn't be offended. But what I was going to say is that the women have lots of denim, and are very adept at sewing new clothes; it's almost like making a paper airplane for them. Or maybe a little bigger of a deal than that. But you seem to be laboring under a sense that since the Amish are such backwards people, they aren't allowed to have a sense of humor. Were you surprised at the sense of humor they had?"

"Filthy sadist!"

"So did you get bored with nothing interesting to do besides surf the web through your cell phone?"

George said, "Filthy sadist!" Then he paused.

Fr. Elijah sat back and smiled. "George, I believe you have a question."

George hesitated.

"Yes? Ask anything you want."

George hesitated again, and asked, "When can I come back?"

Fr. Elijah just laughed.

George walked around, and had a few chats with Abigail on campus. She started to occupy his thoughts more... and George wondered if he really wanted to dismiss all of the literature of courtly love.

He tried to put this out of his mind the next time he saw Fr.

Elijah.

He thought he'd pay a visit, and knocked on Fr. Elijah's door.

Fr. Elijah said, "I'm glad you're here, George. Did you know that a man-eating tiger got loose on the campus of Calix College?"

George stood up and immediately pulled his cell phone out of his pocket. "Do the police--"

"Sit down, George, and put your cell phone away, although I must commend your gallant impulse. This was before your time, and besides, George, it starved."

George said, very forcedly, "Ha ha ha."

"Sit down, please. Have you had any further thoughts about your holiday with the Amish?"

"It seems a bit like King Arthur's court. Or at least--"

"Why would that be?"

George sat for a while, and said nothing.

"Are you familiar with Far Side comic strips?"

"Yes."

"I expected so. You like them, right?"

"Yes, but I haven't read them in a while."

"Do you remember the strip with its caption, 'In the days before television'?"

"Can't put my finger on it."

"It shows a family, mesmerized, sitting, lying, and slouching around a blank spot where there isn't a television... I think you've had a visit to the days before television. You didn't even need a time machine."

George sat in silence for a moment.

Fr. Elijah continued, "If you want, I can show you the technique by which the Bible is censored, and how the translators hide the fact that they've taken something out of the text. But do you know the one line that was censored from the movie production of *The Lion, the Witch, and the Wardrobe*--the Disney one, I mean?"

"I didn't notice that anything was censored."

"Well, you're almost right. Now it seems to be religion that is censored, Christianity having replaced sex as the publishing world's major taboo, and Disney did not censor one iota of the stuff about Aslan. But there is one line of the book that almost gets into the movie, but then Father Christmas merely makes a smile instead of verbally answering the question. Do you know what that line is?"

"What?"

"'Battles are ugly when women fight.'"

"Um... I can see why they would want to smooth over that."

"Why? Battles are ugly when *men* fight. There is a reason why Orthodox call even necessary fighting 'the *cross* of St. George.' '*Cross*,' as in a heavy, painful burden. I've dealt pastorally with several veterans. They've been through something rough, much rougher than some people's experience with, say, cancer. And it is my unambiguous opinion, and that of every single soldier I've spoken to at length, that battles are ugly... whether or not women fight. Therefore, battles are ugly when women fight, and you'd really have to not understand battle, think it's the same thing as a violent fantasy or watching an action-adventure movie, to deny that battles are ugly when whatever group fights.

"So why make such a big deal over a single line, 'Battles are ugly when women fight?' Why is that one line worth censoring when Disney has the guts to leave Aslan untouched? What's a bigger taboo in the media world than Christ?"

"Umm... I can't put my finger on it."

"Ok, let me ask you... What do you think of the Amish women?"

George tried not to stiffen.

"I'm sorry, George, I meant *besides* that... When you're my age you can forget that for women to dress very modestly can--"

"Then what *did* you mean?"

"Imagine one of those women in a fight."

George tried not to make a face.

Fr. Elijah said, "My understanding is that they're strong and hard workers, probably a lot stronger than many men you know."

George said, "Um..."

"Would you deny that they are strong? And tough, for that matter?"

"No..."

"Does it bother you in the same way to imagine an Amish man having to carry a gun into combat?"

"No. He'd be pretty tough."

"But the women are pretty strong and tough too. Why does it bother you to think about one of them entering combat and fighting?"

George said nothing.

"The women strike you as stronger and tougher than many men that you know. So they're basically masculine?"

"Fr. Elijah... the women there almost left me wondering if I'd met real women before, and the men left me wondering if I'd met real men before. I don't know why."

"I think I have an answer for why the idea of an Amish woman fighting in battle bothers you more than an Amish man fighting in battle."

"What?"

"I've been reading through *Brocéliande*. Let me read you a couple of passages." Fr. Elijah returned momentarily, and flipped through *Brocéliande* before reading:

> Sir Galahad he rode, and rode and rode, until saw he a dragon red. Anon the wyrm with its tail struck a third of the trees against the earth that Sir Galahad they might slay. Anon Sir Galahad warred he against the wyrm.
>
> The dragon charged, and anon Sir Galahad his horse trembled, and Galahad gat him down to earth. The dragon laughed at Sir Galahad's spear which brake to-shivers, and breathed fire red as Hell.
>
> Sir Galahad gat him behind his shield, and then charged with his sword, though it should break as rotted wood. Anon the dragon swept him, though his helm saved

> Sir Galahad his head from the rocks.
>
> Then Sir Galahad, who his strength was as the strength of a thousand because his faith was pure, leapt him and wrestled against the beast. Anon the beast turned and tore, against the knight, until the knight he bled sore. Never was such combat enjoined, but the knight held his choke until the dragon his death met.

Fr. Elijah pulled the bookmark out, and found one of several other bookmarks:

> Rose the smoke of incense, of frankincense pure the garden did fill. 'Twere many women present, that hyght Lady Eva, and Lady Elizabeth, and Lady Anna, and Lady Martha, and Queen Mary. Sang they a song, 'twere of one voice, and in that song kept they a garden: in the garden was life. Queen Mary a radiant Child gave suck, and others gave life each in her way.
>
> Verdant was the place of their labour.

Fr. Elijah said, "I think you're missing the point if you're trying to tell if there are differences between men and women by asking who is tougher."

"Why?"

"It's like asking what the differences are between apples and oranges, and then thinking you need to justify it with a measurement. So you may say that apples are bigger than oranges, until you realize that navel oranges are the size of a grapefruit and some varieties of apples don't get that big. So maybe next you measure a sugar content, and you get really excited when you realize that maybe oranges have a measurably lower Ph than apples--a scientist's way of measuring how sour they are--until someone reminds you that crabapples are so tart you wouldn't want to eat them. And all this time you are looking for some precise scientific measurement that will let you scientifically be able to distinguish apples and oranges...

"Is it simply a measure of some difference in physical strength that makes you not like the idea of an Amish woman in battle? If you knew that the women were equally as strong as the men, identically strong, or tough or whatever, would that address..."

George hesitated. "But..."

Fr. Elijah sat silently.

"But," George continued, "the idea of an Amish woman in battle... I know some girls who wanted to go into the military, and it didn't bother me *that* much. And the Amish women *are* pacifists."

"So if those women were gung-ho military enthusiasts, even if they weren't soldiers, then you wouldn't mind--"

"Ok, ok, that's not it. But what *is* it about the Amish?"

"George, I think you're barking up the wrong tree."

"So what is the right tree? Where *should* I be barking?"

"When people notice a difference with another culture, at least in this culture they seek some 'That's cultural' explanation about the *other* culture."

"So there's something about *this* culture? Ours?"

"George, let me ask you a question. How many times in the Arthurian legends did you see someone invite a man to be open about himself and have the courage to talk about his feelings?"

George was silent.

"We still have the expression, 'wear the pants,' even though it is no longer striking for a woman to wear trousers. It used to be as striking as it would be for a man to wear a skirt."

"Um... you don't approve of women wearing pants?"

"Let's put that question on hold; it doesn't mean the same thing. Abby wears trousers all the time. I wouldn't want her to do otherwise."

"But..."

"George, when have you seen me at the front of the church, leading worship but *not* wearing a skirt?"

"Um..."

"But I wouldn't want you wearing a skirt. The question of

wearing a skirt, or pants, or whatever, is like trying to make a rule based on size or tartness or whatever to separate apples from oranges."

"It's the wrong question, then?"

"It's *fundamentally* the wrong question... and it misleads people into thinking that the *right* question must be as impossible to answer as the wrong question. Never mind asking who is allowed to wear pants and who is allowed to wear a skirt. We're both men. I wear a skirt all the time. You shouldn't. And, in either case, there is a way of dressing that is appropriate to men, and another to women, and that propriety runs much deeper than an absolute prohibition on who can wear what. And this is true even *without* getting into the differences between men's and women's jeans, which are subtle enough that you can easily miss them, but important."

"Like what?"

"For starters, the cloth is hung on men's jeans so that the fabric is like a grid, more specifically with some of the threads running up and down, and others running side to side. On women's clothing, jeans included, the threads run diagonally."

"And this is a deliberately subtle clue for the super-perceptive?"

"It changes how the cloth behaves. It changes the cloth's physical properties. Makes women's clothing run out faster, because it's at just the right angle to wear out more quickly. But it also makes the cloth function as more form-fitting. On men's jeans, the cloth just hangs; it's just there as a covering. On women's jeans, the cloth is there to cover, but it's also there to highlight. This, and the cut, and a few other things, mean that even if men and women are both wearing jeans, there are differences, even if they're subtle enough that you won't notice them. Men's jeans are clothing. Women's jeans are more about adornment, even--or *especially*--if it's something you're not expected to notice."

"So we do have differences?"

"We do have differences despite our best efforts to eradicate them. We want men to be sophisticated enough to cultivate their feminine sides, and women to be strong enough to step up to the plate."

"Um, isn't that loaded language?"

"Very. Or maybe not. But one of the features of Gnosticism is that there keeps popping up an idea that we should work towards androgyny. Including today."

"Like what?"

"Um, you mean besides an educational system that is meant to be unisex and tells boys and girls to work together and be... um... 'mature' enough not to experience a tingle in the relationship? Or dressing unisex? Or not having too many activities that are men only or women only? Or not having boys and men together most of the time, and women and girls together? Or having people spend long periods of time in mixed company whether or not it is supposed to be romantic? Or an idea of dating that is courtly love without too many consciously acknowledged expectations about what is obviously the man's role, and what is obviously the women's role? Or--"

"Ok, *ok*, but I think there was more--"

"Yes, there is much more to the Amish, or the Arthurian legends, than what they hold about men and women. But there is also much more *in* what they hold about men and women--all the more when they are telling of Long Ago and Far Away, so that political correctness does not apply to them, so that men who go on great quests can be appreciated even by a woman who thinks men would be better off if they would just learn to talk more about their feelings and in general hold a woman's aspirations of conversational intimacy. And the Amish are 'technologically impaired,' or whatever you want to call them, so they're allowed to have real men and real women *despite* the fact that they are alive today. But the pull of men taught to be men, and women taught to be women, is powerful even if it's politically incorrect, and--"

George interrupted. "Is this why I was trying to keep a straight face when you were asking me to imagine an Amish woman carrying a gun?"

Fr. Elijah thought. "For an Amish man to have to fight in battle would be bad enough. An Amish woman entering a battlefield would be something that would cut against the grain of their life as women. It's not so superficial as the women being dainty and not strong enough to hold a gun."

"The men seem stronger and tougher than the women, though."

"Yes, but is it only a matter of being tougher? Is what you observed simply a matter of the women being tough but the men being tougher?"

George was silent.

Fr. Elijah looked at his watch and winced. "Always when I'm having a good conversation... George, I'm sorry, but I've got someone coming over any minute, and a bit of preparation. Sorry..."

George picked up his belongings, and Fr. Elijah blessed him on his way out. Then George stepped out, and Fr. Elijah momentarily opened the door. "Oh, and by the way, George, I have some more of that paper, if you want to write her a love note." He closed the door.

George scurried away, hoping that Fr. Elijah hadn't seen him blush.

It was not much later that April Fool's Day came, falling on a Sunday. George did not feel brave, and paid a visit to Bedside Baptist. The days seemed to pass quickly with Abigail in the picture.

On Earth Day, George listened and was amazed at how many references to Creation he heard in the liturgy--not just the reference to "his mother, the earth," but how plants and trees, rocks, stars, and seas, formed the warp and woof by which the Orthodox Church praised her Lord. The liturgy left him wishing Fr. Elijah would put off his preaching and say something to celebrate earth day...

Fr. Elijah stood up.

In the Name of the Father, and of the Son, and of the Holy Ghost. Amen.

Today is Earth Day, and I thought that that would provide an excellent basis for my preaching today. The very opening chapters of Genesis are not about man alone but man and the whole Creation. There are some very interesting suggestions people have made that when Genesis says that we were told not only to "be fruitful and multiply," but "fill the earth and subdue it," the word translated "subdue" is very gentle, almost an embrace, as a mother nurtures a child. Which is a very lovely image, but is absolute hogwash.

The word translated "subdue" is the word Christ uses for exactly what Christians must not do by "lording their authority" over other Christians as the heathen do. The book of Genesis tells of this beautiful Creation and then has God charge us with a charge that could much better be translated, "trample it under foot." And what better day than Earth Day than to talk about why we should trample the earth under foot, told to us in a text that is resplendent with natural beauty?

Many people today call the earth 'Gaia', and that is well and good. Today one calls a man 'Mr.' and a woman 'Miss' or 'Ms.' or 'Mrs.' if there is no other honorific, and as much as adults all bear that title, in Latin every woman bears then name of 'Gaia' and every man bears the name of 'Gaius.' And if we are speaking of the earth, it is well and proper to call her Gaia; only someone who understands neither men nor women would think of her as sexless!

If you are dealing with a horse, for instance, it helps to keep in mind that they are prey animals with a lot of fear. Never mind that they're much bigger than you; they're afraid of you, as you would be afraid of a rat, and need to be treated like a small child. But you can only deal with a horse gently after it is broken and after you have made it clear that it is you holding the reins and not the horse. You need to be able to treat a horse like a little child if you are to handle them... but if you spoil it, and fail to establish your authority, you have a terrified small child that is stronger than an Olympic athlete. You *do* need to be gentle with a horse, but it is a gentleness that holds the reins, with you in charge.

There are a number of fundamental difficulties we face about being in harmony with nature, and one of the chief ones is that we are trying to be in harmony with nature the *wrong* way. We are trying to take our cue from our mother the earth, perhaps instead of taking our cue from technology. And it is excellent to treat Gaia gently, and perhaps technology is in fact quite a terrible place to take our cue from, and something else we absolutely need to trample under foot, but there is something mistaken about the rider taking his cue from the horse. In Genesis we are called to rule material Creation as its head: we are to give it its cue, rather than following. Perhaps you have seen the *Far Side* cartoon that says, "When imprinting studies go awry" and shows a scientist last in line with ducklings follow a mother duck... which is very funny, but not a recipe for a life well lived. We are made from the same clay as horse and herb, but unless we are deeply sunk into the even worse cues we will take from technology when we fail to rule it, we do not serve our best interests--or the earth's--when we ask her to dance and expect her to be our lead.

But enough of what is politically incorrect in the West, where we say that men should not lead and mean, in both senses, that humans should not lead the rest of Creation and that males should not lead females. I could belabor why both of those are wrong, but I would like to dig deeper, deeper even than saying that lordship applies to every one of us even if we are all "a man under authority," *including* me.

Patristic exegesis of the rule over Creation is first and foremost of a rule over our passions and over ourselves. We are not fit to lead others or Creation if we have not even learned to lead ourselves; "better is a man who controls his temper than one who takes a city." If you are following a Western model, then you may be thinking of a big enterprise for us to start ruling Creation which is really beside the point. If you save yourself through ascetical mastery, ten thousand will be saved around you. Never mind that this is mystical; it is a matter of "Seek first the Kingdom of God, and all these things shall be added unto you." You become a leader, and a man, not by ruling over others, but by ruling over yourself.

We are in Great Lent now, the central season of the entire Orthodox year, not because it is about ruling others or about ruling Creation--it isn't--but because it is about ruling ourselves. We are not to seek a larger kingdom to rule outside ourselves; we are to turn our attention to the kingdom within, and rule it, and God will add a larger kingdom outside if we are ready. The first, foremost, and last of places for us to exercise lordship is in ourselves, and our rule over the Creation is but an image of our rule over ourselves, impressive as the outer dominion may be.

We bear the royal bloodline of Lord Adam and Lady Eve, and we are to be transformed into the image of Christ. Let us seek first the Kingdom of God, with all that that means for our rule over ourselves.

In the Name of the Lord and Father, and of the Son who is Lord, and of the Heavenly King, who is the Holy Ghost, Amen.

After his Sunday dinner, George thought it would be a good time to wander in the wood.

In the forest, he found himself by a babbling brook, with the sound of a waterfall not far off. George brushed off a fallen mossy log and sat down to catch his breath.

George began listening to the birdsong, and it almost seemed he could tell a pattern. Then two warm hands covered his eyes.

George tried to look up, remembered his eyes were covered, and brought his own hands up to his face, briefly touching a small, soft pair of hands. Then he said, "It's definitely a man..."

Then George turned. Abigail was sticking out her tongue.

Abigail's dress was a rich, deep, deep red, the color of humble earth seen through a ruby. A pair of bare white feet peeked out from beneath a long flowing skirt, a wide, golden straw hat sat atop her locks, and dark, intricate knotwork lay across her heart.

George looked down at his own feet and saw his own worn combat boots, before looking at Abigail's face. She smiled and said, "Boo!"

George said, "What are you doing here?"

"What are you doing here?"

"Taking a walk, as I do from time to time."

"Must be pretty rare for you, if this is the first time I've seen you."

"You're in the woods more often than I am?"

A squirrel darted out, climbed across Abigail's foot, and scurried away.

George asked, "It wasn't afraid of you?"

"Most of them aren't, at least not that much of the time."

George looked at her, and she said, "It's not such a big deal, really. Read any good books lately?"

"No, and--ooh, I told Fr. Elijah I'd read C.S. Lewis, something or other about 'glory.' I need to get back to him."

"Maybe it's a box you're not meant to open, at least not yet... if I know Grandpa, he's probably forgotten about it completely."

"But I should--"

"You should leave it a closed box, if anything. How are you?"

George looked at the forest--how like a garden it looked--and then Abigail. He was at something of a loss for words. He looked down at her alabaster feet, and then her face. "Having a good day."

She smiled, and a sparrow flew between them. "There's a hawk in here somewhere, only it's hard to find. You can spend a lot of time exploring this forest. I'm having a good day, too."

George sat for a while, trying to think of something to say, and Abigail said, "You're being pretty quiet now."

George said, "I've been looking at majoring in math."

Abigail said, "Um..."

"You know how to tell if a mathematician is an extravert?"

"Nope."

George looked down and said, "He looks at *your* feet when they're talking to you."

Abigail giggled. "Have you heard my Grandpappy's theory on how PMS got its name?"

George said, "Um..."

She giggled again. "Something about 'Mad Cow Disease' being taken."

George stiffened, and looked for something to say.

Abigail said, "Stop it, George. Just stop it. Don't you get it? Don't you stand and listen or sing the hymn where the the Mother of God is honored as the Ewe that bore the Lamb of God and the Heifer that bore the Unblemished Calf?"

George's mind raced. "I suppose that if, in the same breath, Christ is called--"

Abigail interrupted. "Next time you're in Church, listen, really listen, as the Mother of God is honored, then listen as Christ our God is worshiped. There's a difference. Don't try to analyze it or even put your finger on it. Just listen, and... George, do you understand women? At all?"

George looked for something to say, but found nothing.

A dark cloud blew across the sky, and cold rain began to fall more heavily until it poured.

George said, "May I lend you my jacket?"

Abigail said, "I'm fine."

The rain grew colder, and began to pelt. George and Abigail both rose and began scurrying towards campus. George took off his jacket and started to place it around Abigail's shoulders.

Abigail said, "I don't--"

George looked down and said, "I'm wearing boots and you have bare feet," and wrapped his jacket around her shoulders. Then a gust of wind tore at Abigail's hat, but George caught it.

Then they ran back, with George shivering under his threadbare T-shirt. When they got back, he went to his dorm and she to hers. George called Abigail and confirmed she was OK, took three long, hot showers, and spent the rest of the evening sinking into a lounge chair in his bathrobe, sipping cocoa, and thinking.

Tuesday evening, George found time to visit Fr. Elijah. He wanted to talk about another subject. Definitely another subject.

"Fr. Elijah, are you busy?"

"I hope not... come in."

"After all this, I still want the Holy Grail."

"Excellent thing, my son... the chief point of life is to search for the Holy Grail."

"But will I find it? I mean... I'm not sure what I mean."

"May I show you something old?"

"As far as material age goes, it is much older than the Holy Grail."

The old man opened a desk drawer, and fished out a small box.

"I thought this might interest you," he said, and took something out of the box, and placed it in George's hand.

George looked the item over. It looked like a piece of bark, not much larger than a pebble, and yet it seemed heavy for a piece of bark. "Is this stone or wood? I can't tell which it is."

"Is it stone or wood? In fact, it is petrified wood... from the Oak of Mambre."

"Oak of Mambre? Should I have heard of it before?"

"You probably have, and if you can't remember it, there is something you're missing."

"What is the Oak of Mambre?"

"I'll tell you in a bit. When you grasp the Oak of Mambre,

you hold the Holy Grail."

"How?"

"The Oak of Mambre is older than any of the civilizations you know; for that matter, it might be older than the practice of writing. Do you know about Abraham?"

"The one Paul calls the father of all who believe?"

"Yes, that Abraham. The Bible tells how Abraham met three men who came to him, and showed the most lavish hospitality, giving them the costliest meal he could have given. And it was then that the men promised the impossible. It is clear enough later that these men were in fact angels, were in fact God.

"From the West, you may not know that even if we Orthodox are big on icons, it's fingernails to a chalkboard when Orthodox see the Father portrayed as the proverbial old man with a beard. Christ may be portrayed because of his incarnation; the same is not true of the invisible Father, who is not and never will be incarnate. Icons of the Father have been fundamentally rejected, but there was one exception. From ancient times there has been an icon of Abraham's hospitality to the three men, or three angels, and centuries ago one iconographer showed something deeper: it is the same three men or angels, but instead of a table with a lamb as in the old version of the icon, there is an icon with a chalice atop an altar. In both the old and the new form of the icon, the Oak of Mambre is in the back, and it is this same oak for which I have shown you a fragment."

"Is it holy because it is old?"

"Being old does not make a thing holier. The pebbles in your yard are of stone ages older than the oldest relic. Though they are, admittedly, part of the earth which received Christ's blood on the cross, and which Bulgakov rightly calls the Holy Grail.

"A thing is kept and preserved because it is holy, and if people will try to keep a holy thing for a long time, it will probably be old to most of the people who see it. Same reason most of the people who have seen the Liberty Bell saw it when it was old because people have been keeping it for a long time, much longer than the time when it was new, so most of the people who have seen, or will see, the Liberty Bell, see it as an old treasure. But back to holy things: a holy thing is, if anything, timeless: when there arose a great evil in Russia and Marx's doctrine helped people try to make paradise and caused a deep, deep river of blood to flow, the communists in the Orthodox heartland of Russia made martyrs, and in that torrential river of blood made more Orthodox martyrs than the rest of history put together. God will preserve saints' relics from that, and it may be that there are more relics from the past century than all centuries before. And they are not the less holy because they are new. But let us return to the Oak of Mambre and why, if you grasp it, you hold the Holy Grail."

"Ok. Why is that?"

"The Church has decided that the only legitimate way to portray an icon of the Trinity is in the hospitality of Abraham. And the Icon of the Holy Trinity is the deepest icon of the Holy Grail--deeper even than an icon that I can show you that shows the Mother of God as a chalice holding her Son. Where is the Holy Grail in this icon?"

"Is it that little thing in the center?"

"In part. Where else is it?"

George looked long and hard, seemed to almost catch something, before it vanished from his face.

"There are different interpretations," Fr. Elijah said, "and the icon conceals things; even the angel is a protecting veil to a reality that cannot be seen. But in the layers of this icon, the deepest glimpse sees the Father on the left, the Spirit on the right, and the Son in blood red clothes in the center, encased as in a chalice, showing the reality in Heaven for which even the Holy Grail is merely a shadow."

George turned the stone over in his hand with awe, closed his eyes, and then looked at the relic he held in his hand. "So I am holding the Holy Grail."

Fr. Elijah said, "Yes, if you look on it with enlightened eyes. Where else do you meet the Holy Grail?"

"In every person I meet?"

"'Tis hard to answer better than that. When you become Orthodox, you will receive the Eucharist and kiss the chalice, and, perhaps, find that the Holy Grail is achieved not by an unearthly isolated hero, but by a community in common things."

"But why do people kiss the Holy Grail? I mean the chalice?"

"If you call it the Holy Grail, even if your tongue slips, you may be understanding it. The Western view is that there is one original chalice and the others are separate sorts of things; in Orthodoxy, what is the same between the Holy Grail and 'another' chalice runs infinitely deeper than what separates them; the 'real' thing is that they are the same."

"But why the kiss?"

"Let me ask you a question. Do you think a kiss has more to do with worship, or with mental calculations?"

"Does it have to do with either?"

"You haven't read the Bible in Greek."

"What does the Greek Bible have to do with it?"

"Quite a lot, but it will take me a bit to explain why. But there is a deep tie.

"The main word for reverence or worship, in the Greek Bible, literally means to kiss. Part of what you'll keep coming to again and again is that the West understands the mind as the thing that calculates, and the East understands the mind as what knows, and is enlightened, because it tastes and even more deeply because it worships. I don't know how to put this clearly, in terms that will make sense to someone who does not know the spiritual realities involved. There is a false kiss--I dare say, the kiss of Judas or a kiss that is hollow like the kiss of Judas--that is nothing more than a calculated act. But there is also a kiss that has something to do with worship, and it is no error that Orthodoxy has things 'with love and kisses.' We embrace icons, crosses, holy books, each other with reverence that includes a kiss. And rightly done, such kisses are connected to worship."

"I still don't understand why."

"Let me make a momentary detour; I'll get back in a moment. Old texts can be at once something we genuinely experience a deep connection to, and something treacherously unfaithful to our assumptions. What would you say, for instance, that the medieval Scholastics are talking about when they use the word that is usually translated, 'intellect'?"

"I try to keep my mind free of preconceptions, especially when dealing with something unfamiliar."

"So you'd be open to anything they'd say about the intellect's ability to draw logical conclusions from one thing to another?"

"They can let the intellect draw conclusions however they want to."

"But here's the thing. They *don't.* It is a fundamental error to read 'intellect' as 'the thing that reasons by logical deduction. Saying that the 'intellect' is what makes deductions by reasoning from one thing by another is like saying that an object's height is what you measure with a bathroom scale, or that its weight is measurable with a ruler. It's a fundamental error; the intellect is precisely what does not reason from premises to conclusions."

"Then what is the intellect?"

"I usually don't use the term 'intellect' for it; the closest English equivalent I can think of is 'spiritual eye'. But even that misses what exactly this spiritual eye connects with. And this spiritual eye was known to the Greek Fathers no less than the Latin scholastics; if anything, the Greek Fathers were more attuned to it. Scholastic theology is an exercise, to a large degree, of that which reasons; the theology of the Fathers comes from another place. The spiritual eye is that which connects with spiritual realities, that which worships above all--and if you want a good, short definition for what 'intellect' means besides 'what IQ is supposed to measure,' use the definition 'where one meets God.' If reasoning deduces what you may not see yet, the spiritual eye *sees*, and knows by what it can see, not by what it can pull from other things it already has. This reasoning from one thing shines like the sun in Western Scholasticism."

"And that's something you don't have in Orthodoxy?"

"We do have it. But reasoning shines like the *moon*: it reflects the light of the sun in each of us, the sun of our mind's spiritual eye. It plays more of a supporting role."

"And what does all of this have to do with your ritual kiss?"

"There was an awful video I heard was shown in one of your college's psychology classes; I don't know if you've seen it. It was talking about one psychological theory, and discussed how reward and such could be used to reduce autistic behaviors. And it showed a scientist, or psychologist, or something, who was patiently training a little girl to not do whatever he was trying to stop her from doing, and the girl lit up when he gave her a kiss. And then, along with a fake-sounding Mommy-ese talking in a high-pitched voice which I *assure* you was not spontaneous, he started to use almost forced kisses to, well..."

George cut in. "Manipulate her?"

"Yes, you found the word I was looking for. The one time I heard Abigail talking about that video, she said there was a bit of bristling going though the class; the students were uncomfortable with something about that video and its one more mere technique, a mere *tool*, for changing a little girl's behavior."

"Is the spiritual eye, or whatever, spontaneous? Is it about spontaneity?"

"I'll have to think about that... I'm not sure I've seriously thought about whether the spiritual eye is spontaneous. But spontaneity is not the issue here. The point has to do with what place a kiss should come from if it is not to be hollow. Have you noticed that none of the icons I've showed you have a signature?"

"Because the iconographers are not supposed to be what we think of in the West as artists, with their own signature style and their big egos?"

"A little bit. Iconography is art, and artistry and talent do mean anything: the iconographer is not a cog in a machine--and may be doing something much bigger than trying to use art supplies for self-expression. There is something self-effacing about iconography--something very self-effacing--but you find that when you bow down and efface yourself, it is you doing something much bigger than otherwise. Writing icons is a form of prayer, a spiritual exercise, and it is said--just like we speak of 'writing' icons rather than 'painting' them--that it is inadequate for an iconographer to sign the icon, because the icon is written, not merely by the iconographer's hand, but by his his spiritual eye. It is ever much more than a merely material process, and when you become Orthodox you may sense icons that have spiritual depth and icons that let you see no further than the wood, and if you receive this gift, you will be responding to the spiritual process out of which the icon arose."

"I have sensed something... the icons still look like awkward pictures to me, but I'm starting to find something more."

"That is good. And your mouth--with which you breathe in your spirit, and show the reason of speech, and will receive the Eucharist--is not that *by* which you may give a kiss; it is that *through* which you may give the kiss that comes from and to some extent is the embrace of your spiritual eye. That's when a kiss is furthest from the hollow kiss that Judas gave. The knowledge of the spiritual eye is something I have discussed as sight, but in the ancient world all people recognized something touch-y about all the five senses, not just one. And this knowledge and drinking are exemplars of each other, draughts from the same fountain, and it is not an accident that 'know' has a certain sense in the Bible between, for instance, Adam and Eve: the spiritual eye knows by drinking in, and it is a fundamental error to think that the holy kiss has nothing to do with knowledge."

"This sounds like a fairy tale."

"Maybe you know your fairy tales, and know that there is something magic about a kiss. As one scholar put it, examples of the kiss as a means of making and breaking enchantments have been found in the folklore of almost every culture in the Western world. Orthodoxy has something more than this enchantment. There is a spiritual mingling, and even the Eucharist is understood as a kiss, and a kiss that embraces others: in the Eucharist, the body of Christ is offered up, including a token of bread for every parishioner--before being distributed. Have you not noticed that the best bishops and the most devout of the Orthodox, give the best kisses? But let me step back a bit.

"The difference in understanding symbol is one of the biggest differences between East and West. In the West, at least in its modern forms, a symbol is a detached and somewhat arbitrary representation. In the East a symbol is connected, cut from the same cloth as it were. The difference between Orthodoxy and various Protestant schools is not whether the Eucharist is a symbol, but what that means--that the Eucharist is an arbitrarily detached token, connected only in the viewer's mind, or whether it is connected and in fact the same on a real level.

"We are made in the image of God, which means that how you treat others is inseparable from how you treat God: you treat God with respect, love, or contempt as you meet him in the person of others. And the things that we reverently kiss in Orthodoxy are all connected with God. We show our reverence to God in how we treat them. And if a person is being transformed according to the likeness of Christ, then it is fitting to reverently kiss that person and show respect for the Lord.

"To give the holy kiss rightly is a microcosm of faith and community. You cannot do it alone, nor can you do it apart from worship. If you look at the things that fit together in a fitting kiss, you have love, God, your neighbor... there are a great many actions that are listed in the Bible, and many of them are holy actions, but only one is called holy: the holy kiss. If you grasp the Hoy Grail in your heart, and you grasp this kiss in its full sense, you will know that the sacred kiss in which our souls are mingled is the Sign of the Grail. It is the eighth sacrament."

George was silent for a long time. "I don't think I know enough to be Orthodox."

Fr. Elijah said, "Join the club! I know *I* don't know enough."

"But you're a priest!"

"And you cannot become Orthodox without entering the royal priesthood. You aren't ready to be Orthodox just because you know a certain amount; you're ready when you're ready for the responsibility, like getting married, or getting a job, or any other of a number of things. You are ready when you are ready to take the responsibility to return the Creation as an offering to God and shoulder a priestly office. And, in your case, I might add, when you enter the great City and Castle called the Church, and are ready for the Sign of the Grail."

"All I know now is my own unworthiness."

"Good. You're growing! Ponder your unworthiness and give it to God. Do you want to take *Brocéliande* back now?"

George gladly took the book back. He returned to his room, and some time later, George began reading:

> The hermit spoke. "Listen as I tell to thee the history of Saint George.
>
> "The King wept sore. 'The land is weeping, the land itself weeps. The dragon hath devoured every damsel of the land, every last one, and now it seeketh mine own. I bewail the death of my joy and my daughter.'
>
> "Then Saint George said, 'By my faith I will protect her and destroy this fiend,' and Saint George prayed and gat him his destrier and armed him and fewtered his spear and rode out and faced the sea.
>
> "And the dragon arose from the sea and his deeps. And venom were in the wyrm his heart, and the grievous stench of death stank all round.
>
> "Then the serpent charged upon Saint George the ever victorious knight, and the dragon breathed fire which brake and were quenched upon Saint George his shield, a grand cross gules upon a field or.
>
> "Then Saint George made him the Sign of the Cross.
>
> "Then Saint George smote the dragon, the great paladin his great spear dove into the dragon his mouth and dolve far beyond that insatiate devouring maw, until the dragon his head were riven asunder from the dragon his body trampled by Saint George his horse. And Saint George hurled the wyrm his head into the dark thrice cursed valley

far outside of the castle.

"That day the King and the whole castle made such merriment as had never been since, for we do not know merriment today. There were jugglers and jesters and a table full filled, and before evensong the King gave George the hand of the King his daughter. That were the gayest of all."

The knight asked the hermit, "Why speakest thou me of this history?"

The hermit spake unto him and answered, "Sir knight, thou hast given me not thine name. What be it?"

"Thou entreatest of me my name? Thou askest what none hath asked of me aforetimes. My name is called Sir Perceval. And now I ask of thee of what I have asked not aforetimes. Had Saint George heard tell of whom doth the Grail serve?"

George slowly closed the book, and put it on a shelf. He momentarily wondered why he treated *Brocéliande* as something to read alone. There was something that seemed just out of his reach.

And then George realized something deep, deep inside himself.

Then it was Holy Week.

Or at least George wanted it to be holy week for him, too.

George found himself standing in Church, in the holiest of surroundings, and struggling to pray. Memories arose; painful memories of stinging things done by those he loved. Voluptuous images sometimes followed. He struggled to pray, but his mind remained locked in earthly struggles. His body ached in the long services: there were icons, chanting, and incense without, and struggles within. He wanted to rest in worship, and he couldn't.

In his mind, he remembered a moment when a beggar had come to him, and wouldn't stop pleading no matter how much he annoyed George. The image filled his mind, and George was startled when he turned and saw the beggar's face on the wall. Why was that?

George was looking at an icon of Christ.

He had fallen short, and not only in seeing that beggar as nothing but an annoyance. Did George really have no common bond with that beggar?

For that matter, did George have no common bond with the civilization that he disdained, the civilization that included everybody he knew from the beggar to his parents, the civilization that gave him everything from his clothing to his language? Was it there for no other purpose than for him to criticize and feel superior to?

Fr. Elijah, moving amongst the congregation, swung the censer before George in veneration.

George barely noticed that some of these thoughts were giving way, and he was aware, with almost a painful sharpness, of something else.

George mulled over Fr Elijah's words about hollow kisses, and then started to see how hollow *George* was.

Unworthy thought he felt, George stood with growing awe and wonder, waiting until Great and Holy Thursday, the one day in holy week where wine was allowed. "Ordinary" wine was allowed, held in honor and in remembrance of the Last Supper, when wine became the blood of Christ and the eucharistic chalice was forever given to men. This day, if anything, was to George the feast of the Holy Grail.

And so he stood entranced, as if he were entering from afar. He watched the Last Supper as here and now, as Fr. Elijah stood "in the flame" before the altar, and then listened as he read the Gospel according to St. John the Evangelist, of the night when Christ loved his disciples to the last, and prayed out from the glory he shared with the Father before the worlds had begun.

And Fr. Elijah read and read, reading until George's body ached from standing.

Then someone walked over to twelve unlit candles, and lit one. The first.

George's heart sank. There were eleven candles still to go.

The readings continued, and became shorter, until the

twelve candles were lit. George began to feel anger at the unending readings--until he heard Christ's words from the garden of Gethsemane: "What, could you not watch with me one hour?" Who were those words spoken to?

And then, when the readings had run their course, the liturgy followed--at once unlike an intimate gathering in an upper room in external appearance, but yet like the place that feels like home though nothing on the outside resembles the home. George thought for a moment about a historical reconstruction of the Last Supper pursued through academic rigor in archaeology... and then realized he needed no such thing. He was watching the Last Supper all around him, and in the words of Fr. Elijah's remark, "You didn't even need a time machine."

Or was this liturgy a spiritual time machine? Certainly time flowed in the most interesting ways, now quickly, now slowly, swirling about in eddies... there was something George could not put his finger on, but he understood for a moment what could make a person imagine a way to turn back time.

And so George found himself almost surprised when Fr. Elijah said, "He gave it to his holy disciples and apostles, saying, 'Take, eat; this is my body which is broken for you, for the forgiveness of sins.'"

Then the faithful sealed this with their, "Amen."

Then Fr. Elijah said, "Likewise, he took the cup of the fruit of the vine, and having mingled it, offering thanks, blessing, and sanctifying it, he gave it to his holy disciples and apostles, saying, 'Drink of this, all of you. This is my blood of the new covenant, shed for you and for many, for the forgiveness of sins.'"

The disciples around him sealed this, with their, "Amen."

George looked in wonder at the chalice that was raised. He thought, "This is it. This is the Holy Grail, forever given, that belongs to Christ's disciples."

As the liturgy continued, and Fr. Elijah proclaimed the Holy Gifts, the people continued to seal the Gifts with their "Amen," and George watched as they received from the chalice, and kissed the chalice in reverence, and (though George paid this little attention) Fr. Elijah's hand.

George found himself basking in the glow of that long moment for as the liturgy continued and Fr. Elijah anointed those around him that they may be healed in soul and body.

As he walked home, he thought, "I have seen the Holy Grail. It has been under my nose. Very soon I will be one of those who share it, one of those the Holy Grail belongs to."

When George got home, he slept as peacefully as he slept in ages.

Then George entered the Church on Great and Holy Friday.

The whole service moved slowly, felt like something great but alien that slipped through George's fingers no matter what he did to grasp it. Around him were some who were silent, some who were singing, and some who were weeping. A great cross was brought out, and a great icon of Christ hung on it with nails.

And then something clicked in George's heart.

Some years before, he had been at a martial arts demonstration and saw a fifth degree black belt standing like a picturesque statue, looking quaint and exotic, holding a beautiful pair of fans. And then, for an instant, there was a flurry of motion as he was attacked by six other black belts with swords. And then, an instant later, George saw a fifth degree black belt standing like a picturesque statue, looking quaint and exotic, holding a beautiful pair of fans, and all around him were six other black belts with swords, on the ground, crying.

That had for long been the greatest display of power George had seen.

Now something was at the back of his mind.

Here was a new image of strength.

Were they the same?

Were they different?

Was the true nature of strength, strength in weakness?

The fifth degree black belt showed strength behind apparent weakness--or at least what looked like weakness to an outsider like George; he had no idea what it would look like to someone who was not a barbarian like him. To him, the martial arts demonstration seemed to show strength, if a show was needed, and a strength great and powerful enough to vastly understate itself. And the One before him on the cross showed more of the same... or was that really true?

Was it?

Something about that did not sit well.

Inside George's heart flashed an icon that had been on his mind--of a Man, his head bent, a purple robe about his wounded body. The robe was royal purple to mock the "pretender," his hands were bound, and a crown of thorns rested atop his bent head.

Atop the icon was an inscription in Greek and in English:

Ο ΒΑΣΙΛΕΥΣ ΤΗΣ ΔΟΞΗΣ

THE KING OF GLORY

George raised his eyes to the crucified God.

This was another kind of strength.

George began to weep.

This was the strength that prayed, if there was any way, that the cup might pass from him.

This was the strength that prayed, "Thy will be done."

This was the strength that drank the cup to the dregs, and shattered it forever.

This was

THE KING OF GLORY
THE KING OF KINGS
THE LORD OF LORDS
THE GOD OF GODS
THE LION OF JUDAH
THE FIRSTBORN OF THE DEAD
THE RESURRECTION AND ETERNAL LIFE
THE NEW MAN AND THE LAST ADAM
THE UNCREATED GOD

THE DIVINE, ORDERING WISDOM
THROUGH WHOM ALL THINGS WERE MADE
BY WHOM ALL THINGS WERE MADE
IN WHOM ALL THINGS CONSIST
THE LORD OF THE CHURCH AND ALL CREATION
THE BRIDEGROOM OF THE CHURCH AND ALL CREATION

Had George ever known what it was to worship?

George stood in awe of the one who was, in truth, the Holy Grail...

or rather, the one for whom the Holy Grail was but a shadow.

And who was George next to such holiness and power?

Unclean and defiled.

When George had thought about going to his first confession, it had looked to him like the least attractive part of the picture of becoming Orthodox. But now, even if he knew even more dread, he wanted, not so much to be unburdened for himself, but to turn himself in and render what was due.

He didn't just think he needed to. He simply knew that it was something that he owed with from the core of his being.

What evil had he not practiced?

He prayed aloud, "Lord Jesus Christ, Son of God, have mercy on me, a sinner," and then in spirit and body fell prostrate before his God and Lord.

George returned home, mindful of his sin, but ever so much more mindful of the greatness of the Lord and Savior.

He spent Saturday in the terrifying struggle to repent of his sin, to face his sin and write the spiritual blank check that he feared in the unconditional surrender of rejecting sin.

When he confessed his sin, Fr. Elijah blessed him, said, "I'm sorry I can't give you the sacramental absolution yet--that will follow your chrismation," and then said, "Welcome home, son. Keep repenting."

And then the vigil was upon them.

It began with George standing in the center of the action as he stood before the congregation and, answering Fr. Elijah, renounced the Devil and all his works, rejecting sin, schism, and heresy, and vowed himself to Christ as a member of the Orthodox Church.

Then Fr. Elijah anointed George with sacred chrism, chrismating him with the fragrant oil of anointing that sealed George as a little Christ, as spiritual prophet, priest, and king, as one of the faithful in the Orthodox Church. This oil of spiritual blessing that worked in him more deeply even as it was wiped away from his skin--the emblem of the Spirit that penetrated like a sword. Fr. Elijah absolved George of his sins, and then the newly illumined servant of God George, stood before the congregation.

Then George faded into the background while the vigil unfolded, and he could never remember all of it--only that it seemed like a treasurehouse from which more and more wondrous treasure was brought forth. George remembered later the incense, the chant of "Christ is risen from the dead, trampling down death by death," the call of "Christ is risen!" and its answer, "He is risen indeed!", repeated triumphantly, in English, in Slavonic, in Arabic, in Spanish... and most of all George remembered the faces around them. There was something more deeply radiant and beautiful than that of someone who had won millions of dollars. The vigil lasted for hours, but though George ached, he barely minded--he almost wished it would last for hours more.

When it was time for the homily, Fr. Elijah stood up, his face radiant, and read the age-old homily of St. John Chrysostom, read at all kinds of Orthodox parishes on Pascha for ages:

> If any man be devout and loveth God,
> Let him enjoy this fair and radiant triumphal feast!
> If any man be a wise servant,
> Let him rejoicing enter into the joy of his Lord.

If any have labored long in fasting,
Let him now receive his recompense.
If any have wrought from the first hour,
Let him today receive his just reward.
If any have come at the third hour,
Let him with thankfulness keep the feast.
If any have arrived at the sixth hour,
Let him have no misgivings;
Because he shall in nowise be deprived therefore.
If any have delayed until the ninth hour,
Let him draw near, fearing nothing.
And if any have tarried even until the eleventh hour,
Let him, also, be not alarmed at his tardiness.

For the Lord, who is jealous of his honor,
Will accept the last even as the first.
He giveth rest unto him who cometh at the eleventh hour,
Even as unto him who hath wrought from the first hour.
And He showeth mercy upon the last,
And careth for the first;
And to the one He giveth,
And upon the other He bestoweth gifts.
And He both accepteth the deeds,
And welcometh the intention,
And honoreth the acts and praises the offering.

Wherefore, enter ye all into the joy of your Lord;
Receive your reward,
Both the first, and likewise the second.
You rich and poor together, hold high festival!
You sober and you heedless, honor the day!
Rejoice today, both you who have fasted
And you who have disregarded the fast.
The table is full-laden; feast ye all sumptuously.
The calf is fatted; let no one go hungry away.
Enjoy ye all the feast of faith:

Receive ye all the riches of loving-kindness.

Let no one bewail his poverty,
For the universal Kingdom has been revealed.
Let no one weep for his iniquities,
For pardon has shown forth from the grave.
Let no one fear death,
For the Saviour's death has set us free.
He that was held prisoner of it has annihilated it.

By descending into Hell, He made Hell captive.
He embittered it when it tasted of His flesh.
And Isaiah, foretelling this, did cry:
Hell, said he, was embittered
When it encountered Thee in the lower regions.

It was embittered, for it was abolished.
It was embittered, for it was mocked.
It was embittered, for it was slain.
It was embittered, for it was overthrown.
It was embittered, for it was fettered in chains.
It took a body, and met God face to face.
It took earth, and encountered Heaven.
It took that which was seen, and fell upon the unseen.

O Death, where is thy sting?
O Hell, where is thy victory?

Christ is risen, and thou art overthrown!
Christ is risen, and the demons are fallen!
Christ is risen, and the angels rejoice!
Christ is risen, and life reigns!
Christ is risen, and not one dead remains in the grave.
For Christ, being risen from the dead,
Is become the first-fruits of those who have fallen asleep.

To Him be glory and dominion
Unto ages of ages.

Amen.

And then the prayers moved very quickly--joyously--radiantly--and the Eucharist was served, George being called up first among the faithful to receive it.

Then the newly illumined servant George received Jesus Christ as his Lord and Savior.

And George kissed Fr. Elijah's hand and the chalice,
forgetting it was the Holy Grail.

And when the liturgy finished, Fr. Elijah announced to the congregation, "You may kiss the convert."

Then the feast began,
a faint fragrance of frankincense flowed,
and a fragrant fragrance of flowers flowed.
Fr. Elijah spoke a blessing,
over a table piled high with finest meats
and puddings
and every good thing,
and the fruit of the vine poured out.
Every door and every window was opened,
and the wind blew where it willed,
and the wind blew where it pleased,
and George settled in to his home,
grateful to God.
Then someone told a Russian folktale,
and someone began singing,
and people began dancing,
and a little boy chased a little girl,
clutching a flower.
And men and women,
children,
young and old,
saluted George with a kiss,

every last one
of his brethren.
And the crystalline light
of a sapphire sky
blew through the window,
and angels danced,
and saints below cracked red Pascha eggs,
red in the footprints of Mary Magdalene,
a holy grail,
and George laughed,
and wanted to weep,
for joy.

Then George and Abigail talked long.

George could never remember now long the celebration seemed to last. It seemed that he had found a garden enclosed, a fountain sealed, filled with every kind of wonder, at once Heaven and home, at once chalice and vine, maiden and mother, ancient and alive. It was the family George had forever wanted to enter.

Then George kissed Abigail--a long, full kiss--and absolutely nothing about it was hollow.

When he stepped back, Fr. Elijah tapped him on the shoulder. "By the way, George... I know this is down the road, but let me know when you two get engaged. I'd be happy to do your wedding."

George looked at Abigail, paused, and said, "Abigail, do you see how the candlelight glistens off your Grandpappy's bald spot? Isn't it romantic?"

Fr. Elijah and Abigail turned to each other and said, "It's about time!"

Then Fr. Elijah said, "Welcome to the Castle of the Saints, George. Welcome home."

www.ingramcontent.com/pod-product-compliance
Lightning Source LLC
Chambersburg PA
CBHW030816310726
48980CB00006B/518/J
9780615202198